MW01680231

Praise for E.V. Legters' **Connected Underneath**

"A potent story that offers an engaging meditation on the most basic desire – to know oneself." – *Kirkus Reviews*

"A gem of a novel, *Connected Underneath* explores the tragedies that ensue when family members hide enormous secrets. I was riveted by the small-town intrigues and heart-breaking characters who struggle to be themselves. Breathless as I finished the last page, I eagerly await Legters's next masterpiece." – Daniel M. Jaffe, author of *The Genealogy of Understanding*, a novel-in-stories.

"*Connected Underneath* is a story about secrets – those we keep from each other and those we keep from ourselves. It is also a story about the damage we can do, both willfully and inadvertently." – *The Lucid Reader*

"There are endless, unseen, silent depths and distance between islands. But of course, underneath, they are connected. This short novel delivers an infinitely large message without sentimentality. Highly recommended." – Susan Rukeyser, *Not On Fire, Only Dying*

VANISHING POINT

VANISHING POINT

a novel

E.V. Legters

Tina — thanks so much for reading VP — I look forward to your review — All best Eve Legters

Vanishing Point

Published in 2017 by Lethe Press, Inc.
118 Heritage Avenue • Maple Shade, NJ 08052-3018 USA
www.lethepressbooks.com • lethepress@aol.com
ISBN: 978-1-59021-647-7 / 1-59021-647-4

Set in Agmena and Steelfish.
Interior design: Alex Jeffers.
Cover design: Inkspiral Design.

LIBRARY OF CONGRESS CATALOGING-IN-PUBLICATION DATA

TK

For Gordon Mennenga

Song

The world is full of loss; bring, wind, my love,
my home is where we make our meeting-place,
and love whatever I shall touch and read
within that face.

Lift, wind, my exile from my eyes;
peace to look, life to listen and confess,
freedom to find to find to find
that nakedness.

— Muriel Rukeyser

Part One

Chapter One

[1] Nothing has changed except Angela Dunnewald. Sustained by a large, rich inner life, she's seen to her husband Ross and his wishes with little trouble for nineteen years, and stayed best friends with Lydia for twelve, but her will, her ability, to care about the things they do has dissolved. For Ross, there's keeping their social calendar full; making sure their housekeeper Ina has hung his carefully starched shirts in his closet by color, buying steaks only from King's. For Lydia, there's her gossip and flirtations and need for attention. Angela loves them, she supposes – maybe not enough – but she's come unglued.

There's this: The very things closing her in and making her feel half-crazy – reminding the gardener to prune the matching crab apple trees afternoons never mornings; answering invitations the day they arrive; getting ready for a Lydia outing – put corners on her days, and give them shape and substance. But then, when Ross is gone, and he's often gone, nerves surface, disorganization, and a sort of self-loathing.

And this: During the first moments Ross is out the door, she'll feel weightless, free, and open to possibility. She'll garden, read, get a full night's sleep. She'll have a party, invite friends in for lunch, or see something new at the galleries on Newbury Street. But she doesn't. She walks from room to room, window to window, waiting for morning, waiting for Ina, waiting for Lydia to call with an idea as to how to spend the day, defenseless against pellets of nervous energy that skid under her skin like metal balls on a metal tray.

[2] Lydia, at Angela's to take her to a benefit brunch, this time the ballet, calls through her open car window, "Hurry up. We're already late."

But Angela has seen something dart through the hedge at the corner of the house near the study. "What was that?"

"What was what? Come on."

"But what was it? Didn't you see it?"

"No, dear. Get in."

Angela looks, and looks again, but nothing; nothing; the hedges are bare. Her nerves?

Lydia talks and talks about one of her husband Jack's real estate deals and about a cruise they might take – "although he doesn't like water" – but Angela hardly listens. Ross is gone, and the metal balls skid, and for the last few days she's had the unsettling sense of a second self, or perhaps a premonition. Maybe Lydia will crash the car – she braces herself against the dashboard when Lydia comes to an abrupt stop – "Don't you trust me?" – or maybe Ross is ill. Cancer? A heart attack?

Lydia finds their places at one of the two dozen round tables dressed with pink linen tablecloths that fill the hotel ballroom. Reflections made by the tiny chandelier lights sparkle among the tall crystal wine glasses and silver spoons. Above each setting of china stands a figurine, a flat-footed ballerina, about five-inches tall, leaning forward slightly, as though the two or three forget-me-not blossoms she carries are a burden. Made of plastic, with black dots of paint for eyes, Angela touches the skirt.

Susan and Hillary and Joan are already there, and the matriarchal Mrs. Althea Smythe, with her dark, dark hair piled high, and her pale powdered cheeks. She wears a red collar that rises up like an Elizabethan ruff around the richly textured skin of her neck, and above her proud bosom. The ruff matches her lipstick.

"I haven't seen you in months," Angela says.

"I've been caring for Harvey. He's been so ill."

"I'm so sorry. Harvey is...?" Her husband's name is George, and her twins, who must be in their forties by now, are girls.

"My Chin."

"Your chin?"

"Yes, my Japanese Chin."

"Oh" – a dog? – "and you need to..." Angela imagines daily shots, intravenous bags, rehab.

"Walk him."

"Walk him?" He must have bad hips.

"Poor thing was terribly depressed all winter. Now he won't rely on anyone else."

Angela concentrates on the napkin in her lap for fear of laughing.

Conversations swirl: A tennis match, an apricot diet, Pilates and spinning, an arc of laughter, Hillary asking Susan about a new job she has that has to do with kids; Susan says she likes it, but Hillary keeps asking how it leaves her with enough time for herself.

The eyes of her ballerina stare out at slightly different angles and Angela wonders if she can see more or less that way. All figurines in all the places are also staring out in different directions.

"Maybe I'll find a job."

"Are you kidding?" Lydia says. "Doing what?"

As waitresses in black and white uniforms serve a green confection for dessert, women at the head table give themselves speeches, congratulating each other for all kinds of things, such as having gathered all of them together at one time, even though these are the same women they all see day after day, week after week, at the club, at other benefits, at shops in town. Angela wants to jump out of her skin, but sits, carefully still, only tracing the folds of the ballerina's skirt, over and over, from waist to hem, with her fingertips.

"Honey, stop," Lydia whispers, even covering Angela's hand with her own, as though disciplining a child. "What's the matter with you today?"

"I should have asked for wine."

"Let's go shopping after," Lydia says. "Oh, there's Evelyn. I need to..." And she's off. Lydia, almost as thin as Angela, but with more luxurious hips and breasts, always seems near bursting. There's an energy about her, some part always in motion. Her clothes, although they fit perfectly, never seem roomy enough.

Someone behind Angela asks, "Does anyone know anything about the ballet? I haven't been in years."

Lydia's hefty red and gold necklace clunks as she slides into her seat.

"Is that new?" Angela's small hammered silver pendant with the off-center stone, the one she bought in Venice during her and Ross's only trip to Europe, sits quietly at the base of her throat. "Buy gold, for Christ's sake," he said. "We're in Venice!" The woman in the shop had no name for the stone, but it resembled opal, and in it Angela could see layers of color, pale, opalescent, color within color, like veins running through it, like music.

Lydia leans in. "You look strange. What's going on?"

"These speeches are forever."

"Hang on. We'll go shopping."

They stand to leave before the applause subsides. Angela puts the plastic ballerina in her bag.

"You're keeping it?" Lydia decides on Genevieve's on Elm. There, saleswomen display silk scarves across their arms, and suggest dresses Angela doesn't want, and suits she doesn't care to see Lydia in. Sitting down on a settee with gold painted arms, she says, "There must be more than this."

"Well," Lydia says, looking over a shoulder at herself wearing bright blue in the three-way mirror, "we could try Mitchell's. They usually have more silk."

Chapter Two

[1] As a member of the town's welcoming committee, Lydia showed up at the Dunnewalds' new big house twelve years ago, alongside the moving men and packing boxes. She and Angela sat on crates as men situated sofas and chairs and tables around them with their knees nearly touching. Lydia offered maps, and a basket of pears and pomegranates, and settling-in suggestions, the best dry cleaners, the best restaurants, the only club to join, hers. She later admitted that the welcoming group's true function was to screen new arrivals. They decided which new people, if any, would be allowed access to what the committee considered the preeminent social circle, and which would be left to try to prove they were deserving. She later said she hated the idea – after all, she said, she'd been raised as a liberal – but that it did in fact save time. "Don't laugh. You adore me." Adore was a bit much, but Angela would have been lost without her. She'd had no experience with preeminent social anything, but was accepted without reservation, possibly because as an attorney Ross might prove useful. With Lydia four years older than Angela, she also took it upon herself to play big sister, always available to clear the way, even when Angela saw no obstacles. She's still steadily generous with advice, rarely asking for any, and rarely taking it when she does. But she's entertaining, and keeps Angela busy, and takes up most of the space when they're together, which is fine with Angela. Lydia's assumptions grant her privacy; Lydia's providing answers to who she is or what she's thinking without ever really asking – like Ross – has enabled Angela to keep her private entertaining inner self intact, the inner self she discovered as a child, and has relied on to keep safe distances, from Ross, from her marriage, from the very social circle Lydia has drawn her into. But this self seems unmoored – no, not unmoored, exactly; attached, but to something jagged.

After Mitchell's – neither bought a thing – Lydia turns into the Dunnewalds' street, the long, curving street close to, but safe from, Boston, one of a number of streets with houses like theirs, all huge, all new within the last twenty years. "Don't be late for garden club in the morning."

"Am I ever?"

Smaller, more modest houses, houses which had probably produced and protected perfectly good families, have been demolished to make room for this sort of grandeur. Those on the Dunnewalds' street are meant to resemble Italian villas or English manners or Scottish castles, and all, Angela thinks, seem embarrassed by their size and how out of place there are on a suburban street in Massachusetts. The house Ross picked for them has the blankest of faces, with a wall of small windows set in pale stone, meant to suggest something found in the Tuscan hills. Ross, hating the noise of hardwood floors, immediately had carpeting installed in every room and hallway, so that silence is entombed. Angela feels the chill from a distance.

This time, stepping out of the car, she's certain there's something in the hedges.

"You have to have seen that."

"What?"

Angela looks more closely. "I saw..." She looks, and looks again. Nothing. "I'm sure..."

"You're seeing things, hon. Call if you need anything," Lydia waggles her fingers out her window and drives off.

Inside, the full weight of the house comes to rest on Angela's shoulders. The two-story foyer and all that open space. To the left and right, the library and living room, dark as grottoes. The stairs sweeping up in a curve seem to go nowhere. She leaves her bag with the ballerina on the mahogany table in the center of the foyer; she'll move it before Ross comes home late tomorrow: he insists personal objects left out are like dirty laundry. She stopped arguing about things like this long ago because he takes less notice of her when there's nothing to notice, and not being noticed can be useful. She's not afraid of Ross and never has been; she's afraid *for* him. She senses he could – someday will – disintegrate, and she never wants to be the reason.

In the study at the back of the house, she straightens a window shade. Between the gardening shed and the hedge in the far corner of the yard stands a man.

Thin, twenty, maybe, his clothes brown, worn; she imagines stains. She watches him light a cigarette and sit down on the little gardening shed step as though he's familiar with the yard, or even works there. Pulled low over his eyes is a hat with a brim. She wishes she could see his eyes, but he's too far away, and his hat droops down over his forehead.

Ross would go to the phone, call the police, remind them how much he pays in taxes. But she stays where she is.

The man extinguishes the cigarette on his boot sole and gingerly puts what is left in his pocket, then lifts a pack, a brown shapeless thing, and walks towards the house, towards her. Thinking he might be coming to the door, she panics, but he keeps going, walking so close to the study he might as well look in. His face is almost delicate, a little older than she expects. When he glances up at the house, at an upstairs window, it seems, she sees that his eyes are dark, and narrow. She follows him by going from room to room, ending up by the low window near the front door. She has to stoop down to watch as he heads for the driveway and disappears down the street.

[2] With all lights off, she watches from the centers of rooms – there's nothing to keep the man from coming back to stand in the yard in the dark, or from ringing the bell, wanting to be inside. She's always been afraid to go near the windows at night; the house is set back from the road, and she can't see her neighbors' houses through the trees, but she often feels someone is watching and judging, especially lately, and especially when she's home alone. It's ridiculous, but a spell hard to break. In the kitchen, she opens a bottle of wine – the Barolo Ross asked her to buy then rejected – goes to the study, and the living room, and the library. Trees and bushes, gray and black at this hour, dance in the outside lights.

Going to bed well after midnight, she can't sleep. She's had too much wine, as though celebrating. Her head aches, and she keeps hearing things, and can't tell if the sounds are inside or out.

She wonders what the young man's voice sounds like and how he can be so completely in possession of himself, how he can seem so much more comfortable in her yard than she's ever been.

[3] "No breakfast, thank you," she tells Ina in the morning. Her stomach feels as if it's floating. Ina's sure she's coming down with a cold. "No, nothing like that."

Only a few women of the garden club members still touch their own soil, but they have strong opinions and have decided the town property around the band shell needs re-landscaping. Angela, known to be reliable, has been put in charge of finding out what rules and regulations might stop them, and has spent a day and a half on the phone, mostly on hold, trying to track down the right people. The papers she needs for the meeting are on the desk in the study.

The young man, huddled under the shed's short roof. It's raining a little. He pulls the collar of his jacket up around his throat. He takes off his hat and hits it against his leg and looks up at the low sky. His hair is thin and pale and fine, like a child's. He puts his hat back on with a tap and gazes steadily at the house. She steps back. He can't possibly see her, but maybe her shadow. Or her eyes.

When the phone rings, she jumps.

"I'm between meetings," Ross says.

Angela feels giddy having him on the phone while watching a stranger stand in their backyard, as though she's getting away with something illicit.

"Angela? Are you there?"

"Of course.

"Confirm the Plagets for dinner. It's important."

The man sits down on the step, lights a cigarette, rests his arms on his knees. She likes it that he smokes.

"Anything else?" she asks Ross.

Ross talks on and on, "just so you know," but she barely hears him. The man has gotten up and is now walking, slowly, a few yards this way and a few yards that, his collar hunched up under his hat brim. She needs to find Ina. She doesn't want her calling the police.

"Bye then," she says to Ross, not altogether sure he's finished. The man's still pacing, but with no sense of urgency. He touches the rake propped against the fence, looks up at the sky, puts his cigarette out by holding it under the rain drops.

She's reluctant to lose sight of him, but needs to find Ina. She isn't in the foyer, or the kitchen, thank goodness, with all those windows across the back, nor is she in the laundry room, or the library. The living room, polishing window locks.

"Why not take off today? Go on. Go shopping or something. Have some fun."

"But I'm not finished." Ina looks as though Angela has told her she's fired.

"Let me take your apron."

Ina unties the strings at her neck and at her waist, but won't hand it over, instead clutching it to her chest and frowning.

"Your things are in the back hall?" Angela says. "I'll get them. You stay here." She retrieves the purple cardigan, the shopping bag with extra supplies – she never thinks Angela has enough cleaning cloths or Clorox Clean-Up – and the big black bag.

Pressing these things into Ina's hands, Angela all but pushes the squat square woman out the door. "Your car's out front?"

"But I haven't done the shirts yet."

"There's always tomorrow." Ina wouldn't have been more shocked than if Angela had said she was painting polka-dots on the foyer walls. Angela shuts the door, but through the low window can see Ina still standing there. "Go, go," she whispers. Finally, Ina turns and leaves, and in a moment Angela hears her Honda start up.

She races back to the study, but the young man is no longer near the shed, or the hedge, or the fence along the back. "You ought to be ashamed of yourself," she says out loud, but is still peering out, hoping to see him.

After nearly an hour, she can't put off leaving for the garden club meeting any longer. Reaching into her purse for car keys, she finds the plastic ballerina. Cheap, badly made, she nearly throws her in the trash, but sets her on the kitchen windowsill, to gaze through crooked eyes instead.

Chapter Three

[1] "Angela. You're so late," the chairwoman says. Both Angela and Lydia call the woman Rose, though her name is Dana. Lydia, down at the far end of the table, points to the empty chair next to her, but Angela choses one near the door. Lydia pouts.

"We're already discussing plans for the band shell," Rose says. "I believe it should incorporate gardens of roses, lovely little circular beds, but Emily wants... what is it you want?"

A number of them had been inside Emily's house not long before; in it, everywhere, were huge vases spilling over with anthodium, flowers with thick single petals the size of plates with the long, interior stamen sticking out, unsheathed. Sitting amid all those dozens of phallic protrusions while Emily served tea had been unnerving, even for Lydia. Now, however, Emily is advocating simplicity, as though this is the very idea they've been searching for.

"What do you see as 'simple'?" Lydia wants to know.

"White, all white, everything white, and only one or two species, three at the very most. It would make a statement, and an appropriate backdrop to any sort of music, a counterpoint. I hear there're going to be rappers this summer." She shudders.

Angela imagines sheets of white impatiens, or tulips, maybe, but their heads are already drooping, so impatiens stretch as far as the eye can see, and then these flowers begin to fade, wilt, until there are only vast fields of brown.

Where's the young man now?

"Well," Rose says. "I suppose we could add that to our list of possibilities. It's unique. What else?"

Lydia catches Angela's eye and looks heavenward.

"How will we decide? Will we all get to vote?" someone asks.

The discussion drifts off to vote-taking procedures, and whether there is any precedent, and whether the chairwoman's vote counts for more. Emily sighs, exasperated that her idea hasn't pushed every other one off the table. Now riotous color replaces the brown field in Angela's mind. Rose is likely to get her rose gardens.

"Angela," she says. "What are we up against?"

"The town council..." She begins with good intentions, but, in the middle of her third or fourth sentence, gets so bored with the project and the details, she feels ill. While on the phone with this or that official, she'd inked blue and black patterns on her notes, first intertwining a few words with circles and squares and then putting leaves and other asymmetrical shapes down the margins. Speaking now, she adds to these with her red pen. Then, without knowing she will, says, "I'm sorry, I can't continue with this. I've taken on something else which will fill up all of my time."

"I don't see how..." Rose is saying. Lydia cocks her head, expecting a telepathic message.

But all she has is, "I'm late now. Here, you can have my notes. Everything you need to know." The papers are passed from hand to hand until they reach Rose, who looks at them with suspicion, at which point Angela gets up and leaves. Halfway down the hall, she hears Rose call after her. "I can't read these. They're covered with doodling. Are these ideas?" Her voice grows shrill. "Some festoons you had in mind? These don't even look like flowers."

They'll turn to Lydia for an explanation, who'll shrug, feign amusement, but be peeved, and equally mystified.

Her hand shakes as she tries to fit the key in the ignition. She knew she'd leave early, before the final motion was made, and before Lydia could suggest shopping or some other little filler, but she hadn't known she'd stand up even before her part was over. Lydia has followed her to the door and is waving and calling out as Angela pulls away. She pretends not to see her, drives through a stop sign, and almost hits a truck. The face of the driver seems comical, his brow all wrinkled, his mouth distended. She waves an apology. He gives her the finger.

[2] The young man is standing in a small group of trees across from her driveway. She has to drive right in front of him; this excites her; she feels larger than life. She tries to act as though she hasn't noticed him, but wonders how she looks and glances in the rear view mirror. How dark her eyes are, and how fierce! Parking the car in front of the garage, instead of pulling in, as Ross requires, she walks from the car to the front door of the house, boldly, but also a little stiffly, as though being followed. She knows his eyes are on her as she unlocks the door and steps in. She heads for the study, hoping he will come around to the backyard. She fingers her pendant. She waits. She stands in the middle of the room. She watches.

The phone rings. Lydia. The ringing stops, but starts right up again, Lydia, wanting an explanation, complaining she's been left hanging, and dying to ask, "What in the world is about to fill up your time?"

Angela drags her wicker chair with its big cushions across the room and up to the window, and sits there, feet on the sill, a clear view of the shed.

At the end of their wedding ceremony, after Ross lifted her veil, four bridesmaids waited, and four ushers, and behind them, parents, aunts, uncles, grandparents, sorority sisters, Ross's friends from law school, all waiting for Ross to kiss her. But he wasn't looking at her. Instead, he was gazing into the distance over her head – only for a moment, but the moment grew long. She had to shift her weight under the full skirt of her dress to get his attention. He said, "Oh," saw her, and kissed her then, but missed her mouth and kissed her cheek. The audience finally had their chance to applaud, but at the moment of their union, he'd forgotten she was there.

She wheels the bar cart in from the library across the carpeted foyer to her wicker chair in the study; on it are bottles of scotch, soda, the ice bucket. She never drinks this early, but feels she might want to. She hurries, afraid she might miss something outside, and settles into the chair to watch.

The phone rings a third time, with greater urgency. Lydia, or maybe Ross, worrying that she's forgotten the Plagets. She has.

As the clock strikes four, she allows herself scotch, no water. She's considering the burning sensation at the back of her throat, trying to think of just the right words to describe it, when her young man appears from the garage end of the house. It surprises her, even though she's expecting him, hoping for him. She feels perfectly safe. The scotch heats the inside of her belly and the lining of her brain. The fellow walks to the far side of the shed and, putting his hands in his pocket, leans with his back against it, not facing her. The scotch enlarges possibilities and he becomes something other than a stranger who shouldn't be here. He is like a prodigal son, or a returning lover. The skin on the inside of her thighs tightens. She pretends to be younger, freer, and never nervous.

And she wills the stranger to come inside, on his own with no intervention. The idea embarrasses her even as she follows it through to various ends; he might whisper and touch her. Or he might hurt her. He turns just then, and leans against the shed, facing the house straight on.

She wants to know his name.

The clock ticks. A car passes on the wet pavement. A squirrel scurries up a branch. Small things in the house shift, a flower in a vase, an ice cube in the bucket.

She stands absentmindedly, possibly planning to check Lydia's voice mail, or to call the Plagets, or get something to eat. Instead, she goes directly to the back door and opens it. Now the fellow is sitting on the shed step, barely out of the drizzling rain.

"Do you need anything?" she calls out. With the shed more than a hundred feet away from the door, and the sound of the rain, she doubts her voice carries.

But he stands.

"Are you lost?" she asks.

"Excuse me. I don't mean to bother anybody."

His voice is a surprise, light and lyrical; it reminds her of something both urgent and distant.

He takes a few steps towards the house. "I got a job with your landscaping crew, but the truck, the boss, never showed up."

"We have no crew. Just one man. You must have the wrong address."

"Oh." His shoulders are bent slightly forward, and he holds his hat in his hands as though a supplicant, safe, even as she knows that his standing in her yard, against her shed, with no shred of self-consciousness, means he's neither supplicant nor entirely safe. "I could hitch hike...but with the weather and all."

"Is there someone you could call?"

"No, not really. Well, yes. Maybe."

In the confines of the back hallway, he smells damp and unclean. But he's slender and seems fine, like china; how odd someone like this is out in the rain alone.

In the kitchen he stands at the phone; Angela hears it ringing; there's no answer. She picks up the kettle to fill it for tea.

"Seem to be out of my luck this week," he says.

Hanging up, he crosses the room to her, not quickly, but without hesitation. His hands in his pockets, he leans back against the countertop, not two feet away, while she fusses with the teapot. She doesn't understand his coming so close, even if it is what she's been wanting. She keeps her head down for fear he'll notice she's been drinking. He seems closer to her than anyone has been for years; even Ross, in their bed, has never seemed as close as this. Still, she steps away until it feels more appropriate, until she feels an invisible cord between them break. At the stove, she watches the orange coil glow, her back to him, unable to think of anything to say. He seems content, however, the only tension in the room hers.

"Some tea?" Her voice wavers. "Have a seat. You can try your call again later." It crosses her mind that he might soil the white cushions. "What's your name?"

"Daniel." His voice is not much more than a whisper. His eyes are wide now, less sure.

He reminds her of a small injured rabbit she once found and cared for in that kitchen, a mild, slightly frightened thing that was happy to get out of the damp, chilly air, but not so happy to find itself with people. But then, when healthy, and released, it had hesitated before disappearing.

"Mine is Angela." She feels the scotch buzz disappear as though she's discarded clothing. "Excuse me. I'll be right back." She takes her teacup in to the bar cart and splashes more scotch into it, hurrying for fear what she's doing will become clear.

Back at the table, the smell, his smell, seems fur-like and damp, but she no longer finds the scent unpleasant. Instead, the kitchen seems obscenely pristine – the tile too white, the copper pots too clean, the flowered borders on the walls silly in their symmetry.

"I have to go," Daniel says, suddenly standing.

She hadn't expected anything so definite at that moment. "But you're not dry yet, or warm."

"You've been unusually kind." He practically whispers.

She feels herself falling down some Alice in Wonderland place; the place and the falling are both frivolous and frightening. If Ross were to call, or Lydia, she'd be unable to talk to them; she wouldn't know who they were.

"I was just about to build a fire. Come." She's lying, but Daniel follows her into the library.

"Let me," he says, and crouches by the hearth to build a small fire with the logs and kindling there. When he finishes, he holds his hands out to warm them. She's worried about what sort of conversation to have, but Daniel looks around and says, "I've never seen so many beautiful things in one place." He studies the wooden objects – Ross has a few carved wooden puzzles, a cylinder, a globe, an animal or two – and the silver statues and crystal and lamps and vases. "My mother always said money wasn't everything. But we had so little, I never knew what she meant." He touches, and then picks up the most intricately patterned wooden puzzle, the globe. Different colored woods have been carved to fit together in a certain way. Around the globe, a silver equator.

"Where are you from?"

"Up north, above Portland, Maine. I'm really just passing through, but I picked up that job. Or thought I did." He puts the puzzle down; when it tips, he sets it straight. "I shouldn't have hung around, but I was tired. I'm surprised no one called the cops."

"Cops? Nothing much ever happens here. We meet the same people, over and over again, people who say the same things, over and over again. Maybe it's not like that for you. Here you are, traveling."

He shrugs. "I have different problems. I should be on my way."

She keeps her voice in slow motion. "Why not freshen up first?" If she talks too fast, she might scare him off, and at the thought of being left alone, nerves surface; she can feel tiny metal pellets at the edges. "There's a guest bed and bath just up the stairs."

"Oh, no, no, I couldn't."

"I'll find you something warm to put on." Angela expects him to resist, but when she stands, he follows, and one after the other, they go up the stairs.

She shows him the guest bedroom with its own bath, and gives him big soft white bath sheets and a clean shirt and a pair of pants from Ross's closet; shorter than Ross, he'll need to roll up the cuffs. She leaves him fresh soap and bubble bath. She gathers up his clothes and takes them down to the laundry in the small room next to the kitchen. There, in that windowless corner of the house, she buries her nose in the folds of the clothes, almost hating to wash the smell of them out, his smell, which is animal and basic. But she does; she washes and dries the clothes and folds them as though for a lover, or perhaps for one's child.

She waits for him in the library, pokes at the coals, thinks she hears him on the stairs, but stopping to listen, hears no sound at all. She pours a little more scotch but doesn't drink it as she sits by the fire pretending to read. Ross rises up in her mind as a body bear-like – dark and dense, a drawing from a childhood fairy tale. She snaps her book shut. Daniel still isn't down, so, tiptoeing up the stairs and by his room, planning to peek in the door, as if on her way somewhere else, but peeking just to see, just to be sure he was still there, she stops. Daniel's asleep, naked on the bed, as though on an altar; he's white and still, his hair now clean and fair. She goes in. She'd like to kneel there.

Instead, she turns away. As she does, she's sure Daniel opens his eyes, but, no, his eyes are closed. There's silence.

Back downstairs, passing a window, she sees that a car is parked at the foot of the driveway with the headlights off. She catches her breath. Police? She steps back. Another car drives past; its bright lights show Lydia. She steps back further. What has Lydia seen? When Ross is gone, she sometimes barges right in without so much as knocking. Angela's heart sinks and rises and seems to flutter out through the top of her head. She doesn't move a muscle until Lydia drives away, and then Angela pulls all the blinds down in every window. Lydia.

There's a man asleep upstairs. By the lamp near the fire, she searches for guilt, but finds nothing like it. She does feel thin, like a wire. When at last Daniel comes down, and takes the chair across from hers, facing the fire, on the other side of the lamp, he's transformed. The bath and the clothes and the rest have changed him completely. "I didn't mean to take so long."

Looking away, she says, "It's late. You might as well stay the night."

She feels a stirring that isn't sex, but feels like sex, in that it is a low, inner, agitation that seems to need satisfaction. It isn't the jittery metallic feeling, it's more hopeful than that, more promising. She presses her head against the back of the chair so that her face is away from the light.

Daniel gets up to tend the fire. Watching him through the fabric of her husband's clothes, she thinks of him as naked, as an animal is naked. He's no longer like the rabbit; he's some lean-flanked, fine-boned thing. A deer. Or a wolf. Her mind is caught up into entanglements, people and animals coupling in strange ways, swans, she sees swans, and satyrs.

"Are you all right?" Daniel asks.

"I think so." But her eyes are wild; she's afraid of scaring him away. But he comes to the back of her chair and touches her hair. "Angela," he says.

She isn't herself, or she's herself for the first time in a very long time. She doesn't know, she doesn't care, if she's larger than life, or in proportion with her life finally. She often feels dwarfed and out of place and even angry. She isn't angry now, and there are no metal pellets.

She lets him lead her up the stairs to the guest bedroom, as though it were he who lives here, and when he undresses her, it's as if for a ceremony. They lie side by side in the bed she's made with white pillows and sheets.

They sleep.

[3] Angela wakes up to find herself naked and alone, and she isn't used to being naked. Her ivory blouse, her breasts bare beneath it, feels like profanity. She finds her skirt on a chair, puts it on, tucks in the blouse, pulls up the zipper, and buttons the buttons as though the day before.

The night seems half real, half dream.

In the library, though, are the real remains of the fire, and the glass with the scotch she'd left there. She hears a sound, the tea kettle perhaps, but the kitchen is empty, quiet, hollowed out.

Walking to the shed, she can't ever remember feeling air this fresh on her skin. She turns her palms out to catch it.

On the small broken step are Ross's clothes, carefully folded. When she picks them up, she catches Daniel's scent, and that of a cigarette. She calls out his name, once, twice, a question. She doesn't know what to do with the silence. She's bothered by what she's done only when she pulls away from it, but even then, she doesn't feel the expected things, embarrassment, or shame. What bothers her, and then frightens her, is feeling so little.

Back inside, she goes up the stairs to the guest room and sits on the edge of the bed. She can see herself in the mirror of the dresser. The dresser is across the room, and the mirror is tilted, so that she looks off-center, distorted, as if she has a headache, and the headache is visible.

Downstairs, the phone.

At the Boston Public library, a central staircase rises up through a large open space. Not long after they were married, Angela happened to be at the top of those stairs about to descend. Near her was a middle-aged man. It crossed her mind to push him. Maybe it was the wide open space which gave her such a dizzying thought, but that the idea had occurred to her, and that her body had tingled, was frightening, but also exciting. She'd stepped out of herself, or another side of her had darted out. Afterwards, when she was safely away from the stairs and in the street, she couldn't help but wonder where the urge had come from; she tried to analyze it, discard it, cure it. She feels that way now, sitting on the bed, looking at her cockeyed self in the mirror.

The phone's still ringing, or ringing again.

She checks herself for guilt as though checking for an injury, but all she finds is wonder; there's no open wound. The night stays with her like a visible thing, a new coat of armor, but translucent, different. All night they'd lain limb to limb, touching, skin to skin, but hadn't so much as kissed.

Four messages from Lydia, worried, she says. And Ross, angry that she "never picks up." And Rose, Dana, rather, about her report, or lack of one. And Vicki Plaget, confirming the dinner she's forgotten. She should call Lydia back to keep her from worrying, or dropping by, or thinking she's seen something. But Lydia, too much a busy-body intrusion; instead of checking in with her, Angela goes back out to the yard. A gray cat weaves in and out of the bushes. The day already feels old and tired. She and Ross had spent one or two nights undressed, but only when they were first married, and only by mistake, after sex, and it is the thought of Ross as she stands in the yard that feels like betrayal, a weed.

The possible consequences of what she's done are alarming, but still there's no shame. To protect herself, she tries to find the woman she was the day before, the woman to whom nothing like this would ever happen. And there she is, thin, reserved, well-dressed, discussing flowers, twirling her pendant with well-groomed fingertips.

In the shower, she puts her hands where Daniel placed his; she presses her palms to her belly, traces the vertebrae she can reach with her fingers, to see if she can tell how she felt to him. For her, there was a place on his breastbone, beneath the base of his throat, where her hand fit perfectly. There had been passion in the night, passion, and comfort, but no sex; he hadn't asked, and she hadn't been willing. What they, or she, had experienced had nothing to do with what she'd come to expect from intimacy, her flesh against coarse flesh. Instead, her hand on the bones of Daniel's breast, which in the dark had seemed birdlike, both steely and fragile.

For their last anniversary, Ross gave her a diamond on a gold chain. When she opened the box and saw the diamond sitting there in its velvet, she was polite. She doesn't like diamonds, and has told him more than once. His not knowing things like this, his not hearing her when she said she found diamonds cold, that she likes her coffee black, that she wishes, or used to wish, they would make love more often, his dismissal gives him an edge over her. She doesn't know, doesn't want to know, if it's on purpose. "What is it now?" Ross asked, the velvet box with the diamond resting open on her palm.

She didn't complain about the necklace. She even wore it once or twice, to avoid hurting his feelings. She understands that if she exposes his failures, allows him to see what she knows, he will fall apart in some way, crumble, and leave her nothing to be married to. When he neglected to kiss her while she waited under her lifted veil, she shifted her weight to get his attention, but never said you nearly missed kissing me. Never said you missed my mouth, what were you thinking, where was your mind. In that moment she decided not to say any of this, but to protect him, because while she considered the world as largely and reasonably solid, she understood he saw the world as shifting, and risky.

[4] Already in the forefront of his mind by his eleventh year, Ross fully realized who he was and what he might accomplish. From then on, he told her, he only looked ahead. During a moment of unusual vulnerability, he'd added he'd fallen short of one goal by not becoming valedictorian – or salutatorian either – both girls – but attended as good a four-year school as anyone in his class, and the best law school he could afford. The rest she'd guessed: His choice of a wife, a calm, quiet woman, self-contained, not much bother, easy enough to like, reliable, if not quite interesting, certainly not as interesting as he, was not likely to stand in his way. He'd never considered a woman as help-mate, much less soul mate. He would do nicely on his own, with no one to thank.

His reduction of things to low common denominators, his clearing away of ambiguity and shades of meaning, made him an excellent attorney; he'd helped turn his firm into a small empire. But his tendency, or need, to see things one-dimensionally makes their marriage paper thin. She sees this, but also sees that his habit of mind is his refuge; he believes it holds off the dogs, the doubt, the uncertainty that even he must know surrounds them. But, then again, look how well he's done. What more could she ask for?

Chapter Four

[1] The house is always so clean it rarely looks lived in, but Ina is vacuuming, vacuuming again, the library, the living room, the foyer. Angela sits in the study listening. Finally, the high-pitched whine dissolves into thin air. Ina looks in.

"Tea?"

Ina comes with a tray. Angela tries to sit quietly, unobtrusively, but can't keep from tugging at her sweater and fingering her pendant and pulling and pushing the pillows behind her. And she can't keep herself from checking the back yard. The air coming through the open window is still fresh from the rain. The tea's so close to the top of the cup, and the slice of lemon floating so brightly, she has to put it down, certain she'll spill it. The cup clicks thinly in its saucer. The tea spills. Together they watch it spot the carpet. Angela apologizes and blots it up while Ina says please stop, you're making it worse.

When Ina goes up the stairs, Angela follows, Ina's nylon stockings hissing between her thighs. Ina's plaid cotton dress is too short; veined creases show through the nylons at the back of her knees. Angela follows her into the guest room; she wants to be sure the sheets aren't changed. She explains she slept there the night before, although Ina hasn't asked. She reaches out to help Ina adjust a corner, saying there'd been a lot of wind, that it had bothered her, a tree branch had kept hitting the window in the master bedroom.

"Maybe we should rearrange this room. The bed might look better in that corner," she says although the notion had never occurred to her before. She fusses with things on the dressing table, a hand mirror, a brush, things that are never used. When Ina goes into the bathroom, she follows her to the threshold, and finds herself talking about a crack in the tile when she sees that wet towels are draped over the side of the tub.

"Who left these?" Ina says. "They'll never dry."

"Ross, must be. I remember now he came in here."

"He came in here? And left towels?" Ina sniffs them. "I'm surprised they're not mildewed."

And Angela follows her when she goes down the hall to the master bedroom.

"Is something wrong?" Ina says.

"Of course not."

But Ina glances at the untouched bed, opens the blinds on the windows one by one and looks up and around for tree branches but doesn't find any. Angela goes to the closet and pretends to be interested in picking out a dress for dinner with the Plagets.

"I don't remember any wind," Ina is saying.

Having her in the house makes Angela's skin feel too tight on her bones. She keeps thinking of Daniel's hand here, there. His words spin round and round.

"Would you mind pressing this?" She hands Ina a pale gray dress that hangs limply from a hanger.

"No, but not much to it," she says.

As she's leaving for the day, she tells Angela about her plans to sort through the linen closet or some such chore. Angela nods and says yes and closes the door behind her, as though shutting out a foreign object. She double locks the doors and runs up the stairs. She takes off her earrings on the way. She takes off her rings. She takes off everything. She slips into the white guest room bed.

At dusk, just as the light begins to go gray, she puts on her heavy robe, pours a glass of scotch, takes a cigarette from the silver box kept for guests. She barely sips the scotch, no longer wanting or needing her perceptions altered. She sits there all night, in the wicker chair, watching the shed, waiting, reliving her moments in greater detail. Her brain has found small doors to open. But Ross will be home. She lights the cigarette.

[2] The sun is bright, brighter than it's been for days. She has to squint into the glare, as though every piece of dew is a prism. What will keep Daniel from showing up the same moment as Ross? She'd have to make up some excuse, say she offered him a job, or even pretend she's never seen him before. She isn't sure she could lie in front of Daniel. Doesn't ever want to.

When the phone rings, she answers without thinking and immediately assembles reasons why she can't talk to whomever, even Lydia.

"What are you doing now?" Daniel asks.

She doesn't know what to say, or, for a moment, who she is. She feels disembodied.

"Angela?"

She'll meet him safely outside, find out more about him, where exactly in Maine he comes from, possibly even what he thinks about what happened between them. She doesn't expect to feel the same as she did. She's prepared for disappointment. Dismay. When she sees him in the light, she'll probably find he looks nothing like she remembers, but poorer, or less good. She doesn't want to find him that way, doesn't want to find out she was mistaken, or simply drunk, or lonely.

He comes through the hedge at the back of the yard and hesitates by the shed, but as he comes toward the house, he has a sure step, a sleekness. Spare, nothing about him inessential, no wasted motion, no wasted words. The fabric of his shirt is thin; she can feel the texture of his skin underneath it.

"Did you think I would stay away?" he says.

They kiss then, and she's inside out, and the taste of desire rises up and her mouth and lungs become full of it.

What a curiosity, undressing completely in the middle of the afternoon for a man not her husband, for a man she has known a single day. They'd already been together one night, but there had been something mystical about it, almost predetermined, and something pure, nothing carnal, and there had been the night, and the darkness. Angela pulls down the guest bedroom shades, but they are translucent, and light filters through. Daniel stands at the threshold. "Can you close the door?" she says. She doesn't want to be able to see out into the hall, towards her bedroom, or towards the stairs, or the life below.

She doesn't know what to do with her clothes. Her impulse is to fold them neatly, and she doesn't know if she's supposed to undress all at once. She wonders about the etiquette. She starts to unbutton her blouse, but slowly, waiting to see what Daniel will do. But as she hesitates, he comes to her and kisses her forehead and her cheeks and then her mouth and he finishes with the buttons himself and slides the blouse down her arms and unzips the back of her skirt. She undoes his belt, fumbling, never having undone a man's belt before. It's funny, she nearly laughs, this need to take care of these things; it's awkward, but also frightening, the undressing part, because it's so definite. When they sit down side by side on the guest bed, she still has on her bra and panties and he his undershorts, and she has to remind herself that they have already been side by side naked, but it's so long ago, a whole journey. They are so tentative now it seems not to have happened or to have only happened in her imagination, replayed all night and all day. She folds her hands into fists in her lap, wanting composure. Daniel, calm, gently kneads her fingers away from her palm; he's patient. She's worried Daniel will see she's too old, that she has parts he can't tolerate, that even with the shades down it's too light, he'll be able to see her much too clearly, but as they kiss, and as he takes her in his arms, he doesn't seem to be aware of her body, not in its various parts; he seems instead to take her as a whole, as something complete. She's slowly consumed; it's as though his hands are covering all of her at once; she couldn't get away, even if she wanted to. She's familiar with her interior restlessness, and she's used to a little anger now and then, with an undercurrent of impatience, with Ross, with the ladies' luncheons, with her hollow days, but she's not used to this. Her desire's out of hand because it's original, intact; it has never been plumbed or experimented with. Daniel seems to know this, and yet he also seems matter of fact; he will please her, but keep her whole even as she cries out, and it's important to her, to feel whole, because she does think she could visibly fray at the edges, some insanity seems possible, and what would Ross think of that? And Daniel understands, for he doesn't in any way belittle or humiliate her, although he does smile once, when she thinks she's about to lose her mind, and says so, and then she, too, smiles, as she comes back into herself a little; she rises up above him and then leans down to kiss his mouth. They roll over, and with her head more safely on the pillow, she can look at him; she isn't afraid anymore; his hair falls around his face and is light-colored and ethereal in the half-light. She touches it. He speaks quietly: Are you all right? Do you love me? He whispers little things but she's unable to answer. Suddenly, Daniel shuts his eyes and arches him back, and he seems to separate himself from her, and even to leave her out. She becomes tentative because she's scared; once taken over that edge into that particular and peculiar unconsciousness, once taken to that singular distant site, she might be unwilling or unable to come back.

Chapter Five

[1] Lydia knocks on the back door but bursts in without waiting. Angela will lock every lock after this.

"It was so embarrassing. Storming out of a meeting? Where were you all day yesterday?"

"Hardly storming."

"Rose was furious. Everyone assumed I knew what was going on. Why aren't you answering your phone? What is that?" She's pointing at the ballerina.

"I like her eyes."

Lydia picks up the doll. "Her eyes."

Angela takes it out of her hands. "Yes."

Lydia plops down in the chair Daniel had sat in to eat his small meal. Angela wonders if she will feel him there. Lydia becomes unusually still. "Out with it. What's going on? Did Ross do something? Like that time he had the cherry tree that you liked so much cut down?"

"Why didn't you come in last night?" Ross had said the cherries dropping stained the flagstone. She came home one day to a stump. She'd loved its blossoms; their first spring in the house, she took a dozen pictures of them, and had one framed for the study. Ross said the flagstones were more important, and that he hadn't known she cared about it. He never apologized.

"Come in when? What are you talking about?"

"You were out in the driveway."

"Not me."

"Of course it was you." If she saw something, Angela needs her to think it was imagined.

"Come on. What's going on? No secrets between us, remember?"

No secrets? Angela considers shocking her.

"I've got it. You're looking for a job," Lydia says. "Like Susan."

Angela doesn't say no.

"You didn't get one already, did you? What would I do without you all day? They're looking for somebody to run the Alzheimer's gala. Want to do that with me? That would keep you busy."

"I don't think so." The women they know believe, or pretend to believe, that their husbands' careers free them to do the things other women, women who "have to" work, don't have time for, and that they contribute to society by not working. Angela has never been convinced; she doesn't believe Lydia is, either. "You have to admit, we've never used our college educations for anything. And you have so much energy."

"Please. We've been through this. Nothing wrong with volunteering."

"Not in and of itself." But they couldn't quite ignore stories about women holding down full time jobs, raising five kids, three foster, or disabled, plus volunteering – Lydia has one completely healthy child raised, in part, by a nanny, a child now in college. Angela secretly suspects they use their husbands' careers to free them from being. "Why do we do so little? What are we afraid of?"

Lydia shifts in her seat, crosses and re-crosses her legs, checks her nail polish, smoothes a cuticle. "Then do the gala. If not you, who? Somebody has to, and everyone else is so hard to work with."

"Honestly, why didn't you come in the other night?"

She watches Lydia consider lying again. "I thought I saw Ross."

"Why didn't you say so?"

She shrugs. "Debated coming in, to make sure you were okay, but I wasn't in the mood to explain anything to him." She frowns. "I was surprised. I thought he wasn't coming home till today."

"I'm just tired of meetings." Angela pretends to need something from a cupboard. "They never accomplish very much."

"Well, there wouldn't be any meetings if we worked on Alzheimer's together. Just us. I was thinking we could have it at the art center. That huge staircase for an entrance. Think what we could wear."

"Just once, it would be nice to plan something small. Really allow the money to go to the charity, not the party."

"You have a job."

"Not yet."

"Don't toy with me." But, the next moment, she's off. Jack, she says, some dinner. Angela almost apologizes for upstaging her by leaving the garden club meeting early. "Give me a hug," Lydia says, and brushes Angela's cheek with her lips, gives her a quick tight hug, and leaves with a sweep of her arms. Even her exits come with flourishes.

[2] Angela arranges herself at the desk in the study, pretending to be busy with bills, Poppy's Carpet Cleaning, Port Charles Coffees, others. Waiting for Ross, she draws trees and leaves down the margins, fills in all the P's and C's. The sense of Daniel lingers under her clothes next to her skin. The kitchen door whooshes open on its swinging hinges. Ross.

"Angela," he says from the doorway of the study. She hopes he won't come any closer, but he is, coming closer, and here he is, leaning over her.

"Did you have a nice trip?" She smells a breath mint, the flat flinty air of the plane on his suit, his shaving cream, a thick smell, soapy, filling his pores.

"I hate how you do that to all of our paperwork," he says.

She puts the pages face down.

"Good trip? You reached a settlement?" She feels brittle, and as though she's been startled; even though she's been waiting for him, waiting for hours, his presence, the reality of him, comes as a surprise.

"Just so you know, I'm sick. Feverish." He loosens his tie and pulls his shirt collar away from his neck so that his chin juts out. She has to look away.

"What a shame. A cold?"

"Make me something to eat? Eggs. Toast. No butter." He talks to Ina this way. He might have asked her other things, like how she was, whether she was having a good week, whether everything had gone well in the house, but instead he says toast, no butter.

After she makes the soft boiled eggs and toast he decides he can't eat, and after she's gone to bed in the guest room, saying he'll be more comfortable alone, she listens to him tossing and turning in their bed, restless. He coughs. Changes channels on the television. And every once in a while calls out, "Angela?"

She's naked beneath a thin nightdress; she sees Daniel's eyes, feels his lips. It's dangerous, reliving the afternoon; she relives it. It's painful; she's reduced, raised up.

[3] Ross is still in bed, mostly on the phone, sometimes talking with the thermometer in his mouth. Even when she's at the other end of the house, she can hear, even feel, his voice. Once or twice she hears words like *fraud*, and *cheat*, and thinks he sounds confused. He must be ill; Ross is never confused.

When Ina comes, she tries to involve herself with the things that occupy Ina, like worrying that the iron isn't heating water hot enough, and that the guest bathroom towels are in the wrong linen closet. But she fails.

Lydia calls. "Lunch at the club?"

"Sure. What time? I have to go out anyway." Get away.

"Are you normal today? You haven't seemed normal."

"What time?"

Outside on the bench in the backyard with her phone and her daybook, she pretends to be taking notes and catching up. She has no way of knowing if Daniel will reappear; she doesn't expect him, but thinks she hears him, beyond the hedge. She looks there, and then up at the house, for fear Ross is watching; it should be obvious, even to Ross, that something is different about her. She believes Daniel will be discreet, and keep their meetings delicate and secret. Of course, there's the possibility he won't come back at all, and in that notion there's both dread and relief. Perhaps after leaving her with no place to sleep, he hitched a ride with a stranger. Maybe in the confines of that stranger's car – she sees vinyl seats and a dusty dashboard, and something hanging from the rear-view mirror, beads, or some saint on a chain – they talked about what it's like to have no plans, no roots, and no responsibilities. Maybe the driver said, "I wish I had your life," and maybe he also said, "I don't have the courage." Or, perhaps, drifters still caught rides on trains. She sees him standing in the open door of an empty box car, smoking, thinking of her, at least at night, as he passes through some city he hasn't seen before, its skyscrapers and spires, its fire escapes. How irretrievably far away he might be while she sits on her garden bench. Daniel's free to leave her, and he's free to be whomever he wants on any given day – himself, or someone else, any experiment.

[4] Four plump, white scallops, shiny from some sort of marinade and arrayed on three leaves of romaine, are placed in front of Angela. Lydia's feet look up through the glass table from shoes made of red leather straps. Across the patio, two teenage girls having lunch with the tennis pro laugh.

"He better watch himself." Lydia picks up a long-handled spoon to stir her iced tea. "They're young."

"Haven't you been taking lessons from him?"

Lydia keeps stirring. "He's not that good." Her miniature crushes are just that, she and the others believe, brief flirtations with young men brought to the club to teach golf or tennis, or the lifeguards who come and go. Since they don't bother Jack, why should they bother them?

"Is there someone new?"

"Not telling." She winks. Lydia often talks about the physical attributes of this one or that, and buys new clothes in which to play tennis or sit around the club pool. It's an outlet, she says, freely admitting her need to be watched, hopefully admired, and reassured she's still vibrant. She's only after a certain kind of conversation, she says, a bantering back and forth, foreplay with no complications.

Soon after joining the club at Lydia's insistence, Angela found herself sitting by the pool with the short, paunchy, patient Jack watching his wife engage in a lively conversation with the golf pro at the pool bar. Without being asked, Jack offered, "I knew going in. I'd watched her all through college. She wasn't going to change just because she was married."

Angela smiled carefully. What else could she do?

But then he looked at Angela guardedly, as though not sure how far to go with some line of thought. He finally said, "She has…a big appetite."

"Yes, she does." She sensed he wanted to say more, but she didn't want to hear more – Was he about to reveal some sort of kinky taste? Make a suggestion? – so she changed the subject to something about the temperature of the pool. They both went back to watching Lydia as if she were putting on a play for them. No one was perfect. And no one besides Lydia had paid much attention to her, the quiet, unobtrusive newcomer. It also seemed possible women were a little jealous because there was freedom in Lydia, so gregarious, so brightly colored, while they all followed all the rules.

Until the day she opened the door for Daniel, Angela had followed every rule, probably more rules than anyone else. But she accepts that Lydia sees herself as a good wife, a good mother, a good friend. She's still young at heart, which Jack, she says, never was. Angela thinks that's at the base of it, some private shortcoming on Jack's part that he accepts and forgives her for missing. Besides, they seem happy.

But sitting there, down to her last fat scallop, she realizes how often and how intently Lydia has mentioned Sam: Sam is good looking. Sam is kind. Sam is better than Jack at tennis. She remembers how Lydia insinuated herself into one of his tennis games – she'd assumed her eyes were on the tennis teacher – and Angela remembers seeing her talking to him beside her car in the club parking lot; when had that been? Last week. Both looked serious. Sam's wife, Sylvia, is small and blond and even-tempered.

Angela risks it. "Is it Sam?"

"Sam?" Lydia's voice seems to come up through the glass of the table, as if from her red shoes. "I knew him before."

"Before what?"

"Let's go to a movie. I hear *Carol* is good."

Angela lets her change the subject. "I shouldn't. Ross is home sick."

"Call him. Do you have your cell?"

"Of course not." She rarely carries it, another irritation for Ross. "Join this century," he says. She's tried, but he calls, often, only to say "Just so you know." Just so you know I need this, just so you know you haven't done that, just so you know.

"Use mine," Lydia says.

Pretending there's an inadequate signal, she goes to the small corridor near the ladies room. She isn't interested in sitting in the dark of a movie about two women and unconsummated passion. Lydia's watching her, so she puts the phone to her ear for a moment before going back to the table. "Ross would like me to come home."

"He's no fun." Lydia's eyes suddenly seem shadowed. "Sarah's been texting me. She's having trouble with her roommate. Maybe I'll drive down to help her sort it out. Think I should?"

"At some point she'll have to take care of things on her own. Besides, isn't the semester almost over?"

"You can come with me."

"Why would I do that? Sarah will want you to herself."

"Share a hotel room. Watch movies all night. Have a pillow fight."

Angela imagines white feathers drifting. She's never been in a pillow fight.

Chapter Six

[1] Ross has left one of his hard square notes on the mahogany table: "Office. Back for you at 7. The Plagets, remember. R." Concrete routines.

At 6:30 she changes into the limp dress Ina ironed and sits down on the end of the bed to wait. She counts the large, faint patterns in the carpet between the bed and the doorway, the bed and her vanity table, the bed and the wall. There are twelve, fourteen, and nine. A crow calls, and another bird she doesn't recognize.

Ross, downstairs, calling her name through the house rather hoarsely. His cold must have turned into a sore throat. "Angela? Angela? Are you ready? Where are you?"

At the mirror in the bathroom, she checks her face, and sees nothing in it that will give her away.

Downstairs she finds Ross in the library.

"Did you light a fire while I was gone?" he says. "I smell ashes. Better have Ina clean it out. Or maybe the gardener, he wouldn't mind, just ask him, just ask him to come inside for a minute. I think he did it last year. Or was that the gutter guy?"

Following him through the house, she watches him turn the foyer chandelier on and then off, the light on the mahogany table on, the light above the stove off – "What is this thing?" She wishes he wouldn't touch the ballerina – he fiddles with the lights as though he's never seen them before, or has never quite figured out how they work. Each time, it could just as well be the first time he's been required to adjust them.

"Ross, just leave them. They're fine."

There's an alarm system, but he rarely sets it; he believes the people at the alarm system company are watching; he pictures them sitting before vast control panels monitoring his every move. She doubts his suspicion that they send accomplices to houses like theirs to steal things. He'd rather take his chances with his deadbolts and locked windows and carefully adjusted bulbs.

As the headlights swing over the driveway and lights the small stand of trees across the street, she says, "Lydia's daughter is having some sort of problem at school. She might have gone down to see her."

"I know. I asked Jack to join us," Ross says, "but then he called to say he'd be late, something about Lydia, so I told him not to bother."

"Were you rude?" Lydia. She's picturing her not with Sarah, but with Sam, in a hotel somewhere, lingerie, room service.

"Oh, for Christ's sake," Ross says.

"I wouldn't have minded seeing Jack." He would have kept the evening light. "I was surprised to find you'd gone to the office."

Ross presses the buttons for the little motor that adjusts his seat, sliding back one or two inches and then forward. "Peterson called. There's an accounting problem."

"Accounting? I didn't know you still had anything to do with that." Early on, when the law firm was becoming established, Ross had overseen accounting in addition to handling legal issues, but as far as she knew, he hadn't for years, not since the firm had doubled, tripled, in size. "Couldn't they have called someone else? Who's Peterson?"

"That underling I hired," he says, turning into the restaurant parking lot. Ross doesn't mention work very often; to him, mentions shows weakness, a letting up, an inability to keep his professional life out of his private life, a failure in the separation of church and state. When he does refer to it in any way, she always imagines him at his desk in his office, but it's a desk in an office that in no way resembles the building it's actually in; instead, he floats above the city street, and the dimensions are all out of proportion, the desk as large, larger, than their dining room table which easily sits fourteen, and the office the size of a hotel ballroom. Poor Ross is dwarfed.

"The Plagets are already here, and we're early," Ross hands his keys to the valet. "Must be anxious."

[2] Warren and Vicki Plaget and Ross and Angela stand at the entrance to a large room looking out over a sea of diners whose conversations slow to a stop. In fact, conversations rise and fall according to everyone's entrances, including the waiters carrying entrees and salads. The four of them are led to a table in the very center. There are high ceilings, and bright light cascading down from chandeliers, and one wall is nearly all windows, like an atrium; outside, it's dark, so they can all see their reflections clearly. They're all on display. She finds this funny. As they settle their backsides into their chairs, she looks into Ross's

face, and into Warren's and Vicki's, to see if they notice anything amusing. They don't. Conversations around them resume.

Through the crowd, across some twenty tables, sits Althea Smythe and her husband, a man notable for rarely being out in public. Angela hadn't remembered him having that ring of gray curls around the back of his head, ear to ear. She remembers him as utterly bald. Althea's ruff is purple tonight. Angela waves; Althea doesn't wave back. Perhaps the Plagets are unacceptable.

A woman in a party of four sits with her back to Warren, and draped across her chair is a coat of sleek fur. Angela is tempted to reach out and touch it, to see if it's as sleek as it looks, or if it would fool her, and turn out to be coarse. The table's a light wood thickly coated with high gloss. Her face is reflected in it, and Ross's, and the Plagets. Theirs are upside down or sideways to her, but all of them slide around the knotty wood grains, a fun house slipping under their plates, and she can't stop herself from peering into it, or from shifting from side to side to see what that does to their faces.

"Angela?" Ross's voice startles her. She jars the table; the water glasses jiggle. "The menu?"

A waiter stands at her elbow, offering her a menu the size of an airplane wing.

"Angela," Vicki is saying. "Warren and I were at your club last week. Thursday, I think. Playing tennis. Did you happen to be there?" Vicki is struggling with her skirt, shifting her thighs up and down in an effort to keep the skirt, too short, down around them.

"I have no idea."

The fur coat slips to the floor. She reaches to retrieve it, but a waiter gets there first.

After soup and salad, impatient with Vicki's lamb and Ross's bouillabaisse, she announces she's going to the ladies' room. Warren's and Ross's and Vicki's heads turn toward her, their faces like those huge sunflowers, blank. She touches the fur of the coat behind Warren in passing; it's soft underneath, but coarse at the tips, a fringe of tiny wires.

The Smythes' table is between her and the restrooms; avoiding it would be awkward.

"Althea. Mr. Smythe. How nice to see you."

Althea's cheeks turn scarlet under her powder, and her eyelids hit REM speed making her small round blinking eyes like those of a doll, or those visible in the holes of masks. Mr. Smythe, a man she's only seen once or twice but always thinks of as kind, doesn't look up at all.

They might know about Daniel.

"Well," she says, "I'll leave you to your dinners." She hurries off, bumping into one or two diners' elbows. The Smythes live on the other side of town, but their behavior is so odd, what other reason could there be? In the ladies room, breathless, she perches on one of the three small upholstered stools lined up against one wall. They can't possibly know; they must have been discussing something painful, maybe the dog has died. But then again... A very tall, black-haired woman opens the ladies room door; she stands up to go to the mirror, but the woman goes away. As she leans close to the mirror, some dampness from the lip of the sink soaks into the front of her limp pale dress, but she doesn't care. Her lipstick has worn away. She doesn't care about that, either.

Crossing the dining room, her purse covering the damp spot in the center of her dress, she takes the long way back, skirting the Smythes.

"You all right?" Ross asks, raising himself into a little squat over her chair, a courtesy, a lady has returned. He never does this when they're alone. "Just so you know, you were gone a long time."

"Was I? Sorry. I saw the Smythes."

Ross has already returned to his conversation with Warren, something about an easement on some property his corporation is trying to buy from a company with which Warren is connected. Ross, sacrificing manners for effect, puts his elbows on the table to lean quite close to Warren to give the impression he's concentrating on every word Warren says. But Ross has no respect for Warren, and is probably already wondering who it is he really needs to speak to.

"I can't stand chintz," Vicki says. "Do you like chintz? My interior decorator is pushing chintz. I don't know how much longer I can resist."

"Chintz?" What a curious word. She says it again, more slowly. "It sounds like chain link, or a town in Herzegovina."

Vicki stops with a forkful of lamb midair.

"Herzegovina?" Ross says, turning to ask a passing waiter for more bread.

Vicki stares at her plate. Angela hadn't meant to embarrass her, is only impatient for the evening to end. She's about to apologize when Vicki says to Ross, "I hear you travel a great deal."

Ross will warm to this topic, complain about flight schedules and argue, with himself, that while business men support the airline industry, no concessions towards him are ever made. "They're always worried about families. Cut-rates, package deals, accommodations for screaming babies. I just want to fly in peace."

Angela is sure Vicki expected him to talk about the interesting places he sees, or even how he doesn't like being away from home, how the novelty has worn off, but instead Vicki is lectured on the airlines' lack of customer service. Angela loses track of the conversation, although she smiles now and then.

The first thing, and almost only thing, Ross says when back in the car is, "We don't need to invite them to our party in the fall."

Chapter Seven

[1] From under the bright white and bright green striped awning of Lydia's patio, Angela looks across a landscape of wallpaper sample books spread over the tabletop and down into the little orchard with the bench she's never seen anyone sit on. She would like to be sitting there now, looking up through the leaves and branches, but the bench and the orchard are only for show. She's restless, terribly restless, although, as always, careful to not let it show. But then, "Is cheating – sex, adultery – the only vow that matters?" she asks.

Lydia mimics a Victorian air of fainting. "Why Angela. I don't believe I've ever heard you say that word before."

"What word? Adultery?"

"Sex!"

"What about honor, and comfort, and support. What about all the other things spouses promise to do?"

Lydia shuts a book's large flaps, two books, three. "I'm not seeing Sam, if that's what you're talking about."

"I'm not." She's thinking about Ross, how he failed her in the first minute of their marriage, how she's forgiven him over and over for his failure to love or cherish or support because the failure seems to come from some deep, inner lacking, something he can't fix, simply can't offer. Still, these are all vows that haven't been kept. She's failed to keep only one. "We keep doing the same things over and over. It's amazing how few of us are divorced."

"You of all people wanting to disrupt status quo? What's gotten into you?"

"Curiosity."

"Curiosity?" Lydia's eyes take on an unusual cast; for a split second she disappears into a self Angela has never seen before. "Okay," she says, "since you're curious, Sam's considering leaving Sylvia. I'm someone to talk to. It's irrelevant if he thinks I'm attractive."

"I doubt it's irrelevant. Jack is irreplaceable." Ross's failures have become hers. Feeling sorry for him while asking – while knowing there will be – nothing in return has come to define her piece by piece. "Does Sylvia know?"

"Do you think I'm attractive?"

"I'm not your target audience."

But Lydia lifts her chin and straightens her shoulders and unbuttons the top button of her royal blue blouse and pushes out her chest and makes her waist even smaller. But then her eyes grow wide, so wide Angela can see the mascara caught in the spaces between her lashes. "Are you cheating on Ross?" She laughs, and puts her head back to laugh harder. "What was I thinking?"

But just as abruptly, she stops laughing. "I want great sex. Jack is not great sex. I miss great sex. I had great sex once." Lydia's looking at Angela but it's not clear who she's seeing. "Never mind. You're lucky. You never think about things like that. Well, you must, sort of. You brought it up. But, an aberration." Looking down at her blouse, bold jewelry, white pants, bright shoes, "I do look damn good."

"Yes, you do." Angela's wearing a plain shirt, khaki pants, Keds.

"What would I do without you?" Lydia tucks Angela's hair behind her ear; Angela puts it back. Lydia wants to know which friends cheat. "Hillary? Not Susan. But Emily seems to be splitting her seams. I would be, too, if I were married to her troll. You're lucky. You're immune to sensations unlike us mere mortals. I want movie-quality orgasms. Oh, don't blush." But Lydia's the one who looks away. "Jack and I are opposites."

"Don't hurt him. And don't string Sam along."

"We had lunch," Lydia says. "The day I drove down to see Sarah. That's all. We all need a change every once in a while."

"Only lunch?"

"Even you. Although you don't seem to know it. Miss Predictable. I can't even get you to wear a print."

[2] Daniel hasn't been back. The memories are painful, there are so few, but these few she worries like beads. It would have been better if it had never happened, if he'd never come inside. The short severed memories are like shards.

Coming in from Ross errands, she stops to touch the ballerina on the windowsill, and there he is, leaning against the shed just as he had the first night. As soon as she opens the door, he crosses the yard. He takes her face in his hands and kisses her. She pulls him inside, shuts the door against the cold clear glare of the afternoon, and leads him up the stairs to their room; Daniel sheds his clothing, stripping his shirt, his trousers from thin, bare skin. She strips off her own clothes and leans back on the bed and spreads out her arms, reaching her hands across the white guest room cover, vast and clean, like a freshly cut lawn. She's naked as she's never been for Ross, breasts and hips and thighs all at once. As Daniel comes near, it's not her breasts or hips he looks at; it's her eyes, and it isn't with seduction, it's with concern; he wants to please. And because of this she's able to surrender. Even as limbs entwine and body parts connect, sex remains a gentle dance, a letting go, not a vortex into which she disappears.

[3] Daniel met up with the landscaper and is working fairly steadily now, and staying nearby although he won't tell her where. He says he won't be able to predict when he can see her, when he'll have a few free hours, so she tells him Ina's hours, when Ross will be gone, and how she'll leave the back door ajar a few inches when it's safe. She'll be in the study, or at a bedroom window, trying not to watch for him, pretending not to watch, pretending to be doing something besides waiting, reading, or answering invitations – to which she now mostly says no – but she's always waiting.

He's asked to see a puzzle, the globe. He takes it apart and puts it back together effortlessly; even Ross struggled with it a little the last time he took it apart for a guest to show off. Daniel wishes he had his tools with him, the ones left behind in Portland so that he could attempt to make one of these puzzles himself, even though, "I've never thought about spending time making something that isn't absolutely useful." He might get work as a carpenter, helping to build a house not far off, but it would be a rough job, all two by fours.

"Maybe I'll be able to make something for you some day. Tell me, though, why puzzles? Ross doesn't seem to be someone who would be interested."

"He says they remind him that everything can be figured out."

She talks about the flower shop she worked in when she and Ross lived in Back Bay, how she'd dreaded the cut flowers when they first came in the mornings, from the trucks, in their buckets of cold water, all thrown together in beautiful profusion, their souls cut.

"Ridiculous, isn't it? I sound pagan, but there was something wrong with it, even as I watched lovely arrangements go out the front door, to hospitals, and to celebrate anniversaries and births; I always felt something had been lost."

He listens as she finds her way through new conversations. She's never kept a diary or journal; she's always been afraid to put words together anywhere they'd be visible. Her parents believed firmly in conformity, and that growing up meant ignoring passions, dreams, and nightmares.

Making love with Daniel entails what love making always does, kisses and liquids and body parts – Ross never knows what to do with his legs and arms, is always pinning her down with an elbow, or kneeing her thigh, or pressing her hair painfully into the pillow – with Daniel his skin becomes hers and hers his. They move as though each knows what step the other will take, so there's no awkwardness; she imagines luxurious paintings, with bodies ecstatic.

And she tells him about things like the house, how the doors had been turned into windows. She tells him as if it were a joke, a silly thing, meant to expose Ross, but he doesn't smile, recognizing it for what it is. "I'd make your windows doors, if I could," he says; his eyes harden long enough for her to see he's capable of retaliation.

And she describes the time her parents made her stop dancing. She had stood up and begun twirling in the middle of the room one day when they had company, waving her arms rather wildly, unusually free, above her head to music on the radio. Her mother chided, and her father scooped her up and took her from the room and scolded her for embarrassing them. The next time there was an opportunity to dance, she danced only in her head. Then it came to be that whenever she had the urge to dance she imagined the whole of her hands, both palms and all of her fingers, making huge whirls with finger paints, that striking blue, that brilliant yellow.

And he says, "My mother read everything she could get her hands on. Our house was full of overdue library books. She couldn't afford to buy any of her own, and was loathe to give them up. It was one more thing for my father to hate about her. She was pompous, he said, thought she was better than he was, smarter, just because of those books. 'Stupid as dirt, though, when it comes to common sense, and that's what you really need. Common sense. You fill these boys with fluff.' He meant me. I read her books. My brother never did. I had to sneak, listen for him coming in, or take them off into the woods."

"I wasn't as isolated, but it wasn't so very different for me." Her inner joy trampled, she'd come to accept it as an embarrassing product of a childish imagination. She'd allowed the young sensation of possibility, of creativity, to be educated out.

He'd been learning carpentry from a master up north, the shaping of rough pieces, the paring away of imperfections, revealing inner cores, inner natures, of cherry or maple or even pine. "I've never had a chance with mahogany, like that table downstairs." He likes turning raw lumber into beautiful objects that are good to touch and look at and use. With the master car learning how to build fine furniture – "The man is fussy, exac I wasn't allowed to do more than initial cuts, but he taught me to slow down by showing me things like how to sand by hand, down to the finest grade paper." Daniel runs his fingers from the heel of his palm to his fingertips, as though his hand is the wood, and he's feeling what work is still needed. On his own, Daniel made gifts for his mother, salad bowls – "no seams, each one a little sculpture, almost, forming a bowl out of a rectangle" – and book ends and shelves – "with fancy ends" – for her kitchen. "Once, I even made her a whole porch, a place she could sit." The way he talks about the wood, about allowing the grain to determine the object he'll make, reminds her what she'd read about Michelangelo and his marble, about essence in the raw, solid blocks. Daniel's hands are thin, and the skin also fine-grained; she would have expected a carpenter's hands to be rough and worn, with a callous or two on the palm. Instead, when he touches her, it's almost as if he weren't touching her at all; she has the impression of air, and peace. Ross's hands have become wide and heavy and obvious. If they grope her in the dark, she stays still, pretending they can't wake her.

They had both been tentative at lovemaking early in their marriage, but her hesitation had been from inexperience, while his seemed to be not only from inexperience but also from discomfort with exposure, the naked flash, the naked need. She thought that over time he would become more comfortable and willing to do simple things, like look into her eyes when he entered her, or discover a place she wanted touched, or kissed, like the back of her neck, or the backs of her knees. But instead their lovemaking hardened into the perfunctory; there was, presumably, for him, the satisfaction of physical need, but never the sharing of emotion she longs for. She's never satisfied. When she realized Ross was not going to give in any more than he already had, when she realized the time for her suggesting otherwise had passed, and that they had settled into this pattern – his pattern – she was disappointed in a deep, central place; thereafter, with hope erased, she dreaded sex and always came away from it feeling slightly unclean. With Ross it was an unnatural act, uncomfortable, all that mattered being her genitals and occasionally a breast. She forgave him, and blamed herself, her reticence.

Chapter Eight

[1] The wicker chair is the one thing in the house brought from her childhood. It's a light-colored wicker growing dark with age, and oversized, with wide, comfortable arms and room for two or three cushions behind her. She spent hours in it growing up, reading, dreaming. It was there she'd decided which college to attend, and waited for Ross the first time he came to meet her parents. She left the chair behind during college, but had taken it to their tiny Back Bay apartment, though Ross asked her not to. But when it came time to move to the house in the suburbs, Ross wanted the chair left out at the curb. "Let someone have it who really needs it." When she told him she needed it, that it was where she felt most at home, he said, "doesn't wicker belong out of doors?" She reminded him that he'd have plenty from the house where he grew up, that his mother was giving him everything.

"Yes, valuable antiques, good pieces, not paper goods."

"Ross." He gave in, but she saw in a flash she'd been naïve; his denial of her wishes was not a too-busy-with-law-school, law-career thing; it was Ross. Beginning with that conversation, nearly everything she wanted gradually became too much work to gain, and so she gave in to more and more, telling herself all these petty things didn't matter.

In that first house, the wicker chair had sat near a kitchen window out of the way, so it irked him when she put it in the study of this house; she insisted; it was the one thing she refused to give up, but the quarrel robbed her of some of the comfort.

She sometimes thinks that without it, she'd be completely invisible to him. But being so peculiarly invisible to Ross, and even to Lydia and the others, is how she gets away with so much. No one is looking at her closely enough to notice she has a lover.

Sometimes Daniel seems preoccupied. For the most part he comes prepared to be interested, entertained, concerned, amused, whatever's called for, but sometimes he seems distracted. Still, she longs for the sense he gives her that she's not spinning alone through the dark. The longing makes her impatient, almost to pain, sitting with Ross in the car or across a dinner table, listening to him go on about his successes or frustrations or the injustice of the system that has stopped him in some legal track, while nothing whatsoever about her seems to register on his conversation, on his mind, on his conscience. She fears her longing for Daniel is as visible as her dress, or her pendant, since the longing is palpable and living, but Ross – or Lydia – never see it. When Daniel asks about guilt, she says, "It's hard to feel guilty when no one knows where I live."

[2] Midafternoon, Angela answers the door in her robe and with disheveled hair. Lydia has shown up again with no warning. Her eyebrows rise up above her sunglass frames. Angela tries to smooth down her hair, but there's a thick tangle at the back. Daniel hasn't been gone for more than five minutes.

"Napping?" Lydia says.

"I have a little cold. I'm trying to sleep it off."

"Can I come in?" Lydia flounces inside. "Do you have any wine? I could use a glass. I have a dinner tonight with Jack and his most boring business partner, along with his dumpy wife, easily the homeliest woman I have ever met." Lydia's looking around the kitchen as though she doesn't know where the wine is kept. Angela checks the yard; Daniel's out of sight. She pours Lydia a glass from an opened bottle in the refrigerator, although Lydia would prefer a new bottle. "But you know," she says, taking the glass, "you can tell from the way her husband dotes on her that he has never even noticed she's ugly. I couldn't be seen in public."

"If you were the husband or the wife?"

"Both." Lydia presses her palm against Angela's forehead, which makes her step back. "What's the matter? You do seem feverish. Did you take anything? Maybe I shouldn't stay, I don't want to catch anything. You're not nauseous, are you?"

"Wait here. I'll get dressed." Angela hurries up the stairs and shuts the guest bedroom door as she passes it. In her own bathroom, she rinses off her face and washes her hands and thighs, then brushes her hair and puts on a long, loose, caftan. She goes back downstairs to sit at the kitchen table with Lydia; her best friend is unable to sense or smell the fact that she hasn't been alone, that a man has been in the house, in this kitchen, that not an hour before she was making love. Surely she'd be able to tell if it Lydia had just come down the stairs from a lover.

"I saw Sylvia," she says.

"And?"

"She was on her way to meet Sam, for a drink."

"Or maybe they were on their way to see a divorce attorney. He talked about a mediator. Wine?"

Angela shakes her head. "But they looked okay."

"Why do you keep that thing?" Lydia goes to the window to toy with the ballerina, turning it over in her hands, almost spinning it. She complains that its eyes are lopsided, and that it reminds her of the kind of party favor her mother always bought, "the kind I always hated."

"It reminds me of innocence."

"Two days ago he told me they're serious. Or he is."

"He's not leaving her for you, is he?"

"He finds me easy to talk to." Lydia gives a little shake of her shoulders, pleased with herself, apparently.

"Men rarely leave without someone to go to."

"You've conducted a scientific study?" She puts the ballerina on the sill facing out.

"Common knowledge."

"He's testing his emotions. Trying to work things out."

"Is he testing yours?" With the joy and terror of Daniel seeping through seams, threatening to burst out into sentences, while she, too, tests emotions, she almost says she knows how it feels. Instead, she says, "People are going to end up hurt."

Lydia turns to Angela, arms crossed, belligerent. "Angela. Darling. He's gay. You have *got* to promise to keep this between us. I only told you so you'd stop accusing me. I…I used to be…friends with his sister. For some reason he's decided to confide in me. I can't remember how it came up."

"Sam? Are you sure? He and Sylvia seem, I don't know, together."

"Like Jack and me? Don't know why I said that. He doesn't know how to tell her why he wants to leave. He's miserable. Can't do it any longer. They've got those two kids."

"I don't know what to say." Angela has had no experience with this sort of thing, gay lives or closets or coming out. "I never would have guessed." She can't recall a time Sam didn't seem like just another husband.

"You weren't meant to. He was about ten when he figured it out. But grew up in a hard core Catholic family, with a really strict father. A very conventional mother. Two brothers. Both jocks. The sister, who's also gay, by the way, but she came out, and it was rough. Her parents didn't talk to her for years. So he decided he could do without. That it would be no big deal. But that's not working anymore."

"What changed?"

"Couldn't say."

"Has he met someone?"

"Not that I know of."

"Still. Shouldn't he be honest? Wouldn't that be easier on everyone?"

"Would you admit you were gay and had met someone after twenty years of marriage with two kids?"

"I'd like to think I'd be honest." Angela feels the hypocrisy down near her pelvic bone.

"Despite all the hoopla, all the television shows, all the talk, all the rainbow flags and Supreme Court decisions, coming out might never be easy. Not for everyone. Maybe in some towns. In some families. But a minority's a minority. And there's still prejudice. Hate crimes. Who wants to confess into that?"

"You've thought about this."

"It's Uncanny Valley."

"What?"

"The sensation you get when something is close to human but not quite," Lydia says. "Like a robot. But I think it also describes how a lot of people feel about gays and lesbians and all the rest, the Caitlyn Jenners. You're cringing."

"Only about the robots."

"He says it's us and them. He couldn't see doing what his sister did. He grew up wanting to be us. He got married wanting to be us. If he could, he'd stay us. But he can't. He feels like he's missing."

"Missing out?" Angela would understand this.

"No. Missing. Like he doesn't really exist."

Doesn't exist. "Why you for confidante?"

Lydia shrugs. "A little more wine, please, before I take off."

Chapter Nine

[1] "There was no job." Daniel props himself against the pillows. They are naked a few inches apart under the white sheet. "I lied. I had no job in this neighborhood. I still don't. Not in the neighborhood."

He reaches for her, but she springs from the bed, pulling on her robe. She turns to look out the window even as she thinks she shouldn't have her back to a stranger, a liar. Outside, the lawn is littered with the petals of flowers destroyed by rain. "You should leave." She's more upset than she sounds, but these weeks of keeping her second life from Ross and the others have made her capable of seeming to be in control. She sits down in the small chair by the window. She has the beginnings of a headache.

"It was the only excuse I could think of for being here."

Her clothes lie in a heap on the floor near to him; she wishes she were fully dressed. "Why are you telling me now?" A stranger, he was only a stranger who somehow happened to be in her back yard. "What else don't I know?"

"Nothing. You know that my mother died a while back. After that, I wanted to get away from Portland."

She sighs, or laughs, some sound escapes, exasperation, dread. "And you ended up here?"

"Angela."

She'll have to decide about things, how much is true, and whether he should stay, why she allowed it to happen; perhaps even how she'll recover when he's gone, as he surely should be.

"My father's a terrible man," Daniel says, "and with him the only one left up there, I took off. I'd been on the road for a few weeks, getting jobs here and there, always about to head further south, or west, I was never sure. I got dropped near here, couldn't get another ride, was just walking. I know it's hard for you to imagine, no destination, no car, even. I saw you."

"Saw me?" How pale he is, too pale to have been working outside all this time. Why hadn't she noticed before?

"In the front, talking to a man I figured was your husband and someone else, a workman, the gardener, I think. I didn't want to leave."

"Leave what?" she says.

"You. Hasn't that ever happened? That there was someone you couldn't leave?" He pulls a section of the sheet's border through his fingers over and over.

"How romantic," she says, but her voice is dry, and disbelieving, even as she wants to find some truth in it to keep her from shame and disappointment, from dread and a sour memory. "How old are you?" as if this will explain something.

"You know. Twenty-eight."

"Well, I'm too old for you."

"I know how old you are. Look at me," he says. She does, only briefly, because every fiber of his attention is so keen she feels flayed. "I did leave," he says. "The next day. I got all the way to Hartford, but came back, looking for you. I had no plan, no motive. I wanted to see you. Close up. I had the idea you didn't belong here."

"Oh really. So you were coming to take me away?"

"You didn't seem interested in what Ross was saying, or the gardener. You never once looked in the direction they were pointing. You seemed out of place. I know all about that. I usually feel out of place." He's like a child delivering a speech in a play, words tumbling out; there's a hint of them having been memorized; he's probably rehearsed them, imagined what this moment would be like, but now, words spilling. "I didn't see you for three days. Then, finally, getting into that car, Lydia's."

"You admit to stalking me." She knows she should send him away, but whenever he touches her there's a euphoria, a white light.

"It was fate."

"Sounds more like a fairy tale."

"You can't say you're sorry. I wasn't wrong. I took a chance, coming back here. I took a chance telling you the truth today. I lied about a job, that's all. It's what came to mind when you opened the door. I wasn't expecting you to do that," says Daniel.

"What were you expecting?" He only shakes his head. To put some distance between them, to break the confines of the room, she looks out across the lawn. Unusually warm, not even June, the window is closed and the carefully conditioned inside air feels cold and metallic; the outside air would feel light against her skin. "Am I supposed to trust you now?"

"What else is there?" Daniel leans forward, shoulders crouched, coiled, ready. She looks out. There's the shed where she first saw him, and the hedge, where she first saw his shadow and where the gray cat is weaving in and out now; there's the gap through which he disappears time after time, on his way to places he won't tell her about.

"You need to go," she says. "It's getting late."

"There was something at stake."

She turns her wedding ring around and around on her finger.

"I'll come tomorrow." He doesn't reach out to touch her; he doesn't seem to expect any resolution. He stands, suddenly calmer, the coil in his shoulders gone; as he puts on his shirt, he comes nearer to her chair. "Or the day after, depending on how the job goes. I really do have a job now." He stands close, close, but still not touching her. "All right?"

"It scares me to think you were watching me." There are only a few inches between her hand and the hem of his shirt where it rests against his bare thigh. She nearly reaches out to touch it, but what a giving in that would be, what forgiveness, so immediate, and so promising. She chooses instead to have him suffer, if only slightly, and if only for a day.

"I was afraid it would scare you." He steps away, and there is about him a trace of boyhood; nothing, however, contrite. "But I wanted you to know." He finishes dressing; she can't watch. It seems final, his closing himself back up in his trousers and belt. "I'm not perfect. I never meant to be, or to pretend to be." He lifts his hand to touch her hair but stops. "I'll see you tomorrow. I'll at least stop by." How young he is; how old she feels. "I am sorry."

The carpeting in the hallway and on the stairs is too thick for her to ever hear his footsteps. And the kitchen door is too far away to hear him shutting it tight.

[2] He'd studied her, judged her, while she and Ross talked to the gardener in their own front yard, then watched for her, kept track of her, of Lydia, of Ina. But she's the one who called out asking if he needed anything. She's the one who was impulsive, and naïve. She'd looked out of place in her own yard to a perfect stranger. She's believed that her self-control, her reserve, her privacy, protects her. And she's believed she's in control of the relationship with Daniel, that for once a situation is in her hands, even as she can't predict his comings and goings.

She turns to look for him on the lawn, but she's too late; there's no trace; the cat's gone. People leave to go somewhere mundane, shopping, or lunch, and never come back, seeming, to the people left behind, to have fallen off a cliff. If there'd been no Daniel, would she have found a different way?

Chapter Ten

[1] "Just so you know," Ross says at dinner, "if that Peterson calls here, that guy in accounting, don't talk to him." His square jaws march over words, mangle meat.

She pushes her own piece of roast to the corner of her plate. "Why would he call?" People from the office rarely do. "What would I talk about?" She can't even remember the last time his secretary phoned.

"Just don't."

Rinsing out wine glasses after dinner, she can hardly keep herself from snapping the thin stems. And then, without warning, Ross, behind her; his hands on her shoulders.

"Let's go up early."

She puts the last glass upside down on the thin white towel. It has been too long to say no. She turns the ballerina to face out.

Putting on a blue nightgown that falls to her ankles, she keeps her back to the guest room down the hall, the bed there waiting under its white sheets and freshly plumped pillows

Ross lifts the blue nightgown up to her waist and pulls her on top of him and she has to go through the motions from there. She reaches over to turn off the light; when her hair falls over her eyes, she leaves it.

[2] Ina opens the back door to shake out her dusting cloths. Daniel steps forward. Angela, at the kitchen window, races to the back door to make some excuse about the man in the backyard. Ina stands motionless. Daniel has disappeared.

"You see somebody, too?" Ina says, her eyes on Angela, not the yard. She clutches her cleaning cloths to her chest.

Angela peers out. "I don't see anyone. I thought you asked me something." The hedges are dark and still "That gray cat wanders through here from time to time."

Ina nods slowly. "I hope you're not feeding every stray that comes around." Ina's studying her face so closely she feels "I have a lover" must be written there.

"I don't know it's a stray," she says, turning away.

Daniel never seems to know just what time it was, or to be completely convinced it's essential to stay out of sight.

As though casually, Angela later finds Ina in the library – she's wiping off the wooden puzzles – "If I could get these back together, I'd take them apart. It's impossible getting all the dirt out from all these cracks" – and mentions working one less day with no less pay since there's really so little to do here – but she should have waited; her voice shakes, and she's made it easy for Ina to see that freeing her up will free Angela in some way. Ina's eyes are passive, but she's gnawing her lower lip.

When Ina finally, finally pulls away in her car. Angela stands outside the back door, so that Daniel can see it's not Ina.

"Over anxious," he says, coming inside.

"You scare me."

"Sorry."

"How you get by? Where do you go? I've never known anyone so unpredictable."

"I don't need much." His brown pack is at his feet, a pack she imagines holds his whole life, his few clothes, his hat, what little money he has, perhaps even a map.

"But where do you stay? At night?" It's beyond her, who has never left town, not even as a child, without hotel reservations. She picks up a large ripe yellow pear from the fruit bowl and runs her fingers over its blush.

"Don't worry about it," he answers. "I'm fine. Don't think about me when I'm not here."

"You don't think about me?" She's imagining him in some roadside motel, a few rooms on either side of an office under a neon sign with most of the letters burned out. She sees the bed with its worn chenille spread, the picture on the wall torn from some old calendar, a country road; she sees the doorway to the bathroom, a thin, narrow door, and, inside, a shower curtain that isn't quite wide enough.

"I don't like thinking about you with Ross, and so I only think about you, not what you might be doing."

Her nightgown up around her waist.

"Is it that easy for you?" How odd his ability to sever concrete ties, to think of her only as "Angela," apparently, without her life. She wants to know where he is, what he's like when not with her, what he does. "It makes me feel disconnected," she says.

"It's what we have."

She slices her pear into a white bowl.

[3] He traces his fingertips down her throat and between her breasts. He draws a circle around her belly button, once, twice, and follows the skin to the insides of her thighs. Unseen places are tied and triggered to her skin. When he touches the backs of her knees, her knees rise up. "Angela. Look at me." She bites her lip. "Angela," he insists. Carefully, she opens her eyes; his face isn't as close as she'd imagined, and it's as if to allow her to find her way out of a claustrophobia. But it also seems he wants to draw her through some secret portal, so that she's inside and outside of herself at the same time. And now she is. She starts to turn away, not to shut her eyes against him but to find some anchor in the room, the window, or the vanity table, something other than the self she sees in his eyes. But he says, "Don't." She feels both safe and exposed. His eyes are dark and focused. Safe, she is, locked there. And exposed. More naked than her body, lying here next to this stranger who has said, "Let me." Her soul finally – finally – no longer a separate, isolated, ugly, impatient, improbable and inconvenient thing. The duality, what seems now to have been a kind of schizophrenia, not denial, dissolves. Daniel allows for, brings together, her disparate selves. There is one being, one self, soul and substance, mind and sex. All of her is in the here and now. And in this she finds surrender.

She lets him join himself to her, lets him find his way into her cunt, a word she had only ever thought of as crude, but which now seems so fine. And then, it's no longer for her, or about her; she feels him as if it's all of him inside her, his soul, his self, his eyes, and whether or not she comes to climax is no longer of any consequence; she only wants to feel him, to let him know she knows him as well as he knows her. And so. Her own hips and mind feel fluid and this is not sex, not dry intercourse; this is intimacy.

Afterwards, when they're silent, and the sheen of sweat on her skin has cooled and dried, she finds she hasn't retained the sense of all the parts of her as integrated; her soul, that inconvenient, private and silent self, is already drifting off; she wants to make love again, as if to better sew this ethereal self to her material being.

Chapter Eleven

[1] Dressed for the party at the Philips', she ventures downstairs and into the kitchen. The back door stands open; it's unlike Ross to leave anything unfinished. She touches the ballerina. He's circling the perimeter of the back yard, walking in smaller and smaller circles; he looks off toward the hedge, then at the corners of the house, as though tracking something down. She plays with her pendant on its chain, and busies herself getting a glass of water when she sees he's coming in. He stands very close to her, just about where Daniel did the first night; he opens his palm; on it are three cigarette butts. "Whose are these?"

"How would I know?"

"You must know who stands around smoking in our backyard."

"Well, I don't. The gardener, maybe? His new assistant?"

"He has a new assistant?"

"Yes, yes, he does. Or, you know who else, that neighbor boy, maybe he was sneaking some, so that his parents wouldn't know." She says this conspiratorially, as though bringing Ross in on something with her, trying to make them seem more cohesive. "I'm not really needed at the Philips'." It isn't clear to her why they've been invited, or why Ross is insisting they go. "Why not go by yourself?"

"Don't be silly." He stares at her as though her behavior is outlandish.

"I'm not in the mood for a party. I won't know anyone."

"Of course you will. And so what if you don't? You have to go. What excuse would I make? What's the matter with you anyway?"

[2] The Philips greet them at the door and wave them inside where it's crowded and already warm. It embarrasses her to think there was a time she enjoyed these gatherings, enjoyed watching Ross percolate through them. She'd admired his ease, his ability to make his presence felt. But one evening she realized he saw himself more importantly than others did; she saw it in the looks they exchanged after he'd left a conversation, after he'd left behind his pronouncements about the weather, the stock market, the country's values. Worse, she realized, it was an old joke; she was the last one to know. He'd become one of those men who, despite having been identified as having grown pompous, and

despite having unreasonable opinions, still wields power. She doesn't understand how this could be so, when she wields so little.

She wants to stand alone, off to the side somewhere, near the marble fireplace, maybe, but that would call attention to herself, so she stands next to Ross and pretends to listen to the conversation he has put himself into, something about land rights in New Mexico. When he asks her to go say hello to this "lady" and then that, neither of whom she knows well, she smiles up at him and at the faces grouped around his and moves off. She blends into a group discussing shiatsu, feels Daniel's hand press against the small of her back, dissolves into a different group just as a brightly blonde woman is saying, "Europe would do her a world of good." She wanders off, sipping champagne from a tall, skinny glass, hears someone say, "Have you heard? Althea Smythe has been seen out to dinner with her dog Harvey's vet." So that night with the Plagets, she was worried about her own affair, not Angela's. She keeps moving through the crowd, careful to wear a light, satisfied expression. A young man, a waiter, looks like Daniel. Jack and Lydia were invited but are out of town. The waiter has fine hair, wears a white shirt open at the collar, his black bow tie loose; he's carrying a tray of champagne flutes. Ross insists the party's important because he's hoping to make some progress in some negotiation, and he repeated something about some accounting. She sees the Plagets, then Sylvia and Sam; they all wear smiles. She replaces her not-quite-empty flute with a fresh one from the waiter's tray. Up close, he's nothing like Daniel.

"I'd like to go home now," she says to Ross.

"I can't leave yet."

"I'll call a cab."

"Don't be ridiculous. I'll only be another half hour."

Up the open circular staircase, then, out of the way; she finds a bedroom, empty, apparently a guest bedroom. She sits down on a covered chair in the nearly dark room; there's only the patch of light from the hallway. The chair is upholstered in a tight, polished cotton; she feels perched on the top, and then, closing her eyes, perched on the top of the house, looking down, as though into a doll house. Ross probably wonders where she is; she imagines him checking the powder room, the bar, the banquet table, worrying she's taken that cab.

[3] It's as though Daniel's with her in this different guest room. She moves from the chair to the end of the bed where she sits and runs her fingers

across the fabric of the covers. Even in his absence he's substantial, and significant, more than Ross, or Lydia, or whomever she's supposed to be with. Sounds from the party underneath swirl about her feet.

"Angela?"

Lydia's voice seems to have risen up through the floorboards and Persian rug. Angela finds her silhouetted against the bright hallway.

"Angela, is that you?" She switches on the light. The abrupt glare hurts. "I thought I saw you come up. What're you doing? We just got here."

"I...weren't you...in New York?" Angela stands. "I'm just...it's warm downstairs."

She turns the light off. "Scarsdale. Jack's uncle. Sit down. What's the rush?" Lydia arranges herself on the bed, luxuriously stretching out her arms, lying down, taking Angela's hand, and pulling her down beside her. "Pretty dress," she says.

Thinking Lydia will somehow sense Daniel, Angela moves away. "Are you drunk?"

"Who me? Of course not." She runs her hand across Angela's back.

"I think you are."

"Did you see Sam downstairs? He looks so genuine. So honest. I wonder how he does that. I can never hide anything."

"It becomes habit," Angela says.

"Men can be so tiresome. Don't you wish you could run off somewhere?"

"You are drunk. Not like you to overdo. How much have you had?" Angela inches further away, but Lydia takes her hand in both of hers and plays with Angela's rings. A strange sensation materializes, the same feeling she had one afternoon when she was afraid her mother was going to find her under the back steps with the boy from down the street.

Ross could come up and find them. She stands. "Do you want me to get you coffee? Or find Jack?"

"Can't we just stay here a while?"

"I need to go. Before Ross comes looking. Are you coming?"

"No. No. Stay here. Please. I've hardly seen you."

"I can't. I won't tell anyone where you are." Angela leaves her and heads down the stairs feeling disheveled, almost as though she and Lydia have been together in some way. And there are two Angelas, her light brown dress with narrow black trim carrying the illusion of her as her own shadow; an Angela behind the one that is visible; and Ross is watching: Angela, reserved, and Angela, unnerved.

[4] Ross, quiet while they wait for the valet, quiet while they drive home, waits until they are inside their own bedroom to ask, "Where did you go?"

"Go?" She's sitting at her vanity table, inspecting herself very closely in the mirror.

"What are you looking at?" he says.

"Do you mean when I went upstairs? It was too hot where you were. And then Lydia came up." She can see him in the mirror also. "You should play more golf." His stomach protrudes into a bit of a paunch, making the front of his shirt look full, like a pillowcase stuffed with linen. "Or squash."

"People were asking. You were gone for an hour. It was embarrassing."

"Lydia'd had too much to drink so I stayed with her."

"She told me you stalked out of some meeting. Said you were too busy to stay."

"Weeks ago. Why are you two discussing me?"

"And that you're hardly ever at the club anymore." He fingers his cuff links, starts unbuttoning his shirt. "You'd think you were having an affair."

She pauses, says nothing, but then purposely animates. "Oh, please," she says, picks up a brush, puts her earrings away, looks herself straight in the eye in the mirror. She doesn't look like she's lying.

She slips under the covers, her cheek on the pillow facing away. She listens to Ross washing up in the bathroom, to the water running, a cabinet closing. When, heavily, he gets in beside her, near her, he quietly waits. "No apology?" he says.

But their ability to negotiate small moments has fallen away. She only closes her eyes and shifts away without quite moving.

In the morning as they sit across from each other with their coffee cups, she expects some new reprimand, and plans to apologize, in order to bring him to her side, to quiet any more questions, but Ross only scrolls through his phone and checks things off. He'll be gone overnight, DC, this time.

She turns her spoon over and over.

"Just so you know, the gardener will be here tomorrow," Ross says. "I want those apple trees pruned. Make sure he waits until afternoon. I won't pay him if he doesn't."

Chapter Twelve

[1] During one of the few business trips she took with Ross, she drew doodles on a travel brochure while waiting for him in a hotel lobby. She liked what she'd done, circles, concentric squares, boxes shaded to put them in perspective, cones and cylinders, exercises from a childhood art class. After that, it became a habit to pencil little houses, or flowers, or tiny stick families on the edges of envelopes, or on slightly damp cocktail napkins, while waiting for things, the water to boil, a waiter to bring a bill. It was what Rose complained about on her garden club notes, and what Ross hates down the margins of his newspapers and bills. Now she's doodling all the time, while waiting for Daniel, or just after Daniel disappears, or while listening for Ross, or while waiting for Ina to stop cleaning. She needs it, as if the connection of the pencil point to paper is all that's keeping her stable.

"Do you have to?" Ross asks one morning at breakfast, after she's put a column of faces down the margin of the newspaper's arts section. "What's it for?" He points to a series of concentric circles pierced with arrows. "What's that supposed to be?"

She understands her drawings are rarely as good as a child's; they're self-conscious and stilted. "Why does it bother you?" she asks. Some are pictures of objects, a spoon or a vase; others are designs, shapes, energy spilling out the ends of her fingertips.

[2] Ina's day off; the hedges remain dark and still and maddening. What a shame, spending a morning like this, waiting for a man she doesn't really know, for a conversation with a man with whom she has very little in common. She wanders out to the gardening shed and opens the door a little bit. It's dark inside, damp. Ross's gardener brings his own tools, so sunlight rarely penetrates there. Daniel gives her a sort of center; she's not lonely or at loose ends or rattled when he's with her; she feels natural, connected, even in the midst of the fear of getting caught. She props the shed door open, decides to air the room out. She finds a trowel, work gloves. Outside, in the new bed of begonias she chops at the ground. Daniel says it's the same way for him, but she doesn't quite believe him,

not because she thinks he's lying, but because she doesn't believe she's capable of filling empty spaces.

There's a cot in the attic. She could slip it in here. Along with a few things he might need, soap at the small sink, a towel. No flashlights, though. No candles. No cigarettes. "You'll have to be very, very careful, of course," she'll say. "No lights. Not even a match. But you'll have somewhere to go. Just in case."

Two thick, fast growing weeds on stalks as hollow as bamboo have grown up along the fence and she tries to pull them out, but her gloves are too big; she can't get a good grip and her hands slide up the stems, turning their belligerent leaves slimy. She sits down on the ground. She'd expected Daniel. Leaving the trowel and gloves in the grass, she goes inside, lights a cigarette, breathes the smoke in too deeply.

She drives into town, a place to go, a walk to take; she has no Ross errands. Genevieve's has a new display in the window, all lime green, everything, even the mannequin dog. A few doors down is the art store, a place she's never gone in before, although she'd often noticed displays through the windows, the easels, and the canvases. The bell hanging over the door tentatively announces her arrival. Inside, there are all sorts of things she knows nothing about. A saleswoman smiles eagerly, but she doesn't know what to ask. Everything seems to be in black and white tubes or boxes bursting with reds and greens and yellows and secrets. She'd like to buy something, anything, and is considering this when Emily, anthurium-Emily, fields-of-white Emily, comes into her aisle, asking, whispering, really, "Where are the acrylics? Have you moved them?" The familiar face startles her, as though she's been caught stealing.

"Angela Dunnewald," Emily says, although addressing the saleswoman. "I've run out of pink, there's a certain shade. For my ceramics. You didn't know I painted ceramics? Everyone knows. My little hobby."

"How nice." Angela releases the saleswoman to Emily's pinks, and heads for the door, but on the way down the aisle sees all sorts of pencils lined up in neat racks, chunky pencils with soft leads; she hadn't known there were pencils marked 6, even 6B; their tips feel cool, generous. And there are all sorts of paper, stacks of thick pads, some labeled with information about rag content, what's best for charcoal, pencil, watercolor, and she likes this idea, working on fabric, it's a richer notion than drawing on ordinary paper; it seems possible paper full of threads and fibers will both absorb and reflect. She also thinks it's possible that even anything she draws on such paper will seem fuller, more round, perhaps, and more meaningful. Still, she leaves empty-handed; as she pushes open the door, the little bell ringing, Emily appears at the cash register, her hands full of small glass jars, mostly pink.

The moment she opens her back door, the phone rings. Lydia. "I really wish you'd carry your cell. Want to go with me for a swim at the club? The new lifeguard's gorgeous."

Lydia had played with her fingers and rings. "I just saw Emily at the art store. I didn't know she did ceramics." She'd rubbed her back. "I've been meaning to ask why you talk to Ross about me."

"What's that? Do you want to go swimming?" She hesitates. "Look. Forget about the other night. I was drunk."

"Oh, the Philips'? Don't worry about it. I had too much, too."

"A swim?"

The shifting, chlorinated water would be too much, the glare of the sun, the giggling girls, the lifeguard she'd be required to admire, so she says she has to stay home and wait for the gardener.

"Can't you just leave a note? Ever since, I don't know, maybe the ballet benefit, you've been really strange. Ross thinks so, too."

"You and Ross? I wish you wouldn't."

"Well, did something happen? Why won't you tell me?"

Looking outside for the thousandth time, she sees Daniel by the shed, leaning against it, not even looking towards the house.

"Angela. Angela? Still there?"

"Yes." It's unsettling how calm Daniel is, how he lacks urgency.

"Are we still friends?"

"Of course, don't be silly. But please don't talk to Ross about me. I would never talk to Jack about you." She wills Daniel inside. "I'll call you tomorrow. Early."

[3]

"What really made you stop that first day?"

"I told you. I saw you."

"And?"

"I recognized you."

A chill carves the skin next to her spine. He runs his fingers up her vertebrae, as though he knows this.

"Soulmates," he says.

"Oh, please."

But they kiss. And in the study, with the thickly woven carpet pressing into her buttocks and hips, he enters her slowly, and he loves her slowly as if to music. And as he rises and falls he tells her how the word cunt is his favorite because it means the all of her, there, down there, inside her, all those places he can touch only with his cock. Ancient empty places fill. And they whisper these things, and he whispers feel me, do you feel me finding you there, her thighs and buttocks pressed against the coarse weave of the carpet, as if her body were pressed against the earth.

Side by side on the carpet, still breathing hard, Daniel softly says, "I'm sorry, but I need to use your phone." A rude interruption into their quiet, private life, but she says, "Of course," and, "Is there a problem?" He only kisses her shoulder and gets dressed without saying who it is he needs to call so soon after. Dressing also and following him out to the kitchen, she hands him the phone; he kisses her lips, and turns to go outside; there, putting the phone in the crook of his elbow, he lights a cigarette before making his call. Then he speaks with his back to the window where she waits. She's not sure he knows she's there, but she is there, watching him, watching him have his cigarette with someone else after making love, even as she tells herself it's probably only about his job, or about somewhere to live. Although he stands perfectly calmly, and seems to be looking here and there around the yard – once up at the sky – there's something about him, a slight hunch of his shoulders, a slight hunch over the phone, over the very conversation, which makes her feel the conversation is intimate, about something other than a job. When he comes back inside, he hangs up the phone, comes over and kisses her again on the lips, very lightly. "Sorry."

"Everything all right?" She needs more than a simple answer, but at that instant the phone rings, someone outside coming between them again. For a moment she thinks the call must be for Daniel, but it's Ross, calling out from the old-fashioned answering machine he favors, calling out as though he knows she's there. "Angela?"

[4] In the shed, sometimes a towel is still damp. Or there are dried bubbles on the soap. Or an empty paper coffee cup left on a sill. Once or twice, he's used the cot.

Chapter Thirteen

[1] She read somewhere that Brahms sometimes composed with frustrated women in mind, and so chooses this to hear during dinner. The chords. She waits for Ross to complain, but he's busy with his tilapia – inexpensive – stuffed with crab meat – costly. She hadn't been able to resist this small folly.

As she sits at her place at her own dinner table, in front of the meal she's prepared and presented on her own china, listening to the disc she's popped out from its cover, to all of this, she feels peripheral. Ross doesn't feel the white light or smell the sex; he never picks up on the new scent. Why, she's grown a new skin; she felt the new armor after the very first night. It's translucent but also dense and visible, moving with her, and carrying her in it.

"I waited and waited for the gardener," she says, "and finally left to do a few errands. Wouldn't you know it, that's when he showed up. He couldn't have been here very long."

"We aren't going out enough," Ross says, picking at the skin of his baked potato.

"A change of pace."

"I need to keep up with my contacts."

"I get tired of restaurants."

Ross shrugs. "I still need to keep up with my contacts." He helps himself to another filet. He prefers dishes he can't pronounce. In restaurants, he'll produce foreign sounding syllables vaguely resembling French, or Italian, or Vietnamese, but when the waiter frowns, and says, "Pardon me," Ross will look around the table, even roll his eyes, as though questioning how the restaurant could employ a fellow who doesn't understand its own menu. Then, with a flourish, he'll point at words. She wonders how often he gets what he wants, or believes he's ordered. At home, she makes things he understands, even though he sometimes says, "This again?" When they were first married, he once said, "Make whatever. I'm too busy to notice."

"Do you want dessert? There's cake."

"Cake? Who eats cake anymore?" He sits back, the fish mangled but largely uneaten. "I can't finish this. You didn't want it, did you? People are going to stop asking us, if you keep turning them down." He picks up his glass of wine and swirls the last of it before drinking. "What about our fall party?"

"Oh, soon." And suddenly she sees their friends and associates showing up at the yearly fete in costumes and make-up and masks, completely themselves. Ross, and she, too, dressed as themselves. A masquerade!

"We need to set the date."

"I'm tired." No, no masquerade; convincing Ross would take too much energy. "I'm going up to bed," she says. He checks his watch and adjusts something on it, one of its dials or indicators. He has everything there, the time in four separate countries, a stop watch, the date; she wonders about barometric pressure. "Help yourself to desert, if you change your mind. Ina made it." She stays, though, tracing patterns in the tablecloth with her fingertips. The music stops. Her shoe slips off her toes and makes a dull thud on the carpet.

He looks over the rim of his empty glass, not quite at her, but not quite away.

"Things have gotten so routine," she says. "Suffocating. You never feel that way?"

"Can't afford to."

After leaving Emily in the art store, she saw a blue flyer stapled to a sapling growing between squares in the sidewalk, a sapling someone had thought to leave, appreciating how much work it had taken to be there. A drawing class was starting at the high school; "Even Beginners," it read.

Across the expanse of linen and dirty plates and faded light, she announces, "I've decided to take an art class. At the high school. Tuesday evenings. It shouldn't interfere with your schedule."

"Art class." He laughs a little. "Aren't you a little old for that?"

[2] Ross, propped against pillows, reads his papers in bed; she'd fallen asleep in her thin silk robe with nothing underneath. As she climbs out of bed, the hem catches in the bedcovers, and is pulled away from her body, exposing her breast and thigh to a man to whom she does not want to be exposed in any way. Although she swiftly pulls the robe free and doubles it across her chest, Ross, she knows, has seen. He pretends to be engrossed in his papers, to have seen but not to have cared about his wife's breast, unusually there, bare, though untouched, her thigh, white against the black of her gardenia silk.

Ross's eyes follow her across this room, and it's as if his hands are touching places she does not want him to think about, between her legs, her nipples, insistent as he sometimes is, desperate. She feels sullied, and pulls the bathroom door shut with gentle resolution.

She's thought, sometimes, not of leaving Ross, but what life would be like if he magically vanished (not into death which would mean funeral arrangements and deciding to what degree to mourn.) Since there isn't much to the way she lives, she'd likely amount to the same alone as she does with him. Who can truly justify drifting away from a marriage just because it's a bit boring? There are worse things. Perhaps she was, alone or with Ross, trapped by an inability to rise above it.

For a year or two into the marriage, despite seeing Ross more and more clearly, she'd clung to the belief her marriage would bring some attention to her and her wishes and whims, to the hope that marriage – that grown up thing – would free her from her parents' fear of whimsy. To them – and to Ross – a mind free to dream was a mind open to chaos.

Chapter Fourteen

[1] On the first Tuesday, there are twelve students. Housewives, a plumber, a history teacher, Angela. It had been a long time since she'd introduced herself to strangers. Her voice shakes. "Hello, I'm Angela Dunnewald," and she adds to herself, "I have a lover." When the person beside her speaks, she calms down. She'd mattered only for a moment.

She can't even hold a soft-tipped pencil correctly. The teacher says do this, try that, and what first appears on the paper taped to her easel is exciting, but then it disappears and disappoints, and she has nothing left. She's discouraged. She considers leaving. But the teacher – a man with large features and pock-marked skin and a shirt that doesn't appear to have ever been ironed, blue, rolled up to his elbows, his name Mr. Campowitz; all of the adults call him Mr. Campowitz, never Ed – comes by and tells her that drawing is both easier and harder than it looks.

"Once you get the touch right, you'll think you've taken flight. Try this," and he takes her hand with the pencil in it. She doesn't like his holding her hand. "Loosen up," he says, shaking out her wrist. She feels ridiculous. He turns her hand and the pencil this way and that and suddenly she has a nicely shaded circle.

It's exciting to have the new class to tell Daniel about because she always seems to have so little; he would talk about someone he'd worked with, some thing he'd noticed on the street, some child, or some tree, or how the stars had looked last night, while she has never had anything new, or anyone new, or any new observation, but now she has this.

"There are twelve of us. Everyone but me has a real place in the world."

"You have a real place."

"They have jobs, kids – they all seem to have a stance, a take on things. A vision."

"You do, too. You just haven't said it out loud."

"It'll be interesting to see what we each choose to draw. Even the plumber probably has demons." They laugh, but then he says, "You think people only draw demons? What will you draw? Me?"

"Yes."

Coming to the kitchen window to watch him leave, she's startled to see Jack there, carrying a golf club he borrowed. He's standing absolutely still, staring in the direction of the shed. She opens the window above the sink and calls out, "Jack?" While she was still upstairs, she'd seen Daniel stop to light a cigarette; Jack might have seen him.

"Oh," Jack says, "there you are. I thought you were off with Lydia. Who was that guy?"

"What guy?" She touches the plastic ballerina's skirt.

"I could have sworn I saw someone between the shed and the hedge," he says, reluctantly turning his back to the yard to prop the club against the back door. "I'll leave this here. But keep an eye out. Jesus, don't hesitate to call the police." He faces the yard again, clearly not comfortable with his back to it.

"Don't worry. I'm locked up tight here."

[2] She walks around the shed, and then again, before opening the door wide. Inside she touches the cot, a towel, and one of the four small windows. She rubs a circle into the grime of a pane with the palm of her hand. In a few places along the walls and under window sills, spiders' webs are as thick as silk. But she imagines clean walls, a chair, a table; she imagines herself drawing; she sees a studio. She's tried the study, and the library, but always feels she has to put her things away, that someone's watching, or that Ross will laugh at her efforts. She'd sat with her sheaf of drawing paper in one of the out of the way guest rooms, not the one Daniel and she share, but she'd felt like a foreigner, and couldn't find herself in it. The walls, the color, pink, felt artificial; she was the guest. There's a desk, but a lady's writing desk, an escritoire, with a too-small surface. Everywhere she'd gone in the house made her feel itinerant.

Why not the shed? But the idea of having to explain it to Ross…but then, in her mind, in one swift movement, she moves old boxes and tools and rakes (and the cot) outside. She sees the old things in the yard, scattered every which way, and Ross coming home. He might ruin it for her. She'll wait, then, until sure. But as soon as she's back inside, looking out at the shed over the ballerina's head, she's quite sure, and, by the time Ross comes home, not only are all those boxes and tools (and cot) on the lawn, but she's up to her elbows in soap and water; when he appears in the doorway, she realizes she's been humming.

"My new studio." She blushes, wiping away the wet hair on her cheek with the back of her soapy hand.

"Are you kidding me?" Ross expels some small syllable, shakes his head and walks away, but then comes back to say, "There's no room in the house? How did the cot get out here?"

"I've tried the house," she says. Excited, about to tell him what she plans, forgetting that it's unlikely that he'll cares or listen – not exactly forgetting; she never loses hope that he will – Ross sits down on the broken step. He seems unsure, sunken.

"You could at least have gotten Ina to help you," he says.

"Lydia's between housekeepers. She's over there today. What's wrong?" His eyes dart from the house to the patio to the garden – what does he know? The fact he's sitting on a narrow, cracked step – "Remember that thing with Peterson?" he says. Oh, nothing having to do with her. But here he is, once again, managing to rob her of her moment; whatever's happening with him is more important than whatever is happening with her, and not only more important, but capable of obliterating it. "It's a bigger mess than I first thought."

"Peterson," she says, feeling half-hearted, but trying to show enthusiasm. "You didn't tell me much about it." She always feigns enthusiasm, afraid that if she ever indicates she's bored, they'll have no relationship whatsoever.

"In accounting," he says.

She glances back inside the shed door. She pictures a drawing table, an easel at the window. "Is that the same Peterson, someone's nephew, just out of college, the one you hired a year or so ago?" She'd like shelves, and a chair or two.

"That's the one." How odd, his sitting down like this; she certainly doesn't want to hear he's suspicious about her in any way, or that a young man has been seen in their back yard, but she still half hoped that what he had would have had something to do with her, some money problem, some stock failure, some decision, anything. Lights. She'll need lights. Although the room is already remarkably bright.

"He sneaks around –" Is he talking about Daniel after all? "He got by my secretary, insists there's something wrong with the books. I look, he shows me, but I don't see anything. But he's convincing, he's so sure. Somehow he's managed to make me feel I'm at fault somehow."

"You?" she says. Once, when he'd broken a teacup, had all but dropped it on the floor, he'd blamed the table, saying it was too small. "What kind of problem?"

"Missing funds, what else?" He shrugs and stands up.

Some cheating, some theft.

"It's why I went to our accounting firm party, at the Philips'. To develop an inside track. If something's wrong, maybe it's behind their doors, not ours." He sighs with such force his cheeks puff out.

"What can I do?"

"I'll call someone to cart this stuff away."

"No, about Peterson, the books." The fraud, the adultery.

"What could you do?" And off he strides paying no more attention to her new studio and already looking like himself. She tosses the soapy water from her bucket across the grass. If they'd been in the house, in their usual places, she doubts he would have mentioned Peterson or Philips or his suspicions in quite the same way. It was more likely that, over dinner, or in the car on their way somewhere, he would have turned it into a boisterous announcement, pronounced whoever it was a bastard, and talked about prosecution to the fullest extent of the law. That he'd spoken in this way while sitting on the shed steps made it seem as though there's already something about the shed, the studio, capable of removing them from their practiced lives.

[3] Mr. Campowitz puts out stuffed animals and tells them to pick one to draw. He laughs with them, but says it's an excellent way to discover texture. The plastic or the fur, the cheap ribbons, the felt of the paws, that's what they need to be after, the differences in the surfaces. Angela choses a stuffed bear. When Mr. Campowitz comes by their drawing tables, with suggestions and comments and encouragement, he stays near Angela's a little longer than he has the rest.

"It's pretty bad," she says.

Mr. Campowitz shifts his weight to his heels and rests his hands on his belt. He squints at her and then at her work. She thinks he's going to suggest she quit.

"You don't have much technical experience."

"I know, I..."

"But you always have a dimension that's intriguing. Don't give up. It's important."

With one brief nod, he moves on, leaving her to sit in a small but very bright circle of satisfaction.

Putting her pencil to her paper on her own, with one thing in mind, but accidentally doing something else, she's frustrated by her inability to create with her hand what she sees in her head; nevertheless, the effort is wonderful and visible.

Come winter, the studio will need a heater.

Chapter Fifteen

[1] Lydia, dropping by to pick Angela up for brunch at Beth's, finds her in the gardening shed humming while maneuvering a mop with long stringy yarns into corners.

"I can't believe my eyes," she says. "What the hell are you doing?" A little lipstick's caked in the corner of her mouth. "Ina told me you were out here, but wouldn't tell me why."

Where does Ina put dirt? She seems to be only pushing it around. Ina should be paid more. "The brunch. I completely forgot."

"Well, hurry up. Go get ready. There's still time."

Angela has spent years avoiding being cause for disappointment, even when it left her disappointed. Not today. "I am so sorry."

"You're not coming," she says. "You're not coming?"

"Forgive me."

"I can't wait to tell everyone you preferred to stay home with your mop. Cinderella."

"Maybe I should have vacuumed first." Her bucket of soapy water is brown and full of grit. "Just tell them I'm not hungry."

Lydia stays on the broken step, her hands clasped in front of her, her eye on the mop as though it might ruin her shoes. "Really, what are you doing?"

"I'm going to draw in here. I want a space of my own."

"Well," Lydia sniffs, "better than Henry's wife. She took up trekking and ended up in Nepal. Or Frank's, who's surrounded with astrology charts." She screws up her nose. "But you're really not coming? I've barely seen you."

Angela holds the mop steady. "I'm sorry." And she is, about hurting Lydia, and letting her down, not about finding this place of her own. "I just can't." She attempts a joke. "I'm having too much fun with my mop."

"It's like you're having an affair. I should have one. Then you would know how this feels."

[2] The twelve-feet-by-fifteen studio is the largest space she's ever had without a mother or father or husband in it. New curtains, a small couch, and an

easel with wooden knobs and compartments to accommodate all sorts of brushes and pencils and paint.

A disconnected memory keeps popping up: her trip to Palm Beach, where by then her parents had a condo; her father had been hospitalized for influenza. With his case deemed not serious, he was resting comfortably, she flew home, only to arrive with the phone ringing, her mother, in tears. It still happens that if the phone rings at night she might hear insistent tears intertwined with the real time conversation. Now, as she fixes up her studio, she finds herself replaying the sequence – the hospital, the flight, her mother's tears – over and over, as though there were still something she could do to change it. It's no doubt prompted by Daniel mentioning his mother's death, and the studio is bumping her up against reality. Then, without warning, with a warped sense of time, as if it's about to happen again: a few days before the first anniversary of her dad's death, at the close of a telephone conversation with her mother during which they discussed Ross's job, how big the condo seemed, a party she was about to give, her mother said, "Your father wasn't very old, you know." The day after that, the building manager called and identified himself, but she didn't recognize the name, didn't understand his connection to her, even as he gave the name of the condo complex. "Your mother died in her sleep," the man was forced to say more than once before she understood his words.

[3] She waits on the stool in the studio for Daniel. When he appears, she calls out, "Come in, it's ready."

He never wears all the new clothes she's bought for him at the same time. He'll have on a new shirt one day, but his old pants, or, like today, new pants, but the shirt with the hole in the elbow.

"I like it. Why didn't you ask me for help?"

"I enjoyed doing it. I felt I was building something. Something of my own. I know I can draw here, maybe even paint. And you and I fit perfectly. Ina has instructions not to come out, not to disturb me, the artiste, you know. Ross thinks I've gone mad."

Daniel touches her paper, a pencil, the wooden knobs on the easel, then sits down tentatively, on a light colored chair near the door. "It's like sitting inside you."

When she first tries to draw something there, going out as soon as Ross leaves for work, she's so excited she can't think of a thing to put down on the paper.

She's self-conscious; there seems to be an audience waiting for her to fail. How will she ever justify doing this? What, she wonders, will she call the room after she fails and can no longer call it a studio?

But in a few days she's accustomed to freedom. With the house looming above, she and Daniel make love on the white couch, and in this room, in this studio, it's safe, warm, with her drawings all around, some tossed to the floor, rumpled, torn, evidence of frustration, and some tacked to walls, evidence of success.

[4] Only eight students are left. Both men, and five other women, the quieter ones, not the ones who shared anything and everything loudly. Before classes, they talk about what they've drawn, discovered – often a confirmation of something Mr. Campowitz has said. She likes them all, but especially enjoys Melanie, who has an "Art is Basic" sticker on her car bumper; Angela doesn't know anyone else with a bumper sticker. They sit next to each other at the long table, or at their easels. She's about Angela's age, but with four – four – children, three boys and a girl. She says she's trying to hang on to some thread of herself during these kid-years, but she laughs, which leads Angela to believe that the parts of her life, as wife, mother, friend – she has no doubt Melanie has lots of friends – artist, co-exist quite comfortably, while the parts of her own, wife, lover, friend, possibly artist, are in uneasy competition.

Between Tuesday classes to which she often brings homemade cookies, Melanie calls to see if Angela's practicing the way Mr. Campowitz hopes. "Although you're already better than the rest of us."

And on each Tuesday, Ross asks, "You're doing what?"

For class, she puts on baggy khaki pants, an old shirt of Ross's and a brass and copper and beaded bangle bracelet originally bought for a Halloween party. Lydia is appalled. "Hippie? Hipster?"

Mr. Campowitz puts out boxes, baskets, a rubber ball, a dusty plant. Pick one, he says, and think in terms of contour, not details. And contour, not details, is how she now sees her life.

"Squint," he says. "Watch what the light does."

She feels silly, but squinting does reveal shapes in the shadows.

Chapter Sixteen

[1] She and Daniel aren't always tender. There's a new urgency, or fear, as though time is running out; or anger; perhaps all these things; she doesn't understand what they're looking for or trying to assuage.

Sometimes it doesn't seem to be love they're making. The shed – the studio – has brought out more in each, raw expression; the house defined them more than they realized. Now, he doesn't always release her from sensations that hover between pleasure and pain – teasing her nipples causes her clitoris to swell to near bursting, but he refuses to touch her there – and he refuses to release her, even when she begs him to stop. "You don't really want me to," he says. But she can also take him to the edge with a caress of the thin skin at the base of testicles, perhaps, while touching her tongue to the whorl of his ear. She doesn't stop when he begs, either; it's as though they are under a distinct pressure of time, as though they want to be sure to reach the peaks and depths inherent in every possible sensation before time runs out. They dig their nails into flesh, and drive themselves into each other beyond passion, as if to punish themselves for all they've taken. They never say this. She never says not now, or not today, because however much they seek, more always seems possible. The word passion seems too small, overused, and trivial.

[2] "Why do you lock the studio?" Daniel says, drawing himself out of her and sitting up on his knees. "You never locked the shed."

She covers herself with her hands, shocked by the sudden loss.

"I don't want Ross in here."

"I'd like a key."

"I worry we'll be discovered." She knows it has more to do with a new need for control.

"I feel like an animal, hiding in the bushes."

"You didn't use it that often when it was a shed."

"Often enough," he says. "When we were together in a room in that huge house, it was like a dream, a fantasy." He stretches the length of her body; the sun shines in through the window panes on their skin. "This is so much more real, so much more definite."

"And better?"

"The dream was interesting, but this is good. I want a key."

"I feel more like myself as soon as I come through this door. I can even see who you are more clearly." She sits up and clasps her hands around her knees, aware of her naked breasts, thighs. "I didn't know what to make of your self-possession at first. I envied how you were absolutely yourself and no one else, I was jealous, but I admired it." Daniel rolls over and traces designs down her back with his fingertips.

"I know."

"It didn't seem fair. You were too young to be so far ahead of me."

"There's never been much to separate me from myself," he says. "No money, no clubs, no overwhelming marriage. But when I saw you, I knew who you were."

"Would I ever have on my own?"

She's brought an old fashioned pitcher and bowl from the house from which they wash themselves. She draws the sponge across his shoulders, the cool water, and down his back and between his thighs and then she lies on top of him, body to body, skin indistinguishable from skin; it's painful, close to worship, and sacrifice.

And there, in the mornings, after Ross, and before Daniel, she practices with her pencils and pastels. A corner of the room or something as simple as a spoon. But she's aware of the finite, the edges of that spoon, that room, the dimensions of her relationship with Daniel. It can't last. It won't last, key or no key, not in a twelve-by-fifteen-foot room.

Part Two

Chapter One

[1] Ross is pleased with himself. "You're going to Seattle. Just so you know. First week in August." Just in from work, "Any mail?"

"I'll miss my last art class."

"We haven't done much together lately and I only have two, maybe three, meetings. Rest of the time we can sight see."

"Lately?"

This doesn't sound at all like Ross; he must have talked to someone, Jack, Lydia, about how distracted she is, how obsessed she seems, with drawing, of all things; Lydia might have said she seldom she leaves the house. Angela would rather have the Ross she's used to.

"Can't we do things together here?"

Settled into his wide first class seat, Ross will read her parts of articles she's not interested in, take over her armrest to manage his laptop, complain that his scotch or wine or whiskey is too warm, or too cold.

"You don't wanna go?" he says.

"Of course it would be nice, but you're always so busy, I wouldn't want you to think you have to entertain me while we're there."

"I won't. If I get busy, you can shop."

[2] To calm Lydia, she tries, "Lunch before Seattle? Back Bay? Today?"

"You're breaking up with me and need a public place so I don't make a scene. I can make a scene anywhere. Just do it over the phone."

"Very funny. Pick you up at noon."

On the way, Lydia jumps from topic to topic, none leading anywhere, until she finally says, "Really, what's going on? You've dropped us, all of us. Not just me."

"It's not that bad."

"Oh, it's that bad. One day, Angela; the next, someone else. It's like you're cheating on me. I'm trying not to take it personally. Should I take it personally?"

"Absolutely not. I'm learning how to draw. Paint. Takes time. Concentration." She considers turning at the next intersection to take Lydia home.

"You keep saying that. But I don't think that alone would turn you into a recluse. Jack told Ross he should take you somewhere before you become Emily Dickinson."

"Jack said Emily Dickinson?" A quote from *Business Week*, perhaps.

"I'm saying Emily Dickinson."

"Why shouldn't I have something?"

"In any case, you two haven't gone anywhere in ages. You wouldn't even come with us to Napa last year."

"Ross couldn't free up any time." They'd talked about going, then briefly considered some island or other, but she'd let the idea die. Wherever they are, he only wants her to notice what he does.

"So, Seattle. You can't blame us for being worried."

"There's no reason to be." In Venice, she'd found herself wishing she was there alone, so that she could *see*, but to keep Ross happy she'd had to pretend her perspective mirrored his. And so much of what he sees displeases him. So much makes him uneasy. Hotel beds are too soft, or too firm, or the limo driver drives too fast, or too slow, or the food is too spicy, or too bland. And Venice was, of course, sinking.

"Seattle's nice," Lydia's saying. "Ever been there? Rather gray. All that drizzle. But sort of pretty. Good food. Not the best shopping. What are you wearing? Need something new? Like a raincoat? A bright yellow slicker?"

The raincoat would give then something to do, but – such stiff fabric.

"Wish we were going with you," Lydia says.

"No, you don't."

"I do." She rests her hand on Angela's arm. "Not there, though. I'm tired of busy. Some place to relax. Just us, maybe. Wouldn't that be crazy? Just us at some resort?"

"You'd be off with the scuba diving instructor or some hang gliding guy before I had time for sunblock."

"Would not."

Chapter Two

[1] Ross decides he needs to fly out two days ahead of her. "Just so you know, there's a problem with your ticket. The girl got it screwed up, got you coach, instead of first class. I tried to change it, but it would mean a long layover in Denver, and you don't want that."

He calls once from his hotel room to tell her what the scenery out the window looks like, how he can see water and the needle, and to ask when she's coming.

She's in their bedroom with her open, nearly empty suitcase on the bed, saying "You don't know?" just as Ina comes in carrying hangers of blouses. Angela shakes her head and whispers, "Ross doesn't know when I'm coming."

"Don't worry," Ina whispers back, "you'll have a good time. He's absent-minded sometimes. He's so busy and all."

Ross says "Gotta go," and the line dies.

"Why do we all forgive him for everything? I'll never understand how some people get away with these things. Does your husband ever forget where you are?"

"My husband is not a big man like Mr. Dunnewald. He doesn't have responsibilities. But, no, he's never forgotten me or our kids. He's a good man." She rushes to finish. "Mr. Dunnewald is a good man, too, in a different way."

[2] She nearly misses her flight. The phone rings and she rushes to answer it thinking Daniel, but it's only that Peterson fellow Ross warned her about. (Disappointed, and startled, she hears herself say, "I'm not supposed to talk to you." Peterson splutters something and hangs up.) The garage door won't quite close; she catches every red light; the parking garage's full and she has to take the shuttle from an outlying lot. Finally, neatly-settled passengers watch her push her purse and pull her carry-on up the narrow aisle to 21C. Rising above the seats in front of her are the crowns of two balding men. But there's no one beside her, and only one very young woman in the seat across the aisle. She's looking forward to one of those little bottles of screw top wine.

The young woman stiff arms the seat in front of her as they taxi. On takeoff, it seems possible she'll push herself right through the back of it. Her eyes are scrunched tightly shut. The woman, no more than twenty, twenty-two, wears jeans, and little black shoes and a white blouse with a large, floppy embroidered collar. Her long, dark hair is full of tight curls that shoot out from her head like the endings of nerves. At her feet like a pet is a large, lumpy brown leather bag. When she opens her eyes, she looks right at Angela, who tries to look as though she hasn't been watching.

At this moment, Ross might be sitting in a board room, leaning back, while everyone else leans forward, eager, conciliatory, but Ross, his paunch in front of him, will sit back, on the verge of impatience, or to give that impression.

"Excuse me," the woman with the hair says. "Excuse me, but can I come sit next to you? I'm afraid of flying, I'm too scared to sit here alone right now."

There must be somewhere else she can go, although glancing around, Angela sees no other empty place. "Well," she says, lowering her snack table as if to put it between them.

"I promise not to bother you. I won't say a word." The young woman's voice breaks. The girl does seem unhinged. "For a few minutes." She'll simply ask her to move back, or go across the aisle herself if she has to.

She turns to the window, expecting land or water, a great lake, perhaps, but beyond the scratched pane there are only clouds so bright they seem to be shrieking. The woman moves in beside her, dragging the brown bag with her. "Thank you. Flying really freaks me out. I'm Mary."

Angela nods but in order to discourage conversation pulls out the in-flight magazine. "Borneo Beaches." "Big Ideas for Small Spaces." Cat carriers and lawn sprinklers and perfume for sale.

The plane trembles. Mary gasps. "Are we all right?"

"It's just a little turbulence." Mary's face is white. Angela decides to tell an attendant, and can see two, but they're both in first class. Then, one emerges from the galley with a beverage cart. Mary blows in and out rhythmically as though practicing for childbirth. Finally, finally, the attendant arrives.

"Beverage, miss? How about you, ma'am?'

Mary produces a fistful of dollars. "Yes, two bottles please, two bottles of anything." The attendant hands over two bottle of red wine. "And for you?"

"Wine, white, but more importantly..." The plane shudders and Mary cries out.

"Oh, you poor dear," says the attendant, Diane on her name tag.

"Haven't you flown before?"

Angela is distracted by Mary's blouse. On her side the broad collar is fine, quite normal and flat, while the other is threadbare and cockeyed, its embroidered flowers nearly gone, a few threads poke through, looking picked.

"This turbulence, it's minor. We're above a small storm. We're just fine." Diane says.

"We're not going down?"

"Of course not. Look, when I'm not busy, I'll come back and talk. Flying bothers a lot of people."

"Excuse me." Angela's feeling unsteady herself. But Diane is trundling on with the drink cart. One of the bald men is listening in; she can see his ear pressed against the crack between the seats. "Cheers," says Mary. She pours out one bottle of wine and drinks it down completely. "Maybe I should have had vodka." She opens the second and shivers. "Not exactly vintage."

This woman, the loud clouds, the balding heads with their traces of hair, one weakly brown, the other gray, coffee smelling of yesterday, someone else's tomato juice. She unscrews her own wine and pours it into the small plastic cup. A little sloshes over the top.

That night, after Ross told her they were going to Seattle, after she'd put up her little resistance, he'd added, "Why wouldn't you want to go? It's not like you have much going on here."

"Well, the garden club, a lot of decisions are coming up," she'd said.

"I thought you'd quit."

"I'm undecided. I don't want to let anyone down."

Ross had turned away on his pillow. His hurt seemed genuine during the days that followed, so she'd given in by performing small acts of enthusiasm, like asking what hotel they were staying in, and if they would be leaving the city at all. She was relieved when Ross said no.

The plane creaks. A change in air temperature perhaps. And the engines rev up. Mary's sitting with her eyes closed, moaning softly, with no let-up, a chant, bees, a wire about to go short. The chanting suddenly stops. "What's your name?"

She hesitates. "Angela." Mary only drones on again, a dentist's drill, sports commentary, a car ride that's too long, a day too hot. Angela leans her head back and closes her eyes and tries to think of pleasant things, her wicker chair, her drawing, her studio. And Daniel, but there's a bit of a thorn in that.

"How are we doing?" Diane, dark hair in a coif, dark blue suit with a little dandruff on it, wide red smile, is back, perched on the arm rest across the aisle.

"This woman's seat is actually over there, where you are.. She's not doing very well, and I don't think..."

"Meet Angela," Mary says. "She's so nice. I fly all the time, but I always hate it." Mary pulls at her hair, gathers it off her forehead, forces it into a bun. Angela has to move to make room for Mary's elbows. "Some trips are worse than others. This one is terrible." When Mary releases her hair, it bounces off in a thousand new directions. "But Angela is my Good Samaritan."

Mary fidgets; chaos rises up through Angela's skin. "I have some work to do," she says. She finds a piece of paper in her purse, and a pen, and starts drawing lines, squares, intertwined boxes, trying to make it look like she's designing something, and has decisions to make.

"What was that?" Mary shouts. Angela jumps.

"I didn't hear anything."

"Angela?" Mary's face moves within five inches of hers. "Could you just hold me?"

Hold her? Her hand, surely she means only that. She presses her shoulder against the window. "You'd better call an attendant."

"Please." Mary is nearly in tears, and her face is ghastly white.

"I'm going to call an attendant." She reaches for the call button, but Mary releases her seat belt, raises the arm and falls across Angela's lap. Oh, the head, the body, the curls, how soft, but in her mouth and nose. She pushes the hair down, trying to get it out of her face, trying to say, please, sit up, when Mary says, "Oh, thank you, that's great." She has mistaken Angela's gesture for a caress.

"The turbulence is over," she says. "You can sit up now." Mary only trembles.

Angela feels Mary's texture, her shape, a doll in an antique shop, a thin kitten too young to take home. Her hair's being parted by a comb of metallic air from the nozzle over her head. She shifts her feet, cramped by their bags, and pulls down the blind to block out the sun, so bright now it's making her head feel dented, but that turns their seats into a box made of cardboard, dimly lit. She has never been this close to a woman, not even Lydia.

The attendants move down the aisle like sloths, delivering trays of lunch in slow motion. Mary's hair smells of apricots and overripe fruit. By the time plates are put on their trays, Angela's so agitated she fears she'll scream, but only says, "Mary, please." The food looks better than expected. Chicken in a white sauce, and long, bright green beans; apple crumb cake for desert. "Mary. I'd like to eat."

But Mary doesn't move.

"Excuse me, Diane," she calls out, but Mary interrupts. "More wine, two more, here." She fishes dollars out of her pocket without sitting up.

"This isn't right," Angela says.

"Did you request something else? Kosher?" Diane asks.

"Not the food. This woman in my lap." She actually laughs.

Mary clings to her arm like a lifeline, and rocks back and forth. "Don't make me get up."

"We're short-handed today." Diane moves out of reach.

Angela laughs again, not her usual two or three note gesture, but an embarrassed, rather loud laugh.

"Oh God, I'm dying," Mary says.

"Oh, I don't think so." She unscrews the cap of Mary's third bottle of wine. "What in the world are you doing here? Why fly at all?"

"My parents. They don't like Boston, so they insist I go out to see them." Mary takes her mouth out of the folds of Angela's skirt. "I can't tell them I'm afraid to fly." If Angela were to touch the fabric, she knows she'd find saliva there. "They wouldn't understand. They wouldn't even hear me." Mary sits up only long enough to finish off her wine.

During a drive home last winter, Angela slid down an asphalt hill coated with a thin film of black ice. The surface of the road had looked perfectly normal when suddenly it was as though her car wore skates. At the bottom of the hill was a woman with two kids in snow suits about to cross the street. The woman glanced up and saw the car that seemed to be at a safe distance; there was no way of knowing the car, brakes useless, was sliding uncontrollably. The woman, who probably crossed this street every day and had never had anything bad happen before, stepped into the street leading a child with each hand. Angela shouted at her through the closed windows. As the woman realized the car was careening, her mouth opened wide, her eyes, Angela looked on as the children's bodies flew through the air into snow banks. She came to a crooked stop as the car sidled up to the snowbank next to where the children had landed. It took her a moment to realize that they had not been lifted through the air because she'd hit them. She looked at the three of them safely and miraculously on the curb, almost without comprehension. The woman, though, was angry, as though she'd nearly hit them on purpose. Angela lowered her window to explain and apologize, but the woman only pulled the children to their feet and marched them away.

She'd planned to tell Ross about it. She wanted the comfort of sharing the near disaster, of taking the opportunity to spell out the worst case scenario, in order to cleanse the possibilities from her mind. But she knew he'd say, "Nothing happened, what's the big deal?" And so she kept the incident to herself.

Diane retrieves her untouched plate. "All finished here? You had enough?" The surface of the white sauce hasn't even been disturbed.

A movie starts. She doesn't bother with earphones.

[3] Angela wakes up when Mary sits up to put herself together. "I feel better. It happens this way sometimes. I think my body gets sick of being scared."

Angela's lap feels empty with her gone. She brushes herself off as if there were crumbs.

"Do you work?" She hadn't known she would ask.

"Yes. Day care center."

"Really?" Angela had pictured some sort of boutique, with herbs and cosmic pebbles.

When the landing gear drops with a long drawn out grind, Mary grips the arm rest, her knuckles white.

Angela considers telling Ross about Mary. Maybe she can turn it into something funny. It puts her in an odd light, but without it, what will they have to talk about as they drive away in the rented car?

"My father will be glad," Mary says, her syllables overlapping. "I'll tell him you saved my life."

"Hardly that." *Ross, there was a woman on the plane, she says I saved her life.* No. *Ross, the most extraordinary thing happened...this woman.*

The plane dips; an expressway comes into view. Ross is probably on it, seeking the right exit, or maybe he's already looking for a place to park. *This woman, she was young, she jumped – shrieked – at every sound the plane made. She leaned on me, Ross, she was practically in my lap.*

And you let her? he would ask.

Chapter Three

[1] Seattle, beautiful, is surrounded by water, more than she's aware of in Boston, even though it, too, is nearly surrounded. There's a greater sense of room, of things that don't end, of an infinity. She wants her drawings to feel this way. But when she thinks of home, of her drawings, of her studio, there's Daniel, but also Lydia: something different about her, no, something emerging, seems to be closing in; Lydia used to help her look outward. No more. Or less often. Or maybe it was never true.

Awake in the expanse of the hotel bed, she listens to Ross breathing, but hears Daniel's voice. He's not talking about love or reassurance, though; she hears dark edges like the burned edges of parchment. In the way he says her name sometimes, or tells her where and how on his body and cock – he likes the word cock, says it goes well with the word cunt – to put her fingers or the palm of her hand or her tongue. Or he'll dig his own fingers into the flesh of her buttocks, pulling her so close she can't move. The sound of his voice frightens her, excites her, and makes her jealous; his passions, his ability for passion that still feel pale in her. There's relief in the distance between them. She loves him, but her physical need for him just now isn't sexual, or not only sexual. It's a hunger to be more than a woman in a hotel bed yearning for an absent lover. She curls around her hunger, a viable, palpable thing; the hours spent airborne with Mary have changed her.

[2] She and Ross board a ferry boat for a tour around the harbor. She looks out across the water and the city with her back to Ross so that she'll have a memory of it without Ross. Ross drives them around the city in the rented car, talking constantly, pointing out what it is she's supposed to be interested in. They have dinner with his business associates, during which one of them, a Bill Something, periodically looks over at her and winks. She's assigned shopping while Ross has a meeting, but she goes to a café and has two glasses of wine and draws pictures on the napkins. Profiles and tree limbs and sliding shapes.

They go out alone on their last night.

A waiter introduces himself. The restaurant's dark, the clientele young; she's overdressed, has on too much makeup, or not enough. She takes off her wedding ring and slips it into her black silk purse.

"Why did you do that?"

"It's bothering me."

"It's so damned damp here. You probably have a rash." Ross concerns himself with some seed, or piece of bread, caught between bottom teeth; he worries it with his tongue before saying, "Just so you know, this thing with Peterson. I'm going to have to notify the others on the board. I was hoping to find out on my own who it was, for containment purposes, but whoever it is, they're damned smart. Peterson can hardly keep quiet, he's so excited. He thinks it's going to earn him a promotion. Probably will."

"I forgot to tell you. He called just as I was leaving." She now knows that Ross signs off on the books – he mentioned it out of the blue, out of context one afternoon – but that for years this is all he's done, signed the sheets, without ever taking a look.

"I hope you hung up on him."

"Why would I do that? He was persistent, though, wanted to know how to reach you. I didn't tell him. Is it going to be embarrassing in some way?"

"Why should it be embarrassing? It's not big enough to hit the news, if that's what you mean." A waiter wheels a tray of desserts past them. Ross looks them over saying loudly so the waiter can hear, "I expect better in a place like this."

She hadn't been thinking about the news. "How much money's involved?" As he sits there, a little hunched, his eyes almost darting about the room, clearly avoiding her, he seems guilty, caught. "Is it a lot?"

"Thousands," he says. "Not hundreds of thousands, though. You think a situation is watertight, but then something like this. Embezzlement, fraud, under my nose – you have to wonder." He waves in the direction of a waiter. "The service here isn't much better than the dessert tray."

"Wonder about what?" An impression, a sensation, leans in, Lydia, something about Lydia leans in, and then there's the way she tossed the word queer around last week and the burgeoning need Angela feels to protect herself as if Lydia were a stranger.

Chapter Four

[1] An empty coffee cup sits on the sill next to a few ashes from a cigarette. Daniel. In the corner of the drawing pad resting on her easel, her name written three times. He's been here.

She'd made clear when their plane would land, what time Ross was likely to leave for work, that she was giving Ina the day off. But hour follows hour. Then, day follows day. From the house, she watches the hedge, the studio, the lawn at the back. She paces, twirling her pendant on the chain; when the silver piece falls to her hand, it takes her a moment to realize she's broken it.

He's left her. She missed the signs. He'd probably even said I'm leaving you. But she hadn't heard.

Just as well.

Rather cruel, though, only her name.

But in the doorway, Daniel.

"I'm sorry. I got another job. More yard work."

"You should have called." Her voice sounds old.

"You told me not to." A kiss, but not the peaceful one she'd imagined. She takes his lip between her teeth and bites down; he flinches. Taking hold of her shoulders, he pushes her onto the couch. "I thought that while you were gone you'd think about what we were doing, look back at things here and hate it."

"No."

She imagines telling him about Mary, considers sharing the discomfort, the folly of the experience, the impossibility, how nothing like that has ever happened before. She considers telling him her new question about Lydia. Instead, looking at Daniel falling asleep beside her, young and inexperienced and so very separate from her, from the parts of her life that have nothing to do with him, and there are so many, she keeps Mary, and Lydia, and the hill of black ice, to herself.

[2] But still she's not bold. She draws lines for the bowl Ross left on the table, and, with two fingertips, dabs at the lines to smooth them; she should be able to show just how the bowl curves, she's practiced long enough, but her fingers only smudge the edges, blur the lines, and make the bowl nothing but

messy. Down the sides of the paper she draws other lines and shadows; there's nothing to lose, the bowl's already ruined, so she runs her fingers, her thumb, her fist over these marks; nothing good happens, until there, and there, at least in these places, there's texture, depth. Different pencils bring different results, a number six, a nine, and by pressing and brushing parts of her hands across these, first hard and then soft, and in-between pressures, and there, that pancake flat circle she's made is now a curved circle, a ball; it looks, to her complete amazement, round.

But she also sees there's still not enough heart in her marks. She's tried other implements, like charcoal, but it's messy and bleak; all the paints seem complicated. Then she tries pastels, chalk, the stuff of childhood. The texture of the paper, the life within, the colors on her fingers, dusting down her clothes; she ties her hair up in a white and blue bandanna. She feels sudden; she feels generous.

And each day, she wants Daniel to come, but later, after, because she's also aware that when alone with her pens and her pencils – and her colors, she loses her fear of color – she's able to enter a sort of trance, and she finds this elevating; also frightening, but she resists the fear. She can't be sure where a trance will take her. It's not unlike sex, in that it occupies similar parts of her brain; she feels her soul become more visible, and real, not some ethereal entity. She wants Daniel, but also wants greater control over his coming and going, because when Daniel doesn't show, she would like to have known he wasn't coming; she would have gotten more done, instead of looking out the window time and time again, expecting to be interrupted.

During longer stretches, when the expectation of seeing him is replaced with the belief he's permanently disappeared, when she only has Ross or Lydia to sustain her, she feels disembodied. Ross might notice the color of her dress, he might complain she's not wearing her diamond, but he never notices what mood she's in, or if there's anything she longs for. It's not just her secret, her secret life, and the demands and delight of keeping this safe; it's not only this which separates her from the sense of weighted substance others clearly feel: They never look confused, or as if they might be floating about untethered, or questioning their own whereabouts, or their position in the here and now. Ross continues to pour himself scotch, Lydia continues to schedule manicures, and Althea Smythe showed up at the club today in a brand new ruff rising above her elaborate blouse; it certainly seems these things are enough for them, and Angela wishes for this for herself, these simple requirements. Instead, she's pointedly aware how Ross and the others fail to make some essential, elemental contact with her – or she with them. It must be her fault, some flaw. Perhaps the flaw is that she's always only seen herself in regard and in reference to others. She's always allowed others, parents, friends, a husband, a friend she calls her best one, to dent, diminish, rob her. But for reasons she wishes she could understand, Daniel does not have this effect on her. And so, when she's finished with drawing or with her colors, he's all she wants.

Chapter Five

[1] "I catch myself counting up the moments I'm happy," she tells Daniel, sprawled on the couch playing with Ross's wooden bear puzzle. "It makes them seem more substantial." He'd asked to see one or two again. She brought him the globe, and the bear, and one abstract shape, a sort of lopsided hexagon; he takes them apart and puts them together effortlessly, two or three times each.

"Happiness is overrated," he says.

"Without happiness, there's not much else."

"My mother said something once." He hesitates. "My father was cruel. He was indifferent to everything she ever said or did, but it wasn't just indifference; it was careful, studied. He was careful to ignore her, he pretended she was nothing. It was his only source of control. He'd failed at everything else. I don't know how she stood it, or why. Why didn't she fight it?"

"Could she have?"

"She could have left him." His eyes are hard now. "Anyway, I was the one who sat by her bed when she was so sick. He would come, but never stay." *Don't worry, Angela, your father's comfortable.* "He never so much as held her hand. If he said anything, it was about himself. He would come for a few minutes and leave. I couldn't stand to be in the same room. I could have killed him." He puts the puzzles aside and stands; leaning against the wall, he lights a cigarette. "That's when I started living the way I do. I would leave for days, stay in the woods, go into town just to see her."

"For days? How old were you?" *I'm sorry, Angela, your father's dead.* And the next year her mother, alone in her sleep. "What about friends?"

"I didn't want friends then."

Ross is indifferent to her, but she's never thought of it as cruelty. "Ross doesn't have time for anything but himself because it's all he can handle." She sees in a flash how true this is. "Emotion, want, need. Anything out of the ordinary, anything that can't be paid for, scares him." She feels a clarity, something she hadn't quite known about Ross, but it also feels like a heaviness, a burden, a marriage in one dimension, a marriage she's considered leaving every now and then, but never with sincerity, never with a plan. And the reason for this is suddenly clear: Ross is needier than she – the word pathetic comes to mind, and she shudders.

"One night." Daniel restless, sits down again, but leans forward with his forearms on his knees, as he does when he has something difficult to say, his cigarette still lightly between his fingertips. "I sat by her bed, stroking her hand, her arm, she was so thin, it almost scared me to touch her. I was ashamed I felt so revolted. But it was selfish, too, because I wanted to remember her the way she was, not the way she was dying; I thought she was dying." Had her father died alone? She'd never thought to ask. "The only light in the room came from the machines, and from the hallway, so there was this glow." She's always pictured her mother at his bedside. "My mother's eyes were closed, but then she said, out of nowhere, 'It's contentment you're after.'"

Maybe not holding his hand, she thinks, but there.

Daniel puts out his cigarette in the small china dish, the tip against the tiny red ashes, as though he's grinding medication, or mixing paint. "I think she was right. Being satisfied with what you have. Happiness is a busy thing that needs to be fed. It flies by. And you can't always be running after it."

"I can see that." She'll never know where her mother was when her father died, and knowing seems important. *It's contentment you want.* "She died soon after?" She can smell the acrid ash of his cigarette, a single ember still burning.

"Might as well have," Daniel says. "A stroke, a coma, it's been months now. For me, she's gone. Her cousin, Hannah, is with her."

"You told me she'd died." Metal balls roll in a metal tray.

Daniel picks up the bear figure and turns it over and over, careful not to look at her. "I never should have said that. I still feel guilty, leaving my mother and all that responsibility on Hannah. I didn't know what you'd think of me." He reaches to take one of her hands.

"No," she says, but he holds on tight.

"You're thinking I lie. That I fail every time."

She wants to pull her hand away. She wants to stand up. She sees herself at a distance. But she doesn't stand up, and she doesn't pull my away. His mother hasn't died after all. "What else don't I know?" But Daniel says nothing, his face utterly still; he only sits there quietly, holding the bear in one hand, her hand in the other. "Never mind, what you did or said before we were lovers isn't any of my business." She says this, and sounds convincing, but something in her lets go, like a boat or a raft slipping free of its moorings.

[2] All evening she's been unable to sit or be still. *Daniel's mother is alive.* When she wanders into the study, Ross follows. "I was sure I left that contract here." He opens a drawer, but she doesn't believe he's looking for anything. "I've been..." He clears his throat. "Why are you so...what are you? Sick?"

"Sick? No."

Ross's tie is loose, his shirt's wrinkled; maybe Ina has stopped doing them. He leans on his hands, his fists, side by side on the desk, all his weight on them, his knuckles white. "But it's impossible to have a conversation with you anymore," he says. "I don't like this drawing thing."

"This drawing 'thing'?"

"No need for hysteria."

No hysteria, but a sour, steely taste rises up in the back of her throat.

"Relax. All I ask is that you keep things organized around here. But you're off somewhere, some other world. I'd hoped it was temporary."

So all he wants from her is organization. "Life with you doesn't amount to much." It shocks her that this has slipped out.

"Careful." Ross straightens up and squares his shoulders as though facing an opponent in a ring.

"Drawing adds dimension. That's all I meant." She mouths "draw" again, just to see how it makes her mouth move. It's a rounder word than she'd thought; she'd always thought of it as thin, like a pencil. "Is that thing with Peterson all over with? You haven't mentioned him lately."

"Don't change the subject."

"I was just curious. It seemed important."

"Your sudden interest in doing artsy stuff, is it some mid-life crisis? Only men are supposed to have those."

She's glad he's said this ridiculous thing; it relieves her of guilt. She feels pristine and calm. "But I've always had an interest. I'm even experimenting with paint now, like I did when I was sixteen."

Ross only meant to bring her back from wherever it is she's gone, not veer off in this new direction. Now he won't know how to end the conversation, and she's not going to help him. He might remind her that he provides them with everything, and ask what sort of life she'd be living without him, if she'd married the guy she was seeing when they met – the what was it, psychology major – he likes reminding her about him and what he considers a vague profession. Or, he could say he misses her, the cool, quiet, efficient Angela, or he might say he doesn't understand what's happening between them. But what he says is, "Well, Angela, you're no artist."

[3] "We argued last night," Angela says. She expected Daniel to apologize for lying, to tell her more about why, but instead she's said this. "I usually go months without crossing words with anyone."

"So do I."

"He wants me to stop drawing." She usually avoids telling him about Ross. She thinks complaining puts her in a very bad light, staying married to him all these years, choosing him in the first place. "Amazing, a man like Ross bothered by a few pencil drawings. So innocent. It could have been worse. Devil worship."

"He's not jealous of the artwork. He's worried about me."

"He doesn't know about you."

"He does, somewhere in his mind he does."

She's about to ask him to explain the how and why of his lie about his mother; instead she allows the woman and her dilemma to slip away to say, "I think Lydia's gay, and I think she's trying to tell me."

"What happened?"

"Not sure. It's confusing. She can't possibly have been performing all this time. Flirting. She's so aggressive that way. Besides, we're supposed to be best friends. Wouldn't she have told me?"

"Hard for someone who's conventional."

"Lydia's hardly conventional."

"Hyper-conventional."

She feels a chill of recognition. "What about Jack?"

"Part of her cover?"

"Wouldn't that be something."

"It would be love."

"I keep remembering, or trying to remember, exactly what she's said, or done. She'll disappear for weeks at a time for some project or..."

"For a lover?"

"No, not that. Well, how would I know? I was going to say that she disappears with no apology for days at a time but my 'disappearance' seems to have pushed her in some way. She says things." *Does things.* "I thought maybe just for attention. But I'm almost afraid to be alone with her."

"Why?"

"I'm afraid of what she might say." *Or do.* "I feel I'm about to be uncomfortable."

"Talk to her."

"How? Talking about someone being gay always sounds like an accusation. Do you think this is a new idea on her part? Is that possible?"

He traces his fingers down the back of her blouse with its alternate ribbons of linen and silk. "Ross is uncomfortable. Maybe he's afraid to be alone with you."

"That's impossible."

"He doesn't recognize you."

"I try so hard to seem natural."

"If Lydia knew about me, she'd wonder how she missed your performance."

"You make it sound like a play."

"Isn't it?"

"Oh, life's a stage?"

"A husband telling a wife he's gay, or Lydia telling you she's lesbian, or your telling Ross or Lydia about me, what's the difference? Exploding identities all look the same."

"I want to paint that. Everything I do is so tame."

"That's because you think Ross is watching. And that he cares."

Her hackles rise up. "People looking at my wild paintings and wondering what they're 'really' about. I'd love that." She lets that scene float for a moment. "I'll never tell anyone about us. What would it accomplish? And I don't believe Ross knows about you, or senses you. What he sees is enough. And he can't imagine there's anything he can't see."

"He sees you're preoccupied. He's not imagining that."

Chapter Six

[1] She assumes Daniel cuts through the band of woods behind the houses on their side of the street to get to the main road, and that it would take about the same amount of time for him to reach it on foot as for her to drive there quickly. But when she arrives at the point he should be, he's not there in either direction; perhaps he goes a different way, or got a ride immediately. She doesn't know if people still pick up hitchhikers, and so can't imagine what sort of person he might be with. A man in a battered pick-up perhaps, with Daniel riding in the back with rusting tools, a wary dog. If she'd found him, though, she doesn't know what excuse she would have made.

Next to Ross in the night, she decides to look for Daniel at his construction site. He said something about Route Six. Ross groans, moves, shifts as though the idea bothers him. She imagines Daniel high up on the peak of some roof, shirt off, hammer in hand, can even hear the rhythm of hammers, see Daniel looking down at her while she smiles up. She'd be relieved confirming part of the real life he leads when he's not with her. She pictures him shy, seeing her at his construction site, but she'll call out to him saying only passing through and wanted to say hello. She thinks he might be angry in some way – he's never been angry with her before – he might feel this isn't the part of his life he wants her to see. But her need for a glimpse of him apart from her studio presses down.

[2] She finds the house, two houses, actually, on connecting lots, one set back. Vans and trucks are parked helter-skelter on what would someday be a wide green lawn, but is now nothing but ruts pocked with stones; she pulls her car up next to a blue van without doors. Work on both houses pauses; her nearly new car looks out of place; maybe the men will think she's the owner of one of the properties, a wife, a person who matters here, but when she gets out of the car, there's a whistle and a catcall. She pretends to ignore these, but hearing them makes her realize how embarrassing her mission. Still, she's determined to see Daniel at work.

The houses seem raw, with only their structural bones, the shapes of roofs and walls but nothing solid between the two-by-fours. She can see all the way from the front to the back; it's like looking through trees in a forest, and she can see up to men working on the roof, straddling beams. She doesn't know on what part of what house Daniel might be. The nearest fellow looks down from scaffolding level with the second floor. His torso is bare, which makes her feel exposed; how thin her white cotton shirt. The carpenter taps the head of his hammer against his palm.

"Ma'am?" he calls down. No one's working now, all sounds have stopped; there are no saws buzzing, no hammers, no yells between workers, not even a catcall.

She tells him she's hoping to find a man named Daniel. She describes him and explains he hasn't worked here long, but the man on the scaffolding starts shaking his head almost as soon as she begins talking. "You must have the wrong building site."

"No Dannys here," someone else calls out, and still another laughs. "Won't I do?"

But the moment he's said that, she spots Daniel standing among the rafters of the second house. She smiles, broadly, happily; she waves. But Daniel, from his perch, is solemn, and shaking his head, no. He doesn't not want to be identified. He's refusing a conversation. He's claiming he doesn't know her.

She tells the man she has the wrong site, sorry to have bothered him; he salutes, lightly touching the tip of his hammer to his temple.

[3] A clatter outside the studio door, and then Daniel's inside and out of breath. "Angela, what were you doing there? I thought you'd made a mistake, or got there by chance. I was so shocked I was afraid to let on." She pretends to be especially interested in a drawing of a nude woman, the result of Mr. Campowitz's new live drawing sessions.

The twenty feet back to her car felt like a hundred, every eye on her, evaluating her, her clothes, her walk through muddy ruts on low thin heels. She'd felt drunk, her body tipsy and pieces of her mind shattered. The hammers and buzz saws started up one by one, reaching a crescendo of cacophony as she opened the car door and got in. "They don't know your name." She'd wondered if Daniel had gone back to his work as nonchalantly.

"Crews don't pay any attention to us newcomers; we come and go."

"Do you use a different name there?" She can't seem to capture the curve of the woman's shoulder. She erases lines.

"A different name? Why would I do that?"

She blows the erasure dust away. "No one knew of any Daniels." She leans down to pet the cat now rubbing itself against her to hide tears.

Daniel shrugs. "I don't know. Maybe they were playing a game."

"A game? Were you playing a game when you pretended you didn't know me?"

"Please, Angela. I was shocked. I thought you'd made a mistake. Us in public. You're always telling me not to take chances. And then there you are. On my job site." He smiles lopsidedly. "Forgive me?"

"I'm not sure."

"Wait till you see what I have. I cut boards from leftover lumber; good quality stuff. They didn't mind. I'm going to make you a bookshelf. Will three shelves be enough?"

"You scared me. I didn't like it."

"Come take a look." He takes her hand and leads her outside as though nothing unusual has happened between them. "For your art books."

"You think I should trust you?"

The lengths of cherry are already carefully cut. The bookshelves might only ever remind her of the walk back to her car.

"I thought we're supposed to keep our separate lives separate. You crossed over with no warning. I'm not sure it's my fault I didn't react the right way."

"I suppose." But, still, a fissure.

"I'm curious about something. This might not be the time. You don't have to tell me."

She's about to ask what he does on the houses, and if he's living with one of those men now, but asking makes her nervous. Answers have been so slippery. "What is it?"

"No children. How come?"

"Oh. Ross wasn't able to. Not impossible, but highly unlikely." Daniel up in the rafters; she wonders if he's afraid of falling. She goes back inside to her drawing; he follows.

"You're kidding."

"No, and he refused to see if there was anything that could be done. I didn't push. I didn't dwell on it. He insisted it wasn't meant to be. We should have talked about it, the way I hear people do, but we never did. His ego was damaged."

"But what about you? Didn't you want kids?"

She shrugs. "I assumed it was the next thing we'd do. I never thought – it was a setback. It never occurred to me I wouldn't have a family. Ross alone doesn't add up to one. I was an only child, Ross has a sister he never sees, and all of our parents have died. It was a blow for both of us but we barely talked about it. We were stoic. I suppose that's how we considered ourselves. And for some reason the failure helped keep us together."

"His failure. Not yours."

"He blames me. He likes to blame me."

"How can he?"

"I don't know. It's what he does. Calling him on it wouldn't change anything. It wouldn't give us children. I never told my mother why we were 'waiting.' She hadn't liked him much. I didn't want to add to that, for her sake as much as mine."

"That's terrible."

"'For better and for worse.' Raising kids with Ross wouldn't have been easy, anyway; since we never discuss anything, how would we have made decisions? Not all his fault. I opt out. Which apartment should we rent? Which house should we buy? What color carpeting? Who cares? We probably would have disagreed about how to raise children, and it would've been hard to stand up to him after giving in on almost everything else. He's decided who I am. I let Lydia do the same thing. Invent me. I can't blame them if I'm unhappy with who they came up with."

"We all make each other up to some degree."

"That's chilling." In her drawing, the woman's breasts don't seem to be part of the torso, but to have been glued on as an afterthought. But there's something in the eyes. Angela tears the drawing in two, discarding the portion with the breasts but tacking the half with the face on the wall. "There are a lot of things worse than some woman not being able to have a baby. Or having a neglectful husband."

Daniel inspects the drawing. "These eyes are so secretive."

"I knew before I married him that he wasn't neglectful because he was busy but because he was Ross. Not long before, but long enough if I'd been brave enough I could have called it off. But would I be any more or less happy than I am now?" She draws three series of very dark concentric circles down a margin. "Marriage is so much more complicated than I thought it would be. The worst thing in my mother's life seemed to be the dandelions in the front lawn. She would attack them with this long-handled prong. It was the only time I saw her upset. I'm kidding. Not really." In pedal pushers and sneakers and a halter top, disdain on her face, her mother would kneel in front of errant yellow flowers. *You have to get the roots out.* "Lydia's marriage might be even more complicated than mine. She and Jack always seem so simple together. So simple I've been jealous."

"I'm sorry about what happened at the site," Daniel says quietly. "I should have come down to talk to you. I could have pretended to the other guys you were interested in hiring me for something."

"It's ridiculous, that it all matters so much. What happens to me, to you. Ross. Our lives. Nothing in the big picture."

"It's what we have."

Chapter Seven

[1] Lydia's in full talking mode before Angela even gets the phone to her ear. "...coming to get you. For coffee at least. You can't say no. Tried to reach you last night but only got voice mail. Again."

"Might have been upstairs reading. Ross is in New York."

"I know. Jack said. Get ready."

In fact, she and Daniel spent the night together on the couch in the studio, side by side in the narrow space, tightly bound. "Maybe later," she tells Lydia. "I had trouble sleeping."

"But my new housekeeper's here. A Napoleon. She marshals me from room to room." Now it's Lydia instead of Daniel needing a place to go.

Angela had felt the sheen of sweat down her back, on the skin between her and Daniel, who seemed comfortable. Her mind kept scurrying off, becoming more and more agitated; she pictured him sitting on roadsides, on cots in large public rooms; she wanted to stand up and turn on the light without waking him, walk around a little, shake wrong ideas from her head; once, there was a nasty sound, a small animal dying, the gray cat devouring a mouse, perhaps. "I do have Ross errands to do," she says, "this afternoon." She's knowingly mistakenly convinced it's her fault Daniel lives the way he does, or the way she thinks he does.

Lydia agrees to the afternoon, but shows up at the studio – "I got bored" – no more than an hour later during a moment Angela's fully engaged with a sketch of Daniel from memory, nude.

"What are you doing here?" she says. "I mean, you startled me."

At first Angela found the proximity to strangers' bodies in live drawing classes – especially to a boy who was no more than twenty – disconcerting – Melanie couldn't stop blushing – but discovered if she only concentrated on bone and sinew and the length of arms and legs, if she didn't try for too much detail, only tried to capture position and gesture, and the shadows limbs made against cloth, there was enough for her to put on paper. But now, trying Daniel, or the impression of Daniel, she discovers she wants the drawing dark, and wild, if she can; she'd expected to try something pleasant, something she could show him.

She blames Ross for the dark overlay, and is in this idea when Lydia appears. She hides the sketch under one of a tulip with the petals falling off.

"Let me see that. It's incredible you do this. I could never concentrate." Lydia's dressed in a pink jacket with the collar propped to frame her face in the particular way she insists upon; if any collar fails to perform, she has a seamstress rip the collar's seams apart in order to insert some stiffening material.

"Advanced doodling. That's all."

"This doesn't look like doodling." Lydia draws the naked drawing out from under the petals. The head of a fair young man is caught in the web of his own hair made of leaves, as though trying to get free. "Wow, you did this? How sinister. What's that art teacher up to?"

"How's Jack? I haven't seen him." She takes the drawing from Lydia's hands and carefully puts it under pastels of trees, things bland.

"Now these are nice," Lydia says. "He's fine. He's always fine. That's why I married him. Do you ever draw women?"

"I'm not really in the mood for a field trip. Okay? Another time? I could make coffee here."

Lydia cups Angela's face in her hands. "What are you in the mood for?"

"For the work." She makes herself sit still for this typical Lydia gesture, although what was typical makes her want to squirm now.

"We're all suspicious. I certainly am," Lydia says.

"Of what?"

She lets go of Angela's face, but Angela still feels her hands. "People act like you are when they're hiding something. Something big. Unless I did something wrong. Did I do something wrong?"

"Of course not. I wanted to major in art in college. You know that. My parents wanted me to do something 'practical.' You know that, too. I let it go. I'm sorry I did and I'm making up for lost time. That's all."

"No one believes 'that's all.'" Lydia is back looking through the paintings and sketches, and even squints at the fragments pinned to the wall. "I think you're thinking about leaving Ross."

"That's ridiculous."

Lydia takes out the Daniel drawing again. "Draw me," she says. "I don't mind being nude. Where should I sit?" She takes off her jacket and starts unbuttoning her blouse. "On the couch?"

[2] "Oh my God, Angela. What the hell happened over there?" Jack's big voice on the phone.

"Over here? Why?"

"Lydia's in the bathroom sobbing. Won't let me in."

"She was fine when she left." Not exactly. *You draw strangers but not me? You don't like the way I look? Breasts make you uncomfortable?* "I'll come over."

"You've been avoiding her. Why?"

"Jack, I didn't feel like going out. It was only for coffee." *Are you a real artist, she said, touching them, touching herself.*

"Only coffee," he whispers. "Hold on." She hears a door close. "Honey." No one but Lydia ever calls her Honey. "Honey. Something about a drawing?"

"I don't know." *Touching herself.*

"You don't?" But he sounds incredulous. "You really don't?"

"No." The irreversible is about to be happen.

"Honey. You're not stupid."

"Excuse me?"

"She thinks of you as a lot more than a friend."

"We were best friends." Past tense.

"Angela." He gives her name a rough edge.

"Jack?"

"She's in love with you."

"Don't be ridiculous."

"You knew."

"What are you talking about?"

"You knew." He's accusing. He's mean.

She doesn't know this Jack. "We're not lesbian just because we're close friends. Why do all men think that?"

"Don't be coy."

Stop, Angela had said, trying to say it lightly, laughingly, to Lydia with no shirt, no bra, skirt pulled off, I won't draw you naked. "What are you doing, Jack? What are you saying?" *How about a portrait? Put your skirt back on. Your blouse.* "Where is she now?" *A portrait? A person cut in half?*

"She had an affair. She never told you? Not a hint?"

"No." *You don't have to be naked, Angela. Just me.*

"With a woman?"

"Never. When?" *She imagines two women, she imagines bare limbs, matching mouths.*

"I didn't see this coming."

"What coming?"

"I was stupid." Pause. "No. I was scared. So damn scared." Then, "And I trusted you."

"Trusted me to do what?"

"She completely fell apart. When it ended. Pure hell. She was out of her mind. Wild."

"Where were you?"

"Really rough on me. But then you moved in. She believed you'd been sent. Divine intervention."

"I don't understand."

"Jesus. She convinced me."

"That's ridiculous, Jack. She's much too practical. You're much too practical."

"She pretends – she believes – sometimes believes – has to believe – you're in the closet."

"Go check on her." *I need to hang up.*

"She fantasizes. Tells me things. Too many things. Explicit things."

Explicit things?

"But then she'll say no, no, just kidding. Just playing around. And then she'll call herself straight. Or bi. Or nothing. Like me."

Nothing?

"Are you still there?" he says.

The question, delicately put. "Why not just come out?"

Nothing, until, "Would you?"

Would she?

"She's said things to you," his voice gentle now, as if to keep it from breaking things. "I've been there. You always pretend not to notice."

"I never do."

"Hard to believe. Remember… Shh. She's opening the door…no, no, she's not. She's still crying, but not hysterical. What happened over there?"

"Maybe she'll let you in now."

"The time she suggested you two skinny dip at the club in the middle of the night. What do you think that was about?"

"She likes to be shocking." She can hear Jack pacing, on hard wood, on slate.

"I told her over and over she was going to get hurt. We argued about it. I begged her. She'd say 'I'm having fun. What else have I got?' But, something changed that. It wasn't playful anymore. I don't know what. I think you do. I'd bet on it."

"I don't." She would like to stop lying. And she would like to stop envisioning the four of them out together, Jack and Lydia with their secret, she and Ross naïve. And she and Lydia, so often side by side, so often so close, always, she now knows, on the inside of pretense. "I must have been an easy target."

"I figured you'd finally caught on and were trying to extricate yourself."

"She seemed okay when she left." Not quite. She'd rattled on about bikinis and something about photographs. Man Ray. Didn't apologize – Angela had, for what she didn't know – but did wave. "She even waved." She seemed fine. "She seemed fine." Angela had come inside to look up Man Ray.

"Fine? She seemed fine? Like she has for twelve years?"

"But she has so many friends."

"What's that have to do with anything?"

"What's she doing now?"

"Ross says there's been something going on, was it this? You were figuring things out? Or maybe she's having a psychotic break. What does that look like?"

"She hasn't seemed any different to me." Until today. Exuberant. Physical. Often insisting on sharing dressing rooms. Sometimes hugging and kissing her on both ends of a visit. "It's like you're talking about someone I've never met." Until today. Linking arms strolling down Boylston, saying it made her feel European. Calling four times a day. Lurking outside that first night with Daniel. Lying beside her at the Philips' party. Making her feel she's hiding with a boy under the back steps. Saying new words, like queer and beard. She'd had to look that one up.

"Don't ever tell her I called. It would destroy her. Unless she already is. Destroyed."

Lydia: "Jack? Jack?"

"Don't say anything," Jack hissed.

"What should I do?"

But he's gone.

[3] Angela's few ideas about women together had taken place on a sort of movie set, with bright lights and a film crew choreographing and recording and judging performances. Women kissing never creates any feeling other than it being none of her business; that and having no understanding. But she hasn't felt she needed to. Now there's talk about gender continuums, but about this she hasn't cared either. Caitlyn Jenner or RuPaul going mainstream. She sometimes doubts the sincerity of female celebrities kissing for cameras and on red carpets. For show? For shock? Some sort of proof they're on some tolerant forefront? Ellen DeGeneres is adorable, and Portia gorgeous. No other famous couples register. To her knowledge, none of her friends have ever been in a gay club, or known a gay couple. The one or two couples in town – there's been some talk about the women who run Genevieve's – are never on display. And, except for Lydia, few of her friends speak openly of intimate details of any kind, even when intimate details go viral.

But now, disturbing images frighten her, if, or how, or when Lydia has thought of her in ways only Daniel has permission. Out loud she says she'd feel no differently if she'd discovered Jack had been thinking of her in these ways for twelve years, but it's hard to tell.

Chapter Eight

[1] Jim and Kathy, George and Carolyn, associates of Ross's and their wives are on their terrace for aperitifs. Angela's tried calling Lydia – twice, admittedly at times she wasn't likely to reach her – a complicated shame – but she's only reached her cheery voice mail message, and only once left a message. Ross, holding his glass close to his shirt front, high on his chest, surveys his lawn, his territory. There's something about him that's unsure, or hesitant. She's had dreams about Lydia; they'll be wearing odd costumes, with strange protuberances that make it impossible for them to kiss, or with Angela in a cabinet of glass. Now, sitting in a stiff wrought-iron chair near Ross, she's inert when she should be offering their guests fresh drinks. The air is pleasant, light, cool for late August. *It's contentment you're after.* Jack's called, but she's afraid to answer. Ross is oblivious to all this even as he seems troubled.

The men and the women speak in low voices about the new rose garden at the band shell that's about to be dedicated, a movie only one of them, Kathy, has seen – "All sex. All gratuitous. As bad as all the violence." – a little politics, the fact that George is supporting the new mayoral candidate, nothing controversial enough to catch fire, but each takes each sentence they say seriously. Angela feels no need to add to the two or three conversations going on around her. But then a tiny red glow in the window of the studio, gone before she can look at it straight on. She smiles at a joke being told – Ross, too, is laughing – she puts her head back, consciously, with the idea of seeming nonchalant, and turns her head to look at the studio straight on, and there's the glow again, more orange than red, small, a dainty circle. She sits up, uncrosses her legs, stands, brings a pitcher of marguerites around with her back to the shed, to her studio, and then, facing the cart with the drinking supplies, the extra glasses, the napkins, the long swizzle sticks, the flame again, rhythmic, predictable.

Turning away, she finds Ina standing in the kitchen window, barely visible in the fading light; her face is mask-like in one of the small panes, her eyes on Angela. She feels a flash of panic; Ina vanishes from the window pane as though she's dissolved.

Later, when the guests are gone, and she's taking serving things back into the kitchen where Ina is washing up, she and Ina exchange a glance, more than glance, a look long enough to hold a whole conversation: yes, Ina has seen the cigarette point, and of course she doesn't approve, but she'll never mention him, tell anyone, or complain.

But later, almost to herself, she says, "I can't see how it'll turn out."

"It'll end," Angela says. "And it will have been nothing."

"I don't know about that."

"It's nearly over now." She puts a few glasses in the sink. "Do you, just curious, do know anyone who's gay or lesbian? Personally?"

Ina barely hesitates. "Besides Lydia?"

"What?"

Ina shrugs. "When my son was a little boy, he had this nice little friend. They played together all the time. Forts and all kinds of imaginary games. My husband and me, we always thought the boy was gay. When he came out, only my son was surprised. But things were okay until this boy started telling my son maybe *he* was gay. He kept saying things like that, insisting on it, until they couldn't be friends anymore. Then in high school, he told me he *wished* my boy Tony were gay. That there'd never be anyone else. I told him no, not to worry. But I saw him a few months ago, and he says yes. Tony says he's out of control. At the clubs and online and all that. I guess being in love with the wrong person can do that."

[2] Daniel doesn't come for four maddening days. When he does, she takes hold of the lapels of his shirt. "I saw your cigarette." *Ina and I both did.*

But all he says is, "I needed you."

"What could I do for you with all those people here? You knew they were coming."

"I would have said I'd broken in."

"You could say that in front of me?" They'd touched on this discussion before, what they might do, but never quite seriously, and Daniel would always interrupt.

"I'll say I'm the gamekeeper, like in *Lady Chatterley's Lover*," he'd suggest. "Or I could say I'm the owner of a big gallery coming to see your work. No, I'll say I've come to buy it all up." Now he says, "Would you have let me say I'd broken in?"

She lets go of him. "I would have had to." Even as she'd poured drinks, watched Ina, sat back down holding her breath, she hadn't known what chances she would take. What chances were available? *Excuse me, Ross, there's my lover, I'll be right back, while blue and red screaming police lights pulsed over and around and all through the house.*

"I shouldn't have come."

"Why make things even more dangerous?" Sometimes she feels like she's trying to reason with a stubborn child. "Why take such big chances?"

"I get so lonely."

"We wouldn't be able to see each other. Ever."

The room feels small; a claustrophobia is setting in; how small their existence in the confines of this room. "Let's go somewhere," she says. "Let's get out of here."

"Won't we be seen?"

"Oh, who cares? You apparently don't." But she feels eyes in every window of every house around them, as though in each one stands someone with a telescope; she tells him to wait a few minutes and then follow, that she'll wait for him in the car. How repugnant, sneaking; it's why they haven't left before, but right now she's only certain of need, a need to be outside the bounds of that room, this yard, for even a short while. Walking to the house, almost running, she worries like a young girl about what it will be like, finally, being in the car beside him, seeing him in ordinary circumstances. What will they say? Where should they go? They are so much defined by all that confines then.

In the kitchen for her keys, she sees him through the window, over the head of the ballerina, sees him in the doorway of the studio, standing back a little, waiting, probably wondering the same thing, together in a car, so ordinary, so extraordinary, how would it be?

She opens the garage door, starts the car, and rearranges her skirt, turns off the radio, and waits. He's taking too long a time. Perhaps he misunderstood, or has lost nerve, or someone – the gardener (or Lydia!) – has appeared in the yard. She's about to go in to investigate, when in the doorway, Daniel. When he turns to shut the door behind him, she thinks he's turning away to leave, that he's refusing to go with her. She nearly calls out. But there he is opening the car door and settling inside, tossing his pack into the back seat. She takes a deep breath and chatters on about how the car hasn't been running quite right, and pulls out of the garage and has to reach over his head to push the remote door control on the visor, and he's so close to her, in this ordinary place, and she feels relief.

"Where should we go?" The man from two doors down jogs by as she pulls out of the driveway; he waves. She doesn't dare acknowledge him.

"Who's taking big chances now?" Daniel says.

She's trying to think of a place they can be alone but together, private but in public. She remembers a coffee shop, but they have such small, rickety tables, and a diner she hasn't been to in years; it smelled of greasy food.

"Where are we going?" he says.

[3] She chooses the diner, the plain cups and the plain silverware, and once she had an egg sandwich there that reminded her of a childhood friend who'd brought egg sandwiches to school every day for years. A new bright red awning hangs over the stained front windows with the aluminum blinds, but neon signs are still sell brands that no longer exist. Inside, everything is just the same, although the awning now blocks out almost all natural light and casts a red glow. The booths are cordoned off – "I'm the only one here," a waitress says without being asked anything – so they choose a small square table set for four at the back near the kitchen. A heavyset man and an even larger woman sit a few tables away watching them. Sitting down with their menus, she and Daniel discuss what they'll have as if the situation were usual, as if they always stopped here – "Coffee?" the waitress asks, already dangling the coffee pot over their table at a precarious angle; Daniel puts up his cup ready to catch what she spills – and as if they routinely debate whether it's breakfast food or lunch they're in the mood for; in fact, they're in the mood for neither. "Just coffee," Daniel says. The waitress shrugs and produces packets of sugar and tiny tubs of artificial cream from the depths of her apron pocket. The heavyset man and his wife are still watching. Angela whispers, "I try to imagine the aftermath of Ross finding you right in his own backyard, but my imagination isn't big enough." She picks up her spoon and stirs her coffee briskly, as if she's put something in it. "Or not brave enough."

Daniel runs the tip of his spoon around the lip of his cup once and puts the spoon down. "He'd have me arrested for everything he could think of."

"More?" the waitress says, already back at his elbow. The woman at the other table and her husband both wear raincoats, despite the sunshine; they keep their coats on while they eat. The woman nods, having reached some conclusion; her husband merely stares at his plate, his mouth full, the next forkful waiting.

"And your marriage as you know it would be over." Daniel shakes his head slowly. "I wasn't thinking clearly."

Angela sees herself as the other woman might: middle-aged, well-kept, expensive clothes, while Daniel, so much younger, wears work boots, heavy khaki pants with wide frayed cuffs, with the sleeves of a thin shirt rolled up.

"How often does anyone? Jack outed Lydia."

"Why? Why now?"

"We accidentally collided."

"When?"

"She got upset. And...Jack told me something else. Ina says she's always known."

"Known what?"

"That she's had a crush on me. More than a crush."

"Jack said this?"

"Couldn't have been easy. Or maybe it was a relief. But I feel stupid."

"You shouldn't."

"Not so much that she's gay. I have no radar for that. I never know. It never crosses my mind one way or the other. But feelings for me? I didn't notice?" That night at the Philips'?

"It's the way she played it. She didn't want you to know. She manufactured something that worked for her. And Jack played along. Until he couldn't."

"He says she harbored all sorts of fantasies. But dropped hints that I ignored."

"You had every reason to take her at face value. Nobody spends all their time looking for flaws."

She hesitates. "Ross."

"Ross."

Angela feels a stoicism, an outer rim, fall away. "I always thought of her friendship as safe. It was always somewhere I could go. Something I could pretend to be doing. But she was using me. I realized how much I'd used her. I cried." She had cried. Ross had come in. "She was lying to me every time she saw me. I wasn't doing that, not for twelve years."

"Why were you crying? Who for?"

She shrugs. "Ross came in. I couldn't explain. All of us?"

"Ross? Sympathy for Ross?"

She shrugs. "We all slid into wrong lives."

"Me?"

"Maybe." She takes a deep breath. "Lydia wanted me to draw her nude. Got undressed. It was a horrible moment. I thought – stupidly – we could somehow pretend it never happened, but when she got home, she fell apart. Hysterical. Jack called. He was angry."

"At you? Why not at Lydia? Or himself?"

"People talk about tolerance. Embrace the rainbow. And we think we do. But what we really do is keep everything we possibly can at arm's length. 'Not me. Not here. Not us.' We do that with everything. We do."

"What if she'd said she had a crush on one of your friends instead of you?"

Angela laughs. "The first thing that comes to mind is jealousy."

"We're so fragile. How do any of us survive?" He touches her fingertips.

"She's always looked down on Ross, and my marriage, and she doesn't know nearly as much as you do about either. I let her. It was an out for me, an excuse for something, but hers can't be any better."

"It's a cover. Like yours."

She pulls her hand away slightly.

"Everybody tries to control what people think about them," he says. "What we say. What we don't say."

The waitress, again. "Are you going to order? You need to order something not just take up space."

"Pie," Daniel says. "Two forks."

The waitress frowns, walks away. Not much of a tip in one piece of pie.

"Are you talking about yourself?" Angela says.

"I want you to like me."

"That entails lying?"

"That entails caution. Just like you're cautious."

Cautious?

"LGBTQ – I never know," she says, "I never know if I have the right letters in the right order." The letters aren't like the puzzles Ross keeps. Those have a shape, an order; nothing to spill over.

The pie arrives. One fork.

[4] Angela has checked cupboards, shelves, under the sink: Her ballerina is missing. Maybe she absent-mindedly carried it upstairs; checks drawers and her vanity table, but no. When Ross comes into the kitchen asking what's for dinner, she mentions it.

"What were you doing," he says, "drawing it?"

No. She'd last seen it just before meeting Daniel in the car.

"I know you don't like it, so I thought you might have put it out of sight."

"Don't blame me for everything. Are you making dinner?"

And right then, the shock of Daniel by the hedge. She gasps.

"What's the matter with you now?" Ross shakes his head, rolls his eyes. "You're a nervous wreck all the time." He's at the refrigerator looking for ice. Daniel is near the studio. "This is all the ice there is? You don't need art, you need medication." Ross comes to the sink, where Daniel will see them side by side. "There's something wrong with the ice maker. Call someone, will you?"

Chapter Nine

[1] She forgets about Ross and Ross errands and about Lydia and even Daniel when she's working. But as soon as she leaves off with work, Lydia seeps in, and the need to see her, and as though nothing has changed, and it's already been too long. And Daniel seeps in, bringing colors, and sensation, and want. Over there, near the door, her back against the wall, he'd pressed his entire body against hers, saying the word love, nothing else. And, once, before he left, he'd sat on the couch beside her, dressed, while she only had her silk blouse, and the light cover drawn up over her, his shirt crisp, unusually crisp and white and the sleeves rolled up, the muscles and cords of his forearms in contrast to the pristine shirt, he'd put his arms around her before leaving her again; she'd touched the place on his chest and there was death there, in the longing, a metallic breathlessness. Or Daniel the one naked, without modesty and without arrogance. She's still much less comfortable with her own nakedness, but about him there's a peacefulness, an acceptance, a patience; even his laughter is slow in coming and gentle.

She sits on her high stool, eyes closed, rocking slightly.

"It looks like you're having an orgasm." Lydia at the door.

"Lydia!"

"Well you do. Or are in some trance. Yoga?"

"I was trying to remember something my art teacher said. Where have you been? How have you been?"

"It looked orgasmic. I should take that class."

"It can be pretty intense." Angela pushes her papers aside, lines up the colored chalks from dark to light.

Lydia kisses the air near her cheek and walks around the little room, filling it up. "Sorry. I've been busy."

"I'm going inside, want some lemonade?" Angela says.

Lydia's looking at her drawings again, those tacked here and there on the walls, but avoiding the nudes. On the easel is a stretched canvas, the paint still tentative and shapeless, not yet Daniel.

"Do you think you'll ever sell anything?"

"Come on, it's hot out here," Angela says. "I keep meaning to buy a fan."

Lydia is reluctant to leave. "Sorry about last time."

"Don't give it a thought. Lemonade. Come on."

Angela goes without looking back, silently begging Lydia to follow. As she crosses the lawn – stray images cross her mind more and more often, like they used to, before she felt herself shredding – she thinks of running through a sprinkler as a child.

The ballerina is back on the windowsill; she has to look twice to understand. She's surprised it's not broken in some way, a missing arm, or a dented skirt.

"How about a gin and tonic," she says when Lydia finally comes inside. "Does that sound better than lemonade?" The neighbor girls and she would put on pink and blue and pale green bathing suits and run through the sprinkler as it swept back and forth in smooth, predictable – and yet never quite predictable – arcs: it would spray her face and thighs at unexpected moments, cold on hot summer skin; she can hear herself squealing on that far off summer day, and see herself and the other little girls trying to outrun it, pretending to try, but getting caught at the sweeping edges, before racing away but never quite far enough, the cold unexpected spray now on their backs.

"Angela?"

She's surprised to find herself in the kitchen and Lydia at the table, she'd been so completely in that childhood backyard.

"What are you doing?" Lydia shakes her head. "Another trance? Are you in love with that art teacher?"

"Gin and tonic. Sound good?"

"Sure." But she's frowning.

The high arching fan of water moves away from Angela. She's not doing anything about the drinks. She'd have to leave Lydia to get the gin, where is it, on the bar cart; she doubts there's a lime.

"Ross asked me to talk to you."

"About what? Why doesn't he just talk to me?"

"I think he's afraid to be alone with you."

Angela laughs. "Afraid of me."

"Afraid you'll go off the deep end if he says the wrong thing. Wants you to see a doctor. A psychiatrist."

"Me?" Lydia's the one sobbing in a bathroom. Her heart skips beats.

"He thinks I'm in cahoots with you. I could be if I knew what for."

Something similar to a hallucination is coming on so strongly Lydia should be able to see it; Daniel is almost visible. "Ah… Ross? If Ross and I can't talk about Ross, we have nothing to talk about." Jack's conversation seems to be sky-written in the air, easily seen if they'd only look up.

"Most men are like that."

"No, they're not. Jack's not."

"A little."

"Very little. Ross, I've been interfering with…his schedule. It irks him." Her instinct to protect Ross – to protect Jack, to protect Lydia, to protect – settles down like a blanket. "That's all."

"He wonders where you've gone off to."

"I'm right here."

"No. You're not." Lydia shakes her head with a sort of bad news sadness. "Forget the g & t. I need to go." She pauses by the ballerina. "This awful thing." She picks it and puts it back down, first facing in, then turning it to face out.

The sprinkler spray hits Angela's calves, her thighs, her lips, her face, and rises above her head.

"He also wants to know if you're working on your party yet."

"He could ask me."

"Well, are you?"

"Of course." But, no. The details she should be attending to by now in order to give one more identical fall party drift into her head, but she lets them go like strings on balloons. The house on the night of the party will be imposing, impossible, no, it doesn't have to be the usual. There could be candles this time, dozens of them, in each window, and luminaries along each path. There could be costumes. Masks and capes and fake weapons.

When Lydia is nearly to her car, Angela opens the door to call out, "Masquerade! This year, the party's a masquerade!"

"Afraid? Why should I be afraid?"

Women and men, swirls of guests not recognizing a soul, then seeing in a flash it's because they're all dressed in large hats and unusual clothes, lace and satin, even the men, and there are masks, the elaborate sort found at carnivals, in New Orleans, or Venice, during the festival.

She shuts the door and runs up the stairs. In the guest bathroom she strips off all her clothes and, turning the shower on high, climbs in, but finds it too sparse. She wants immersion, her bathing suit wet from the sprinkler on the lawn. She draws a bath, and pours in foaming crystals, so that under the full force of the water, bubbles rise up above the rim of the tub.

A masquerade.

[2] Untying his tie, Ross says, "Just so you know, we're having dinner with Peterson and his wife. Here."

"Here?" She feels she could sleep right there at the vanity, through the night and on into next year.

"We're gathering forces."

"Gathering forces? What's Peterson's first name?"

"Hank."

In the night, her sleepy mind briefly considers moving closer to Ross, to be nearer his safe bulk, to possibly even make love in order to feel the security she once did, the belief that nothing, really, would go terribly wrong as long as he was there with her.

[3] "I'm covered with paint. I shouldn't come in." Daniel's at the back door. Ina is just now pulling away in her Honda.

Angela laughs, he's so spattered, flecks of white paint on his hands, his face, even his lips. "What have you been doing? Let me see if I can help."

"I'm painting a house. Don't worry, it's a small house."

None of her pretty soaps do any good. The specks on his hands, his face, only come into a relief she finds appealing. "Come here." She watches his paint speckled hands on her thighs, her breasts, right there in the downstairs powder room. Sometimes sex seems cold and futile because it doesn't quite accomplish all she wants, even as they both cry out and collapse, laughing, on the powder room floor, her flesh tasting of cold porcelain. And this time, there's Lydia, and her hands seem to be where Daniel's are, and her lips, and her face.

"I'll make us your tea," he says, and, while finding the honey, adds, "I need to tell you something. You'll think I failed you again." A hardness, a chill, runs down her arms, across her chest. What new fabrication? What new mask of forgiveness will she have to hide behind? "I did some yard work and never got paid," he says. "So I took some money. Last week. Remember when we went upstairs after the diner so you could change?" Her hands feel numb; her fingers tingle.

"You should have asked. I would have helped."

"I'm sorry. I can be stupid."

She hesitates. But what choice? "Most of us can be."

"Sometimes I'm ashamed to be so poor. Here. I have twenty dollars. To start paying you back." From the depths of his pocket he takes some creased bills.

"Don't be ridiculous." She imagines Daniel standing at Ross's open dresser drawer.

"Angela, take it."

Chapter Ten

[1] John and Hillary Brown. Sebastian and Emily Dwyer. Judith and Lisa and their husbands. Lydia and Jack, of course, and the Smythes. A dozen others, more. Rose and her husband. The stack of invitations grows, a tidy accomplishment, squares as gray as cinder blocks sitting on the desk; she writes the names of acquaintances, friends, all those people expecting to be asked to their sixth annual fall Dunnewald party. She wants to ask Melanie and her husband, but, how can she, the threads of their lives separate except for painting once a week. She writes the cards out by hand because it's more intimate, as if the people she's inviting are actually friends, and not only names on invitations. The small lamp at her elbow is lit. She's turned the patio lights on, also, because the house feels huge, peculiarly and particularly emptier than usual even though Ross is only at the club, not out of town. The Rothkos. The Hillyards. Ross. *Do you remember when we were in Venice, in that gondola, near that villa? It was getting dark, we peered in at that gate, through those grand wooden doors with thick carvings that stood open, and we saw all those people in costumes. There were torches* – but now the invitations seem like a school girl's assignment writing her name over and over on a blackboard – *flickering light. Remember how striking? A scene from a ballet, an opera* – women in satin, long dresses, bustles, lace, men in short pants, like Shakespeare, like ships' captains, plumed hats, and, inside there would have been opal colored punch in huge, cut crystal bowls and white cake – *masks for one night, no cheating, imagine doing that here, for one night, pretending to be someone else.* Not quite. It would not help to suggest Ross be someone else. The invitations had seemed elegant, but now she doesn't even care for the feel of the shiny gray paper. The lights outside flicker; the wind must have picked up. She wishes she had bright invitations, yellow, or better yet, ones with a multitude of colors, swirled and exhilarated, instead of these, subdued and oh so very decent. Ross will ask if she wants canals and gondolas, too. She writes everyone's name, her own, and Ross's, in unusually large script, along with the word *Masquerade!* No peeking out from masks will be allowed, and no peeking in. She even writes Daniel's name in her smooth, even script on an invitation she'll never let him see. News will travel fast, what the Dunnewalds are up to. Daniel, of course, can't come. She won't tell him it's a costume party.

Upstairs, she brushes her hair, puts on a nightgown, a robe, watches the late news – every night, it seems, there's a house, a duplex, an apartment somewhere, tragically burning, with a child trapped inside – Ross still isn't home. She goes back down the stairs, and it's like a hotel, her own foyer feels like a hotel into which she's descending wearing a nightgown. No sign of Ross. She peeks into the garage, half expecting to see his car, half expecting to discover he's come in without looking for her.

[2] "I have an idea," she says at breakfast. Ross didn't come in until after one, saying something about poker as he climbed into bed. "The more I think about it, the more possible it seems."

"What now?" Ross looks into the pot of cream to see if any has clotted around the silver edge. What now?

"Remember that night in Venice?" She's nervous; he's likely to dismiss her however vividly she can describe the party she wants to have. She's prepared to argue and even to say, *I'm sick of you.* But she keeps on with her description of the festival in Venice. Ross can't, or pretends he can't remember the night as though he doesn't remember being in Venice at all. How could he forget a moment that had made such an impression on her? She'd laughed, made the gondolier pause; she'd been delighted, and it was her favorite moment and he knew it. She bought the pendant the next day.

"A costume party? Out of the question."

"Why?" Plan the party yourself, then. But she also wants to say imagine, for once, something outside of yourself, but you can't, can you? *I'm sitting here right in front of you and you can't even imagine me. It must be horrible living inside of you, that skin, those barriers, your walls.* But out loud she says, "Don't you think it would be a good idea, our doing something different?" *I'll let you take all the credit.*

"You want me and my associates to dress up."

"People would talk about it for months afterwards, years."

He sits looking at her, but isn't seeing her. It crosses her mind to wave her hand in front of his face, doubting he would so much as blink. But he seems to be imagining his friends in costume, the impression such a party would make, the aftermath of success. He might be trying to imagine himself in costume, but that's probably too remote, too hard – he'll put that part last. But he nods. Says he'll think about it, but she knows he can't resist being memorable. "I suppose you'll want canals and gondolas, too?"

[3] Daniel pulls some things from his pack and sits on the couch to sand a small piece of wood that's flat and almost oblong on one end, tapered on the other. She sits near him on the floor. The piece fits into the palm of his hand. She runs her finger along the edge of it. "What are you making?"

He won't say.

She hasn't told him about the masquerade; he only knows there's a party. Brushing the fine dust he's made into a pile with her hand, she traces small circles in it with her fingertip.

"Why aren't you working today?" he says.

She feels drained. "It's hard slipping into some other self to plan a party." She's of two minds about the plans themselves. When she decided on a costume party, she'd felt playful, and a little sly, knowing full well she was playing a trick, setting guests up to reveal themselves at the very moment they would believe they were most covered up. But her reluctance to tell Daniel about it brings her up short. "It's a lot of work. Details."

"Is that caterer you wanted available?" he asks.

"Do you care?"

"No."

The urge towards a masquerade, to play such a trick, to hide her own self behind some costume, some mask, is too close to what he most dislikes: secret agendas, and people needing to make fun of each other so that they themselves feel superior. The only honest act would be to have no party at all. She tries to imagine Daniel at a masquerade; what costume? None. He's too solidly himself.

[4] At lunch at the club, while the others congratulate her on the idea, and toss out suggestions – Emily's is Marie Antoinette with a live bird in a cage in a huge wig on her head, she even has a picture; Susan says, Victor Victoria, "A man dressed as a woman dressed as a man. Or was it the other way around?" – Lydia affects boredom. "Oh," she says. "I haven't even started. I've been too busy planning the Alzheimer's benefit. Alone." When Angela arrived, the woman in the chair next to Lydia's started to move, but Lydia said don't bother. "We don't need to be on top of each other all the time." Hillary, Emily, Beth, Susan and Althea Smythe, and all the husbands, Angela's told, have already considered and abandoned dozens of ideas. Couples argue whether or not to come as a pair – Cleopatra and Antony, Dante and Beatrice, Bill and Hillary – or whether "I'll

be me instead of your spouse." She even overheard in a line at the grocery store – she didn't step out from behind the candy display to see who was talking – that some people are going as far as Providence and New York in their search "to be different."

But something delicately woven emanates from Lydia. She answers Angela, everyone, with one or two words – Beth asks if she's feeling okay – and makes eye contact for little more than a second or two. When Angela suggests they run into Genevieve's, she says no.

Ross grunts at breakfast over his own indecision; he's so far had only two or three ideas – "This is harder than I thought." Steve Jobs, but he wouldn't wear glasses, Kublai Khan, too much brocade; Sir Lancelot, perhaps, but where would one find convincing armor?

She's already been through swarms of choices herself, but her indecision comes from having so many. Ross, though, knows what she'll choose. "You're going to dress up as some artist, right?" he says. "All in black?" She only smiles. When the right idea does pop into her head, she recognizes it immediately: Titania, from Shakespeare's *Midsummer Night's Dream*. She'll be the figure who comfortably rests in worlds of both reality and fiction.

She needs a mask, white, of course, but she can't quite picture it. She tries costume shops and catalogues, and is beginning to worry she'll have to make do with something simple instead of extravagant, when she sees in the window of a shop in Cambridge near Harvard Square a feathery confection. Inside, a squat old woman in a black dress with no shape whatsoever heaves herself from a stool behind an old-fashioned cash register and with a prong on a long handle lifts the mask from a stand in the window. Angela expects the mask to be coated in dust, but it's weirdly pristine.

"I've had it for years," the lady says. Her merchandise is mixed and unmatched, a few magic tricks in the glass-topped counter, magazines on a rack, some with plain brown paper covers, pens, banners with different colleges on them, winter caps, Advil and sinus medications.

"Do you have a mirror?"

The lady directs her to a bathroom at the back, one no bigger than a closet, and there she stands next to brooms and mops and a metal bucket on wheels to peer into a clouded mirror. She holds the white feathers against her face. The feathers are layered and curved and they curl around her cheeks and up over her forehead; the mask fits perfectly, and her eyes don't look lost or small, as they have in some masks she's tried, but large and interesting.

Chapter Eleven

[1] Lydia ambushes Angela on the sidewalk outside Jericho's, the small, popular restaurant in the center of town. "You're going to come inside with me and sit with me and listen to me and act like nothing's wrong."

"Okay."

"Because there isn't."

Lydia brushes by the hostess. "We'll take this one," a booth near the door, waving at two or three of the customers they both know and some Angela doesn't.

Lydia leans across the table to present Angela with a big brittle smile, then tilts her head back, laughing uproariously, as though Angela has just told the very best joke.

"What exactly did Jack tell you?"

"About what?"

"You can't expect men to understand. They exaggerate everything. I was all weepy because I had cramps. Jesus. How he overreacts."

"Is that what happened?"

Lydia smiles and laughs again, and gestures for a waitress. "Water? Lemon if you have it. And bread."

The waitress brings crispy breadsticks. Lydia munches on one.

"I don't know what Jack thought he was doing. Calling you. Saying weird things. Telling you that he thinks I'm queer. He was mad at me for something, I guess."

Wow. "I've never known Jack to be vindictive."

The waitress brings tall glasses of water. Lydia dips her breadstick. "No lemon."

"Ross tells you things. You listen. You believe him."

"Yeah, but Jack goes off every once in a while."

"I don't believe that. I've never seen that." Lydia, sacrificing Jack.

"Don't you think I know him better than you do?"

She dislikes this woman. "I have to say, a lot of things make sense now."

Still stirring her water with her breadstick, Lydia looks around, winks at someone over Angela's shoulder. "Why is everyone attacking me?" The breadstick disintegrates.

"I'm not attacking. Can't we just talk?"

Lydia touches her fingertips to her forehead, a shield for her eyes. "Jack asked me to apologize for him. He was in la la land."

Angela tries again: "Something about you has always seemed just out of reach."

The waitress, asking if they're ready.

"We need a few minutes," Angela says.

"No rush."

"I must have seemed young," Angela says, "and sheltered and shy, when we first met, while you were – " the word *garish* comes to mind – "Opposites attract, you said. About you and me. What did you mean?"

"Don't talk so loud. I never said that." Lydia looks away, begins to take a sip of her clouded water. Grimaces. Puts it down.

"You did."

"No recollection."

"Somebody said personas are made up of what others see. That that's what we use."

"Sounds like Warhol."

"I think Proust. I'm pretty sure Proust." And borrowed personas are those most likely to explode.

"You shouldn't take yourself so seriously. I certainly never did."

"Excuse me?"

"Gotta go. Sorry I didn't have time for lunch." Standing, she dips down to peck Angela on the cheek, in case anyone's watching.

"Lydia."

Chapter Twelve

[1] Melanie, always jolly, always generous, always a pleasure to see, has become addicted to the color yellow, goldenrod and butter and lemon. But all of this, all of her, only serves to highlight Angela's two lives, and their intensely opposed parallels. Neither seems real nor tenable. She tries to believe that everything will work out, that there will be logical answers. And all the while the party comes closer, almost against her will, until it's only a few days away. She's almost afraid, as if things might be unrecognizable after.

She gives Ina an extra day off – she wants a free day before those during which there will be deliveries, extra tables and chairs, huge quantities of tall candles – Ross is anxious, "What would our insurance company say?" – boxes of paper luminaries that the gardener's coming to arrange, and then the caterer will begin delivering china and crystal and serving trays, and on Saturday there will be loads of people in the house all day setting up, including a small orchestra. And she made Daniel promise to come by. When he does, she says, "Let's go somewhere. The beach."

"Are you sure?"

"Absolutely. It's artificial that we only see each other in one place."

"I like that one place."

"But, that day in the coffee shop. We were more a part of each other's lives." She doesn't say she senses change, some sort of premonition, not unlike the day she first saw him. "I don't like feeling one-dimensional."

[2] She speeds up the ramp to join expressway traffic. "I was looking forward to this party. I don't know what happened."

"Slow down," Daniel says gently.

"Everyone streaming through the house..." Her initial vision had been one of extravagance, with capes and great hats and complicated jeweled masks, like Venice, but now this same vision has taken on qualities of a nightmare. "It's like a bad dream." One in which she can't distinguish one guest from another as they swirl around and around her and each other. She expects to be unable to recognize the people beneath the masks, to be unable to see the obvious. "What if I don't know anyone? What if the whole thing is embarrassing? A failure?"

"Seventy's too fast through here."

She cuts back into the right lane too quickly. A driver leans on his horn.

"Do you want me to drive?"

"Are you listening?" she says.

"I'm trying."

But she's also feeling, not haughty, but wise, perhaps. All dressed up, Lydia and all the others will be stripped naked. "It's cruel."

"What's cruel?"

"Parties." Her party. "I haven't handled things with Lydia very well." Soon after Jericho's, she went out of her way to ask Lydia for last minute help with the flowers. An onlooker might have taken them for friends, but it seemed to her a very thin balance beam.

"It sounds like she won't let you."

"It's as if I don't recognize anyone anymore."

Time only allows a beach just north of Boston, the one with the narrow band of gray sand, and a few toppling buildings, a closed concession stand, a life guard station.

They walk along the water's edge toward a breakfront that juts out, all the way to the horizon, it seems. The air underneath the September heat is already cool with fall. Holding hands, they watch children play, while some mothers stand knee deep in the waves, and others sunbathe, one eye on the kids playing in the sand among castles and moats. A boy has a white plastic bucket full of tiny red and yellow soldiers that he sticks here and there in his fortress. Daniel's head is down; he's not looking out over the water as she expected him to, as she had imagined they would, as if looking out would free them. He's unexpectedly retreated to some interior place. The shore's too rocky for them to run along, which she'd also pictured, but they venture out on the breakwater and find a place to sit, the mothers and the kids out of sight, and it's was almost as though they are alone there; only voices reach them.

"In Maine, the ocean was always freezing, even in August," Daniel says. "But I'd dig for clams and the fishing along the little tributaries was good. Sometimes I'd go with my father, but mostly, when I got old enough, alone."

"You didn't like your father, even then?"

Daniel shrugs. "I don't want to think about him." He tosses a pebble; it hits rock.

She thinks about her parents often, not directly, generally not straight on, but as presences, inescapable, even as they've dissolved from her life. Behind her, some children shriek, and one voice rings out over the rest, "Not me!"

"I can't seem to get far enough away from the house," she says, "or from the people I know, before they crowd around and pull me back. The only time I feel free is when I'm with you" – although there's something wrong in this, something not entirely true – "and when I'm in the studio."

In a moment he says, "Should we walk further? Or go?"

"You're ready to leave? I'm not." She doesn't like it that something in her is pulling away from even Daniel now. She takes his hand and leads him further along the beach and away from the parked car.

"I'm worrying more than I used to," he says. "About your being seen and getting caught."

"What about your getting caught?"

"It wouldn't mean anything. It wouldn't make any difference. I don't have to face anyone. But when you go home, you have to pretend you haven't been anywhere, or seen anything, that this view..." and he spreads his arms – "doesn't exist." There's a ship, a tanker, perhaps, on the very edge of the horizon. Off to the right, two or three sailboats, their masts and sails ghostly in the sunlight.

They climb over the boulders of the breakwater and walk along in ankle-deep water, splashing it in front of them, stopping once, he stops, and puts his arms around her, and simply stands, his chin against her hair. She can hear him breathing, and the world is small. Small waves kick up, rhythmically, chilly against her ankles. There's a sudden sadness, and she hadn't expected this, either. She presses her face against his shirt; she doesn't want her sadness showing; she doesn't want there to be weakness, or doubt; she doesn't want this moment ruined, this day, in any way with anything that doesn't have to do with them in the immediate here and now. She only wants the water and the sand and the free hours, nothing else, but emotions rise up of their own accord. He holds her more tightly, and when she looks up, there are tears in his eyes.

"What is it?"

"I don't know." He kisses her. "We should go."

"Not yet." And they walk, even more slowly, and not speaking at all.

Finally, the sun behind clouds, and all the kids and moms packing up, they reach the car. "You drive," she says.

"What if something happens?" But he takes the keys.

"I want to watch you taking care of me."

He adjusts the mirrors and checks to see where the signals are, turning the windshield wipers on instead, along with their spray, which flies over the car. She laughs. She sits with her back to the passenger door, one foot curled up in her seat, so that she can watch him drive her car; he is attentive, careful, responsible, and sexy. She leans over to kiss his ear.

"No, you can't do that. I'll go off the road." He takes her hand in his and holds too tightly.

"Ouch."

He takes roads she doesn't know. Maybe he's running away with her, but she senses he's going in the right direction, or the wrong one, towards her house. "How do you know this way?" Too soon he pulls the car over to the side of a road near an intersection she's not sure about.

"This," he says, "crosses your road at the far end. I can get where I'm going from here." He opens the door, but sits, still holding her hand.

"When will I see you?"

He looks away. "I'll think about that beach."

"We can go back."

He shakes his head.

"Are you leaving me?" she says.

"We could live together."

"What would that be like?" They'd have a bohemian existence, he with his carpentry, she with her pencils and paints, and for a moment she's far, far away from this intersection only a mile or so from her carpeted house, the house about to be filled up to bursting with candles and costumes and bowls of bright punch.

"I'll see you a day or two after the party." He walks away without looking back.

Ross might be home by now; she drives into town to give herself a few extra minutes. She parks in a lot in front of a meter with time still on it, and studies the red flag edging closer to the yellow one in the little pane of glass, twenty minutes, then fifteen, and there's Emily on the sidewalk watching her. Angela waves, shrugs, as though she's simply been caught being absent-minded.

At home, Ross says, "You look wind burned."

Chapter Thirteen

[1] Four workmen will spend three hours installing the portable parquet floor over the carpet in the foyer. The small orchestra will be situated at the end of the foyer she's always wished were enclosed by doors, not windows. Waltzes will be played, and ballroom dance teachers, a husband and wife, are coming in authentic eighteenth century dress to help keep things moving, since Dunnewald acquaintances rarely dance. Vast punch bowls will hold the sweet, heavy punch the caterer suggested, a nineteenth-century French recipe. French or not, she suspects champagne will be more popular and orders two more cases. The whole affair has taken on a decadent air. The costumes people are talking about sound heavy, rhinestones and pearls; some of the men are planning to show up in pointed black shoes and short, satin pants, large capes, Sir Francis Drake, Salieri. Masks have been ordered from dressmakers who have never been asked to make such things before, more used to wedding dresses and outfits for mothers of brides. All the costume shops in the area and beyond have been scoured for the unique. Angela is amazed by how eagerly and thoroughly people seek to be taken outside of themselves for one night. On some days the party seems outlandish, on others, a farce, on still others, self-indulgent, a recreation of a memory from her single trip to a foreign place. The energy of the event is entirely out of her control, but it's the energy itself which delights Ross. He says it's all he hears people talking about everywhere he goes. He sees her in a different light: "I never would have expected this of you."

He's continued to fuss and discuss what he'll wear, even calling her from the office to go over pros and cons of a Rockefeller, a DuPont, a Founding Father. The problem he seems to be having is that all of his choices intimidate him, that he in fact isn't sure he can fill the shoes of a Jefferson, a Pierpont, a Steve Jobs. But what he focuses on is what detail will indicate it's Jefferson, not Washington, Jobs, not Gates. Clearly he wants himself in a leadership role, but isn't sure how to define one. It never occurs to him that they could appear as some historical couple, not that it's what she wants, but other couples are. Louis XVI and Marie Antoinette, Tarzan and Jane, Tristan and Isolde, Romeo and Juliet.

Then he considers the Pied Piper.

"The one who lured rats?" she says.

"Oh, I thought children followed him."

But the next day, at breakfast, he blurts out, "I've got it!" but refuses to tell her exactly what he's got, "Since you won't tell me, either."

She soon discovers a large bag stapled shut with something purple and crimson sticking out the top.

[2] "Just so you know," Ross says, the party less than an hour away, "the caterer didn't bring the appetizers I asked you for." Then he discovers they're low on vermouth. "Didn't I tell you last week?" Only moments before he'd appeared in costume: "Merlin!" he announced, coming down the stairs. "I make things happen." And there he was in a flowing purple and crimson robe and a sloping hat with gold stars – "I refuse to wear the pointed hat that comes with it." His mask is also gold but small and simple, really, and fitting, and looking quite comfortable.

But, with a flourish of these robes, he's cursing the caterers for the wrong appetizers and the missing vermouth – "All this," he says, "with a hundred guests due here in a minute." She thinks it's unfortunate that he, even in his wizard's costume, can't conjure up everything that's missing.

While descending the stairs for the first time in her costume, Ross had looked up just as she hoped he would; she'd expected to make an impression on him with her long, white, flowing Tatiana gown, with the sleeves she liked, also long and flowing with delicate embroidery running from shoulder to wrist. She swished the skirt, feeling a little flirtatious – the skirt with its uneven, handkerchief hem, making it look as if the costume might have been put together at the last moment. The perfect dress for a woman living in a fairy tale occupied by both real people and nymphs. Her mask, too, white and feathery, nearly covering her face, curving around her hair, her cheeks, making her feel like a midsummer's night dream. She expected Ross to be pleased by how pretty she looked and that she hadn't chosen black.

But what he said, just as she made the skirt sway, was, "You said you were wearing black." He frowned. "What artist wears that? What are you pretending to be, a free spirit?"

"Not pretending."

The candles are lit; there are candles on the mantles, the mahogany table, every surface. The usual lamps, crystal pieces have been cleared away to make room for candles or tall metal sconces, and more floor sconces line the walls, and their candles are being lit now; Ross is still worried about fire insurance. Outside, electrical theatrical torches, not open flames – they're illegal – line the driveway, the sidewalks, and the patio at the back; again she wishes there were an elegant route out to it, and catches herself working up fresh anger over the lack. It's a warm night; wandering out to the patio would have been nice. Now Ross stands in the open front doorway, looking pleased with himself.

"Ready?" she says.

Clouds have collected, not enough to be overcast, but enough to give the effect of a full moon through sheer curtains, shining through to torch-lit walks, the candlelit rooms. And there's wind, so that over the house the skies are a shifting chiaroscuro. It couldn't have been more perfect if she'd written the script, except that in her script she would have seen Daniel more recently than Wednesday, and in her script, Daniel would somehow show up, costumed or not. She imagines dancing.

There are headlights; Ross closes the door – "too eager" – and she waits near the mahogany table. Ina is still worrying about the finger towels in the powder room – "not the beige ones" – and the head caterer is chiding the help about the insufficient ice at the library bar, but Angela is finished studying her part. Behind her the orchestra tunes its strings, and a violin separates itself out to play a single bar from some simple melody in a minor key. Ross's robes settle down around him. "We've done a good job," he says. He comes to her, in his golden mask, and kisses the feathers near her cheek.

The doorbell rings, and rings again, and all of a sudden there's Peter Pan and Tinker Bell, the Tin Man, with a red heart blinking through perforations in his metal chest, and the Wicked Witch of the West. Then a dozen people in the house with then, and soon after two dozen more.

Lydia is so well-concealed it takes Angela several moments to recognize her – the fear of not being able to see what is obvious now life-sized: Lydia wears a short, very short dress with silver fringe held up by spaghetti straps, a wig of short black hair, spit curls framing her face, bright red lipstick, her bodice tight, with swaying fringe all round, strappy heels, silk stocking with a seam up the back, a cigarette in a long rhinestone holder, a mask encrusted with fake jewels. A flapper. "You look absolutely marvelous," Angela says. "And completely yourself."

"What are you suggesting?"

Jack is dressed as a clown. "Or a court jester," he adds. "I couldn't quite decide."

Emily, in artist's smock, a soft hat, one bandaged ear: "Slightly mad," she whispers.

Mrs. Smythe in a wedding dress! "I never had one," she explains. "We eloped."

"Where's Mr. Smythe?" She doesn't hear the answer.

The wife of one of Ross's associates, as a geisha, no mask, just a perfectly white face and exaggerated black-lined eyes and red lips. And one other woman without a mask, Carolyn, with a painted face, also porcelain, but with jewels that look as though they've been embedded, and enormous false eyelashes. "I'm a living doll." Her husband is dressed as a toymaker. Susan's husband is George Washington but she's Clara Barton, the nurse, in brown, with a high white collar and plain brown mask. And Dora, the garden club's Rose, but not dressed as a rose, as everyone expected, but in black robes, a lace collar, a grayish wig in a bun.

"You are…?" Angela asks.

"Ruth Bader Ginsberg." But she reminds Angela of the grim reaper, despite the lace.

Everyone waltzes. Angela with Jack, after the teacher shows him how, and with their next door neighbor Josh dressed as a circus ringmaster, and with a man she doesn't recognize dressed in rags; the Count of Monte Cristo, he says, holding her close, far too close, seeing as he won't even tell her who he is, while bringing to life her fear of not knowing what's really going on, or who's under what mask.

The ballroom teachers try to arrange quadrilles, but they come out looking like square dances. The punch disappears as quickly as champagne, and as the heat in the rooms grows, windows are opened, the doors, and masks are pushed onto the tops of heads, briefly, though; they only want a little air, and a little food, no one wants to break the spell, and punch is poured into glasses along with champagne. A cha cha – Marie Antoinette in her enormous hairdo – and a tango – Ginsberg and Santa Claus – and Lydia, of course, wants to jitterbug; Van Gogh, then, with the Tin Man, his heart still pulsing on and off. The Mad Hatter, Alice in Wonderland; a wife in a short wig, her husband in long blond curls: Ellen and Portia. The rooms grow ever hotter, from the dancing; orchestra members mop their faces, and ice water is brought to them; masks are laid aside, left hanging from the banister, on the mahogany table, near centerpieces on bars, stray faces, and the people begin to look headless in their elaborate costumes, their heads so plain.

There are several people she really doesn't know – all from Ross's office – and a few guests choose to stay behind their masks the entire evening. Sylvia's dressed as a ballerina in a long dress that resembles Angela's figurine, and there's a tall man as Lincoln, of course. There are courtesans and counts, and one fellow dressed like a peasant in a large soft brown hat – she wonders for a moment if it's Daniel, but that's absurd. Besides, under the mask that covers nearly all of his face and the wig of long flowing hair, she sees that this guest is a little too jittery, not as Daniel would be under these circumstances. Attractive, though, the high, leather boots, soft brown pants, a white shirt with long flowing sleeves, the ties open, at the neck. She'd see him and then not again, but then dancing with Lydia, and with Emily, talking to Jack, Carolyn, Mrs. Smythe, then Ross, and later, Ross again. They exchange glances, this man, whoever he is; he makes her feel flirtatious, and she flips her skirts and makes them sway whenever she sees him watching her dance. A few people had called to ask if a relative or some other houseguest who happened to be in town could attend. He must be someone's houseguest.

Ross's head suddenly seems hugely disproportionate and all the women's teeth too bright. Perfumes and the smell of makeup swirl about rooms that are usually so empty and so taut. She drinks champagne; she even splashes the wine over ice, but however much she fills her glass, the splash, the ice, everything disappears, and she's back at the bar set up in the library or the study asking a bartender for more.

She discovers Lydia hanging on her arm, suggesting they do some sort of dance. "Just show them, Angela, just show them what we can do." She can't think what Lydia means, something about a talent show? Oh, yes, years earlier, they'd considered – briefly – doing a Wizard of Oz rendition for some benefit. Whatever makes Lydia think of that now; there's no yellow brick road in this house.

She sees Sam? Or Jack? with Sylvia, heads close, but there's no tension, nothing serious, no argument, and she sees Ross craning his neck to see where she is and who she's talking to, and she sees him shaking his head at her – she can't see why. Then, just for a moment, she escapes through the kitchen to the open air in the back on the patio. If there'd been doors to the patio through the foyer and through the study, others would have been out there with her. As it is, parties are either indoors or outdoors; there's no crossing over. She realizes she's been followed: the man in the flowing white shirt. He'd stayed clear, always moving and dancing towards the other ends of rooms. Daniel, of course, Daniel, after all, the woodsman, the hunter, at her masquerade ball. He takes her hand and they waltz a few moments before she whispers "the studio!" Fleeing like children over the lawn, they go inside, and in the nearly solid darkness, he takes off his mask and lifts her skirts and puts his hands around her bare waist, his cold hands, and he kisses her, and it's not Daniel. She pushes him away, yanking her skirts down. Pulling him into the half-caste light near the window, pulling him with such force he stumbles, she sees Mr. Smythe.

[3] Inside, the party has continued without her; she'd imagined it as stopped, as though under a spell like the court of a dark fairy tale, fingers pricked, her guests waiting for her in static postures, arms raised, glasses to lips, dances paused, no music, even, to come back to life only when she comes back, only to resume their writhing to the music then, her mask in hand. But this isn't the case. Stunned by what she's done, cold to the bone, her arms crossed and pressed across her chest, she makes her way to the library, hoping it will be less crowded there – the kitchen's full up with the caterer's staff, the foyer with dancers, so the library; she'll wallow in humiliation there. Mr. Smythe said, red-faced, "I thought you knew," before he fled. Only a few guests are there, and it's as if they've been strewn: a man in a red cape in the chair in front of the fire with his leg thrown over the arm; a woman in a fancy gown kneeling in front of the man dressed as Lincoln sitting cross-legged on the floor, knees jutting out, both with mouths wide open in a bout of laughter, and – making no mistake this time, no mistake being possible – Daniel, completely at ease, at the table near the mantel. No costume. He's at Ross's puzzles, has one in hand, and he looks up at her, without a flicker of recognition. She has the hallucinatory sense that Ross and Mr. Smythe and Daniel are all the same man, that their images and identities are slipping and sliding over each other and scurrying off into new directions without telling her which way they've gone; she doesn't know if she's expected to follow. As she watches, Ross approaches Daniel, and he smiles, and together they seem to discuss the puzzle, now in Daniel's hand, now in Ross's, Daniel smiling even more broadly. She closes her eyes and turns away, bumping into the Tin Man, his heart no longer glowing.

[4] Guests drift to their cars, too tired for another waltz, they say, but complaining they've had too much fun to think of sleeping. She sees Ross stride through the foyer from the living room. Odd, that in a triumphant moment like this, his head back, and his shoulders, his chest out, his robes flowing, he has the swagger of a man who is, in fact, caught in self-doubt. Mr. Smythe left without coming back inside. She doesn't know how or when her lover vanished. Althea Smythe kisses her cheek on her way out, saying "Lovely evening, darling." The orchestra plays its last chord.

Last to leave, Jack and Lydia are in the living room. Angela stands by the mahogany table watching Ross just as she had hours and hours before. Taillights disappear down the street. He looks as disappointed as he does satisfied. The night he'd looked forward to is over now, but the memories are there, and the knowledge that it's been a success. Her mask is on the table beside her; she touches the feathers; they seem cold. Illusions dissolve; candles burn out. She stopped wanting to hide behind white feathers. After Mr. Smythe – the memory of which sickens her nearly as much as if she'd actually made love – she didn't need to peer out of her mask unknown, unseen, her eyes shaded; after Daniel left, she'd taken the mask off for good, but carried it, appropriate, some vestige. Ross had pushed his mask to the top of his head, and it's still propped there; the elastic stretched, his hair disheveled. He must have forgotten about it. They turn and together join Jack and Lydia in the living room. Ross seems lost; what's he remembering, which costume, what moment? She makes her own mind blank.

Jack pulls up a chair to sit on beside the couch on which Lydia sits, and she's leaning towards him; her posture is luxurious, languid, reminding Angela of an old-fashioned movie still; all she needs is her cigarette lit. "Great fun, you guys," Jack says, without looking away from Lydia. "I think it's time to take this flapper home." He runs his fingers through the spit curls of her wig as though they really belong to her. From underneath her long fake lashes, Lydia looks girlish, fresh, ready for whatever might be next, dancing, perhaps, or champagne drunk from her shoe. They're exhausted, but neither Ross nor Lydia nor Jack are quite ready to let go, are even loathe to let the evening go; what will they hang onto? The fantasy, the stepping out of themselves? Tomorrow will resemble a typical day, and even if she and Ross were to hold another masquerade, this one will never be duplicated; the anticipation will never quite be the same. The effect of seeing their friends and acquaintances in costumes has been a thrill. But held again, it would become a game, a competition, who has the most outrageous, the scariest, the funniest costume. They would have to start giving out prizes.

"Christ, Jack, I can't believe you had the nerve to dress up as a clown," Ross says. "And that Emily looked ridiculous. 'Half-mad.' She got that right. Who was that young guy without a costume? Where did he come from?"

She glances at Ross. He's already looking at her. "Did you know him, Angela?"

"I thought he must be here to give someone a ride home," she says.

"I danced with him," Lydia says. "He was great."

He danced?

Jack says. "Not better than I am."

While she was out kissing Mr. Smythe in the studio?

"He was interested in my puzzles." Ross takes the mask off the top of his head and tries to smooth his hair down, but it obstinately stands up on end. "He took that globe apart and put it back together so easily you'd think he'd seen it before. Talked about dovetail joints. Didn't catch his name." A clock chimes. "Listen to that. Four a.m."

The caterer and Ina come through extinguishing candles, stacking stray plates. "Ina, go, come back tomorrow, whenever you want. No rush. The caterer's not coming back for the rest of his things until Monday."

"I'll just take care of this first," she says, her arms barely reaching around a huge crystal bowl. "Shall I save it or pour it down the sink?" It seems like a big decision. Angela follows her out to the kitchen.

"Did you invite him?" Ina asks. In her black dress and white apron and the piece of square lace bobby pinned in her hair makes her look as if she's in costume herself.

"Of course not. I was shocked."

"Why is that boy taking chances?"

That boy.

"I need to see Jack and Lydia out," she whispers. "Otherwise they might never leave."

Dizzy, she watches them walk to their car hand in hand.

Chapter Fourteen

[1] She wakes mid-morning to find Ross gone; she seems to remember overhearing him, still Merlin, and the Tin Man and Sir Francis Drake discussing golf. When she lifts her head from the pillow, it feels stuffed with white cotton; she knew she'd had much more to drink than usual, but after coming in from the studio, after seeing Daniel with Ross, she'd felt painfully clear-headed. After Lydia and Jack left, she'd waited until Ross was on his way upstairs before saying, "I just want to make sure all the candles are out." She'd avoided any more conversation about strange men or costumes or after effects. Daniel had danced with Lydia. She was afraid if Ross said the wrong thing – *You said you were dressing in black* – she would answer – *Just so you know, I'm in love with someone else.* Crawling into bed beside him, her arms and legs aching, she'd been afraid he'd want to make love; he sometimes did after their parties. But no, he was sound asleep, thank God. She'd considered sleeping in the guest room, had stood in the doorway wanting that bed, could hear Ross breathing, but Ross would question this, and she didn't want to be questioned first thing in the morning. Champagne; she'd had too much, and containing its swirl and sway, the effort of that, must have contributed to the headache; the keeping it all in must have produced this hangover.

Sitting up, she looks out over the lawn, half expecting Daniel; the separation between her lives has blurred; Daniel keeps slipping into this one; perhaps it's permanent. Maybe this is what Ina had meant when she'd disagreed it would turn to nothing. Mr. Smythe's lips pressing against her own. Which life was that? She draws the back of her hand over her mouth, but his pressure there seems to linger. She pushes away the sheets and covers and tears off her nightgown and wraps herself in her black silk robe with large pink gardenias.

She'll change the bed linen today; it smells tainted; she catches the scent of stale punch and staler cigars. The men had retreated to the study to smoke; she'd seen Jack, in his bright jacquard costume and orange wig, sitting in her wicker chair.

Downstairs, remnants; flowers, the food, someone's discarded mask, feathers from a boa, a sash; it'll be all right; Ina will help finish up, and the caterers will be back. But she's impatient for order. She wants all the reminders of the party discarded; more has been lost than gained. She spills the coffee measuring it out, drops her cup taking it from the cupboard; it shatters on the tile floor, its handle sliding halfway to the swinging door. Daniel stood with her husband discussing puzzles. But as far as everyone else is concerned, the party was a success; by the middle of the week, she'll be back in her studio, and Daniel will come back through the hedge, and she'll berate him for showing up, but they'll make love, and act like children getting away with being naughty.

At the same time, exhausted by the artifice, the second life, she wants only one, one in which choices are hers, not Ross's, and not Daniel's, both men free, really, doing as they please. She paces back and forth by the windows in the study. Strides back and forth across the foyer and its strange parquet floor. Her confession to Ross – if there ever is one – won't only be that she's had a lover; it will be that her discontent has grown large. She goes through the kitchen – the broken cup still on the floor – and out to the patio. It's chilly; she pulls her thin robe around her more tightly. Guilt – not the guilt, or not only the guilt that Daniel has been here, looking comfortably at home in their library – but the guilt and discomfort or fear that she can't – won't – live with this any longer. The realization resembles illness; there's also glory, and it's also physical. A terrible triumph. But the truth is also that her lover has been with Ross, in their house when it was full of friends, and not only that. Full of friends in revealing costumes.

Ross might still be home – she hasn't actually looked – in the library or perhaps he's outside, in front, checking the torches. She goes through the house and out the front door, as if ready with a speech. No Ross. The grass is wet, and so cold and so abrupt a sensation on her feet in black slippers that it clears her head. Daniel won't come now, and not tomorrow, but she's impatient; she wants to talk about what he's done, and about what might happen now. She imagines Lydia and Jack getting up together going out to brunch, reading the Sunday paper. Maybe even having sex. They must sometimes. There's Sarah.

She'll take a drive. Get away. She pulls out of the garage as if emerging from a cavern and drives away from the house slowly, as though trying something new. She lowers all the car windows; the air's cool enough and wet enough to make her breath visible. She laughs. She turns on the radio. Love songs blare. A man putting out garbage turns to stare. Then, going faster, she drives the way they did that day on the way back from the beach.

But soon she finds herself in an unfamiliar neighborhood; she might have driven through it after finding the construction site on Route Six, but there's nothing definitely familiar. She doubles her robe over her chest, puts the windows up, turns the radio down, peers out the windshield looking for something she knows. Her inebriation feels fresh. Slowing down, she makes herself concentrate, but there's no town, no sign, just trees, and small houses set far apart. She feels ridiculous. She's only been gone a half hour; so how far from home can she be?

She swerves to avoid a young woman on a bike. She's unreasonably nervous, as if something truly bad is about to happen, but all she is is lost.

News comes on through the music. Kidnapping, murder, a dead child.

[2] She turns right, creeps along, looks for street signs, some sort of information. Considers turning back, the road is getting narrow. A pickup truck comes from the other direction; the man inside looks at her.

To her left there's nothing but thin woods and underbrush; to her right a brick house with a yapping dog tied to a stake, and a row of slim trees beside a clapboard house with the stand from a swing set, but no swings; next to this still another house, one with peeling green paint which someone has started to cover with white, but unevenly, and only at one end. A wooden ramp leads up to the door through weeds all grown up very high; there's an old car. The front door opens, a wheelchair emerges, and behind it, pushing it, guiding it through the door and down the ramp, Daniel.

It can't be; the resemblance is remarkable, but just last night she'd thought he was Mr. Smythe. It seems she can no longer recognize her own lover.

She stops, backs up, goes too near a ditch, feels the car dip. Wildflowers sit on stalks as high as the windows. Daniel lifts a frail woman from the wheelchair. He works to fit her dazed arms and legs into the front of the old car.

He glances up then, and sees her. He shakes his head, and runs his hand through his hair, but looks neither surprised nor upset, only, she thinks, disappointed.

She gets out of the car, but what does she think she can do, standing in the road, in her silk robe caught on weeds, her heart climbing out of her body by way of her throat?

A car comes up, slows, moves away.

Daniel closes the door for the old woman, the mother he'd told her has died, told her he'd sat with, told her he'd left behind in a coma, up north, all of which had turned him into this wanderer, without a home, and what he wanted.

But this is where he lives, where he goes, to this horrible house, this ill-kept place; he told her he's lazy. It's the only thing he told her that she hadn't believed.

The front door of the house, a door with white paint peeling like lace, stands open, propped oddly back, as though the hinges aren't working right, and she sees a different woman. In slow motion, another woman comes out of the darkness of the dank little house, a woman not much older than a girl, but tired as an old woman, as used; she must be the relative, the cousin or sister, the Hannah he'd talked about. She stands at the door, holding it open, wearing a green colored shift, a dress of no shape, of uncertain material.

Daniel raises his hand, and calls out to Angela what seems to be a benediction, a sort of quiet incantation; she can't hear his words. He's beautiful. She's aware of her hands holding the top of the car door, her pale, narrow hands, a cracked nail, and a woman's voice on the radio singing a song about auto repair. Daniel crosses back to the girl, the woman standing there, and kisses her, oddly, on the top of her arm, and all the while this Hannah watches her. Daniel gets in the car beside the old woman and backs it down the driveway. His mother's face and head come near her, on her side; the mother, leaning against the door, cheek pressed against the glass, doesn't appear able to identify anything. Her head and face pause next to her, while the car shifts into forward, muffler roaring. The mother's face has fallen in on itself.

The cloth of her silk robe seems transparent and is cold, cold against her bare skin; she might as well be standing there naked. The girl at the door is still there.

She leaves the car at its tilting angle in the weeds that now seem to be growing up through the floor of it, and walks up the shabby gravel driveway, if it can be called gravel; there's hardly any left, only a few stones here and there.

She walks up to the front door, as though still drunk, certainly she's drunk now. The girl stands up just a little straighter, but Angela feels no sense of threat. She's determined to introduce herself to this cousin.

"May I come in?"

Hannah says "No" but Angela goes in anyway.

The house smells. There's sickness, and old food, and a dampness, as though it's been raining inside, and there's wet dust; she breathes this in deeply; there's something about it she likes and feels satisfied by.

"So this is where he lives. He told me he lived nowhere in particular."

The girl has a band of black vine tattooed around the top of her arm, although it looks like barbed wire. There's also blood there, as though the tattoo itself has managed to cut her.

"And you're a relative? A cousin? It's Hannah, right?"

"Cousin?" Hannah runs her hand over her arm; she seems to be trying to smooth down the black vine; her nails are short, but filed to points. "I'm his wife. Who the hell are you?"

The floor dissolves, and her knees, and she sees it's remarkable that she's still standing. "I must have misunderstood." She's hoarse, as though she's been screaming. The girl, the wife, presses a sharpened nail against the wire vine circling her arm. Blood appears. She says, "He told me I was imagining things. But I knew he was seeing somebody; I wasn't expecting somebody rich, or old, but I knew there was somebody."

It's as though her skin has been shed; all that was safe, and there wasn't much left, vanishes. She watches the blood on Hannah's arm, horrified, but also removed, as though the blood might be fake.

"He steals," Angela says.

"He only takes what he needs." Hannah's face is still now, but tears have appeared like sudden rain; her cheeks are wet with them. "Get out," she says.

"I didn't know he was married."

"Would it have made a difference?" When she doesn't answer, doesn't automatically lie and say yes, Hannah says. "Aren't you married?"

She turns her hand against her thigh so that her wedding ring wouldn't gleam in the dark.

"That didn't matter," Hannah says "not to either of you two." Blood drips down her arm.

"His mother – it is his mother?" she says. "I hope she recovers. She was dead, and then in a coma, it was confusing."

"Get out."

She feels rooted there, as though staying will change the outcome of the story.

"Get out." Hannah takes a step towards her.

In her robe of pink gardenias, she glides back out the door. She walks to her car through the grass, and the dew soaks through her thin slippers. "He loves me," Hannah yells out across the beaten yard. "Me!" She's pounding her chest. Angela tries to drive away with some grace, but discovers she's stuck in mud. The front door of Daniel's house closes. Softly, afraid now, she retries the gas, but the car doesn't budge; she panics, and jams the gas pedal to the floor. The car lurches backwards across the road and sideswipes a tree. She shifts into drive, lurches forward, hears metal being shaved with sickening clarity.

[3] They'd moved into their house early in the summer, when a large patch of day lilies was just coming into bud. She'd go out every morning to see how they were doing. Any day could be the day they burst into their orange bloom.

One morning, looking out, she thought she must be mistaken; what she saw didn't register. Each bud had been snapped off, or, as it turned out, eaten. By deer, she was told. One by one the deer had stood in the night eating their fill of her orange hope.

And when she was a little girl, a cousin once stayed at their house. This cousin, she knew, was adopted, and she knew, or sensed, that the cousin was trouble, that the parents didn't know what to do with her, that they seemed to think if the girl's genes were theirs, they would automatically have answers. Angela was eight or nine years old the night the girl, fourteen, tried to hang herself from the guest room light fixture with the sheet from the narrow guest room bed. But, silly, the sheet was too long, the light fixture too low, and too small. The girl's weight pulled it away from the ceiling, only wires held it. Angela saw it, the sheet still attached.

Her wedding veil rises up, she feels the whoosh of it, over and over again the wedding veil rises, and Ross is not there, or he's there, but doesn't see her.

Finding debris, a tipped over chair, she thinks there must have been an intruder, completely forgetting about the masquerade. Upstairs, she stands in front of her closet full of clothes, unable to decide what one wears for a day like this. She thinks she hears Ross. He might be home, or home any minute. She'll say she's hung over; she tries saying it out loud, hoping a hangover will excuse everything. Ross isn't there, and by the time Ina arrives, she's dressed in the clothes she normally wears to art classes – baggy pants, white shirt – and arranged in her wicker chair. Feverish, she tells Ina, please leave me alone.

"What a shame," Ina says, standing too near. "It was a wonderful party. How about coffee? Advil?"

Angela thinks Ina might be mocking her, but when she looks, Ina is simply waiting for an answer, patient in her purple cardigan. Angela runs her nails along the soft underbelly of her arm. "Not now."

She expects, half expects, completely expects Daniel to show up, to ring the front door bell, to come, hat in hands, with some impossible explanation. She hopes he will; she doesn't care what Ina would think. It's more important that she not suffer alone, but time narrows; Ina leaves, Ross comes home. When she hears the door, and feels the air leave the house, she runs up the stairs, and climbs into the shower with all of her clothes on. She feels baptized.

[4] Ross is calling through the house for her; he wants iced tea on the patio. Feeling as though all her nerves have been stripped, but then, in the very next moment, as though double and triple sets of nervous tissue has been pushed in under her skin, she lurches from minute to minute.

She spills the tea as she fills their glasses; she sits on the patio while Ross talks, hears nothing. "It seems I'm hung over," she says more than once. Ross glances at her but offers nothing. The afternoon is really too chilly to sit outside; the goose bumps on her skin feel like thousands of pinpricks, but she doesn't complain.

For dinner, she sets the long dining room table formally, placing herself and Ross at each end. She will do penance.

"Not much to look forward to, is there, with the masquerade over," Ross says, taking a sip from his water glass. A droplet falls to the table. She watches the small glistening dome on the thick white linen. The masquerade seems eons away, as far as the one she'd witnessed in Venice. Ross eats his fish, his new potatoes, his salad, his blood orange sorbet. She cuts her portions into the smallest bits possible and pushes them to the extreme edges of her plate. She lets the sorbet melt.

"You look nice tonight," he says.

She's quite sure she's never looked worse; she put on a red dress, one she's never liked, one Lydia pressured her into buying. Ross tells her how well he played the ninth hole – the one he usually slices off to the right – really well, especially considering how tired he was. She smiles, nods, chews the skin on the inside of her cheek. They're behaving as though they've only met a few times.

The liquids from her melting sorbet separate into clear and opaque swirls of pale and paler orange.

Afterwards, after Ross has put his napkin on the table and pushed himself away, she takes his hand and leads him up the stairs.

"What's this?" he says.

She undresses ahead of him and in front of him and gets into their bed and touches him in places she'd only ever touched Daniel, intimate places deeply hidden between thighs, the thinnest skin; touching there, Daniel says, releases spates of sensation so intense he's afraid she'll tear him apart. She tries to make Ross Daniel, but a Daniel who has never lied. And she tries to find pleasure as she has with Daniel. She becomes rough with wanting to find that pleasure, and Ross laughs uncomfortably, says stop, but she doesn't know what he means. There's no pleasure. Only dismay. Ross's shoulders are too large and his stomach soft and big and his hair is dark and he seems so coarse underneath her. When she puts her hand on his chest where on Daniel it fits so perfectly, on Ross this place only feels like flesh. She gives up.

Ross must think she's tired; climbing on top, he finishes himself off. She remembers the damaged car in the middle of the night. She can't think of a thing to tell Ross. She supposes it could have happened while parked somewhere. *But just where were you yesterday?* She doesn't have the courage to go to him first, tell him something happened, something close to what really happened but made up. She drifts off thinking that when she wakes she'll have to perform some sort of experiment; that the morning will be some sort of experiment. But she can't quite put the elements together, something about half-truths, and half-lives.

She hears Ross leave in the early half-light. He might see her car. Amazing he missed it yesterday; he must have been thinking about the party. It might take him a moment to recognize damage, to name it, so out of place here. He'll be confused. He'll feel his own head has been dented.

"Angela. What happened?" She didn't hear him come back up the stairs, and so much time has passed, she assumed he'd left. She had already visualized him pulling out of the driveway while she was still in bed, still buried in the covers, the shape of his head still in the pillow; she'd been just about to punch the pillow, to get the impression of his head out, so that she would be alone in the bed, alone in the house, preparing for a day she knows nothing about, and can't know.

"Angela."

"The car?" She sits upright. After barely a moment, after a hesitation that's barely perceptible, she says "I hit a tree."

"A tree?" Ross's voice is high-pitched.

"Yes. In a parking lot. As I was backing out. I didn't stop to look. It didn't seem too bad, a little paint, I thought. Sorry. I forgot about it."

"A little paint? It looks as though you hit a truck. You didn't call our insurance agent? Have you seen it?"

"It can't be that bad."

"It looks as though you hit a truck. Are you sure it was a tree? How big a tree? What parking lot?"

"What difference does it make?" Maybe it wasn't a tree, maybe it was a mailbox, a guardrail, Daniel's house. She's already back under the covers, tired with the confession, since what there is of it has failed to accomplish anything. She could just as well have lied completely, said she didn't notice, a car must have hit her while she was parked, because taking a little of the responsibility for it feels like taking no responsibility for it at all. What had she been looking for?

[5] She could as easily hold a lit match against her skin as carry on conversations about tables and chairs and what's owed the caterer. She wants to help with the house to hurry it along, but shrinks from being in the same room with the strangers in white shirts, or with Ina, in her purple housedress; there will be no putting the house back in order, ever.

"Do you still feel a little hung over?" Ina asks gently.

"I've had some bad news," but can't tell her what it is, can't even think of a lie.

Lydia calls. "That was fantastic. A fantastic party. Are you free today?"

They're normal now? "Not really. A lot to do to get the house back."

"Isn't Ina there? Want me to help?"

Help? Lydia help with housework? If she weren't miserable she'd laugh. "No, I'll manage. We're fine here."

"Tomorrow then. So much to talk about."

"Maybe the next day."

"There you go. Back to your Emily Dickinson routine."

Clearly Lydia has slipped back into her own; how? Jack must be a miracle worker. Or is it some form of amnesia?

"I just need some time to recover. It was exhausting." Angela hopes Daniel will never have the nerve to come see her again at the same time she's desperately eager to see him; she paces, feels watched, by Ina, by Ross.

Chapter Fifteen

[1] Ross is leaving for somewhere, Chicago, maybe, while she sits in her wicker chair, staring, staring, at the back lawn.

"I have to go," he says from the doorway.

"Okay."

"What are you doing today?"

"I don't know. Have a good trip. You'll be back, when, Friday?"

"Yes, Friday, probably Friday night," but she's paying little attention to her own words, much less his. He seems childish, standing there, as though he's hoping for a moment of a mother's attention. "Will you draw?" he says. After hating her preoccupation, of feeling left out – just once, when he was out with the gardener one morning, he stood at her studio door, and said "This is your work?" And she'd said yes, but saw how his eyes skirted over the surface of her papers, of the sketches she'd tacked to the wall, not once looking directly at the painting on the easel; he'd been unable to make eye contact with any of the flowers or shapes or body parts – but there he stands there now, asking her. She should say yes, I'm going to draw, I have a new project; it would make him walk away. But she hasn't done a thing, not a thing, since she smashed up her car.

"I don't plan to paint."

"Not even going out there?" he's going to be careful and not call it the shed, as he usually does, "What about Lydia? Anything with her?"

"Aren't you going to be late for your plane?"

She might as well have shut the door in his face; it's odd, her wielding so much power suddenly, but not through speech or action; through silence. She says she's not feeling well. It's like no other illness he's ever witnessed; he clearly finds her calmness – he sees it as calmness, because she barely dares move – unsettling. In truth, she's never known a state of such complete agitation. She's still because she's afraid the slightest movement will tear her apart.

"Are you mad at me?" he finally asks.

She looks over her shoulder at him, surprised he's still there; even as she's thinking about him, she'd forgotten him. "I thought you'd left."

"What are you so angry about?"

"Angry? I'm not angry. I'm sick."

"Then go see a doctor."

"Ross. Your plane." She softens her expression, for him, to help get him out of the house. "You don't want to miss it."

Only a few minutes later, a sharp rap at the study window. Daniel? No, Lydia; she must have missed the door bell ringing. But as if a trigger has been tripped, her heart triples its pace. "Ross sent me," Lydia shouts.

"I have some sort of flu," she calls back.

"So he said. Let me in."

Dragging herself to the kitchen, she opens the door, but doesn't even say hello, before going back to her chair in the study. "I have the flu, that's all. What's the matter with all of you, hovering around like this?" She resettles the pillows, but they seem too small or too large, and tosses them to the floor. "I've been sick before and no one noticed."

"This is different. And doesn't seem very flu-like. Maybe you're pregnant."

"Ha." Angela's laugh is short, harsh. "I have a fever. Ina's in and out. There's no danger." She sits up a little taller while Lydia looks her over. "I had way too much to drink at the party. I must have already been coming down with something."

"We haven't even talked about the party. You've been cooped up ever since. Sylvia's ballerina outfit was much too young and Althea Smythe's wedding dress – ridiculous, that huge woman in that wide, white dress," while her groom, as only Angela knew, was in the studio.

"Sam looked handsome, though, in that tuxedo and tails, his baton," – and Lydia raises her hand as though she were in charge of a roomful of musicians – "he says if he hadn't gone into banking, he would have become an orchestra conductor. Can't you just see him at Tanglewood?"

"Has he said anything to Sylvia yet? They seemed pretty comfortable."

"I have no idea. I can't solve everybody's problems."

A flare of anger. Unexpected. Uncontrollable. "We should have a party during which everyone takes turns coming out. We could sit in a circle."

"Coming out?"

"Of all their lies. Our lies. The ones we've told our spouses. Our friends. Our bosses. Wouldn't that be a hoot?"

"What is wrong with you? You really do need a psychiatrist. And meds."

"To make me more or less sad?"

"Okay. Change the subject. Your costume was pretty."

"I'm really tired." Angela's stomach flip flops.

"Did you see me dancing?"

Angela shuts her eyes.

"You should see someone."

Angela feels a bubbling near the surface.

"One visit," Lydia says. "Just to talk. What harm would it do?"

"Please stop." Angela's never going to any of the therapists or counselors or psychiatrists her acquaintances see or send their husbands and children to is partly due to a belief in self-sufficiency – honesty with oneself should produce better results than forced confessions to strangers. "And nobody would agree to just one. They'd want a whole series. They'd want to take me apart." And, left-over from her parents' thinking is the belief that few problems or states of mind warrant such self-indulgence.

"Anything would be better than hiding in the dark," Lydia says.

"You can hide and I can't?"

"I'm not hiding. Here I am."

"Jack told me."

"Told you what?"

"That you've spent all these years trying to wish me into lesbianism."

With fascination Angela watches Lydia's face as a movie camera lens would, watches Lydia's face harden, and then shift into denial, and liberation, and despair, and anger, soft and hard and soft again, with subtle variations, both readable and inscrutable; watches as all that has been extravagant collapses, a party balloon.

"Lydia, I'm sorry. Lydia, I'm so sorry."

But Lydia's gone.

[2] The air is dense and impenetrable. Ross is home. She wants to know when he'll be leaving again, wants him to leave, but is afraid to ask; she'd seem too anxious. It's best to appear normal, so she dresses, leaves the house for short intervals, even if only to drive into town and back, and once or twice pretending to be on her way to see Lydia, and would like to, but Lydia won't see her, and then Jack tells him they had a falling out. "Over what?" Ross asked. "Oh, it'll pass," Jack answered. "Just some benefit." Ross stops asking if she's still sick. But she is still sick. After all these days, nine days, ten nights, since Daniel, since Hannah and the old woman, there's no relief in sight. There's no safe place in

her mind, no room in the house, nowhere in town, no friend to tell; no Lydia. No Lydia. There's nothing. On an occasional morning she'll wake up unaware, but the truth of what's happened immediately seeps back in, and every time it's more devastating to watch each sickening moment accumulate. Daniel in her backyard, Daniel in her bed, Daniel in her studio, her heart, her mind, her body. Then, Daniel at that ugly house with a wheelchair like a prop, as if the scene had been planned, as if some hoax were in place, a hoax it was inevitable she'd fall into. And then Daniel and his ruined mother. And Daniel and his ruined wife.

And her peculiar and painful nostalgia for a Lydia that never existed. They have lost their innocence. Come of age. After a fabricated twelve years. And the mother's face, pressed against the car window, and the smell of the dank green house filling her nostrils, and the bloody vine on that bloody arm. And Lydia's distended face in her hyper-extended camera lens.

Angela looks as if she hasn't slept – her hollow eyes have dark circles – but she does sleep, she knows she does, because she also knows when she's released from sleep, that horrible moment. Then it's as though she's being filled with excruciating liquid, mercury, the liquid both flexible and solid. She's easily shocked by small noises. Ross watches her while she watches the studio.

[3] An ordinary day, with Ross at the office, Ina in the house, the gardener pulling away after clearing away dead leaves; she ventures across the lawn, making an effort to feel safe. In her mind, she wears the dress she wore for the masquerade, the white dress with embroidery and flowing sleeves. She walks as though wearing that, not the narrow beige skirt that stops at her knees. In the studio, nothing has been touched; she'd imagined it otherwise, disturbed, packed up. She'll choose the memories she wants: Daniel the first night; Daniel appearing through the dark branches of the hedge; Daniel with her in their bed, or on the white couch, or that day at the beach. And Lydia, welcoming her, laughing with her, taking her in, walking arm in arm down Boylston Street.

"Angela?" Daniel in the doorway.

A trick, a figment, not a possibility.

But he's there, wearing the clothes he had on the first night, and they're just as dirty, dirtier. He holds his hat in his hands. His hair needs washing. "I haven't been able to sleep," he says.

"You had no trouble sleeping before I found out about Hannah?"

"Were you lost? What were you doing there?"

"Where's your mother?" Anger has been missing. Defeat, humiliation – she'd been a fool – but she hasn't felt the full complication of anger until now, and it's a hard, inner disassembling. "Telling me the truth," she says, "would have given me choices."

"There was truth here."

"Where's your mother?"

"You don't think I love you."

"Did she die?" How flippant she sounds, as if asking him if he's brought in the mail.

He slowly turns his hat around and around by the brim. "Nursing home. Death, without any of the contentment she wanted."

"I would never say someone was dead, unless I hated them."

"Death, marriage, passion, it's not all black and white."

"Oh, please. And lies? What color are they?" Lydia appears to her as chiaroscuro.

"You never asked many questions, Angela." Daniel's voice is harsh, as if the words are edged in black.

"I asked plenty of questions."

"But you never pressed for answers."

"You needed freedom. It's what kept you alive."

"It's what kept *you* alive."

She tosses her drawing tablet across the table. She stands – she wants to push him, knock him right over as she rushes out the door; she pictures him sprawled out on the floor – but instead she only goes as far as her stool where she sits with her head in her hands. She can feel the shape of the bones of her skull under her hair.

"Hannah and I have been together two years." His voice is tender now as he talks about Hannah; he loves her. "But it has never been much of a marriage; it has always been a mistake."

"Two years?" They were together nearly a third of that. What about mistakes? She tries to think if mistakes make a marriage less of one, but all she can see is the bleeding vine on Hannah's arm, and Hannah in that dark, dank house. Unearthly smells, her car, metal tearing metal apart. She punches methodic holes through paper with her pencil point.

"I never should have put you or Hannah through this," he says.

"Don't lump me with Hannah. If I'd known about her… You could have saved one of us." But pressed against the face of her anger is a desire to have him come near her now. She wants him to run his fingers down the pattern on the back of her blouse, or put his hands to her hair; she wants to hear him say "Angela" the way he did the first night as though this will clear the air.

Instead, "We made a decision."

She thinks of the cracked cement beneath his feet and draws that thick, jagged line down her paper.

"What was outside of us wouldn't be a part of what we had here."

"We never said that."

"But that's how we behaved."

Chapter Sixteen

[1] The studio is off limits. Ross keeps his distance. She sleeps in the guest room, even as that's nearly as painful as sleeping beside Ross. She's lost her place. She belongs nowhere. She watches for Daniel. She expects ambush, surprise, while expecting neither. She waits for Lydia to call, forgetting how unlikely. She wakes with a start during the night under the impression she's forgotten to take her pills, but what pills can they be; they seem real and urgent, but she can't name the pills, or their reason. And when she tries to remember, to think, where and what they might be, the idea of them drifts through her fingers like sand. Thinking she's forgotten something vital to her health, or safety, but at the same time, not knowing what, leaves her adrift, and more terrified.

"Angela?" Ross asks in the dark.

She'd like to talk to Melanie, but hasn't been to class, and can't think of an excuse to call her. She has pretend conversations with her in her head. Melanie says all the right things.

Slowly, with nothing to hide, no questions to answer, no responsibility, she begins to find balance, and to recognize safer places to rest her mind. Feeling steeled, she goes to the club and insists on joining the table where Lydia is sitting. Emily says "What happened to you two?"

"Lydia, I saw...Lydia, let's go..." But Lydia is cold. Angela tries to corner her, in the ladies' room, in the hallway, on the tennis court. "Let's talk."

But all Lydia says is "Don't."

[2] Angela, on her own with all she knows, goes to the studio simply to say that she has. She and Ross go out to dinner more, and she suggests they have friends in. She's moving on, even as moving on is moving backwards. She has remarried Ross.

venteen

[1] Behind her easel and canvas of bright broad angry colors, Daniel, at the studio door.

"No." She sounds determined.

But in he comes, shutting the door with deliberation.

"Don't touch me. Don't." Backing away, she knocks over the small lamp; the light bulb bursts and throws sparks. The beach, the house ablaze with light, her white mask. She's against the wall, he's facing her, close, without touching. "Where's Hannah?" she says.

"I love you."

She's not thinking of love. She's thinking of quicksand. "Where's Hannah?"

"She's gone. I told her everything. We couldn't survive; there wasn't enough between us. With or without you."

He leans closer; with both of her hands she pushes against him.

"Please." He stands firmly. "Please. Believe me."

"Why this time?"

"Please."

When she gives in, it's not to love. It's to anger, and hard edges, swords needing to be sunk into flesh. When he entangles his fingers in her hair and pulls her head back, she sinks her fingertips into his chest, just beneath the place where the palm of her hand fits perfectly. Raw, ghastly sex.

And afterwards, she hates her nakedness; they are both too naked. She kneels, hoping to hide her face against his belly, but he kneels down beside her. She sobs, the sound is painful and dry, "How could you?" She's ugly, but he says, "I love you."

In the days that follow, their desire is out of hand. It's pure, but also punishing. They hurt each other with their probing, their needs. She'll sink her nails into the soft flesh of his buttocks or the muscles of his back while she lets him sink down into her; or he might bite her breasts and nipples until she cries out, his fingers deep inside her; whether she cries out from pleasure or pain, she doesn't know, and doesn't much care. It's emotion, and this is all she wants, however raw, illicit or ill-defined.

Part Three

Chapter One

[1] Crouching down on the studio's broken step instead of coming in, Daniel says, "I want to tell you about my mother." He hesitates so long she thinks he might not go on. But then, "She left us. She left my father – I can't blame her for that – but also my brother and me. I was thirteen." He runs his thumb along the door jamb, testing for strength, or workmanship, or flaws. "I thought she must have died – why else would she be gone? – but my father said no, she was just chicken. But I went on pretending she'd died, because it was better than thinking she was a coward."

Angela wants to sit beside him, but he's self-contained and separate.

"But then, a few years ago, I decided to try and find her." He takes a single cigarette from his shirt pocket and lights it with a match. "That's when I met Hannah. She was a clerk up in the main Portland records office. She's the one who tracked her down, found out she was living down here and working as a cook." He sits there a moment, smoking, flicking ash into the grass. "Hannah and I left Portland together, got married, justice of the peace, moved into my mother's house. She'd had a stroke, a small one, but she was already scared."

Daniel sighs, one quick expression of air. "My mother left to look for a better life. Away from my father."

"Did she find one?"

"She would never say."

"So you only imagined making those things for her, the shelves, the porch." What a sad, sad detail.

"I did make them," he says, standing up. Perhaps he'll come in now. "I thought it would make her want to come home. Some impossible telepathy." He taps his hat against his hand. "When I told her, she said she wished she'd known. She would've liked to have seen that porch." He leans down to press out his cigarette against the step; she starts towards him with the little ceramic dish he uses, but he puts the leftover end in his pocket, saying, "That's enough."

She can't convince him to stay.

Later, on a day they've been unusually quiet, almost solemn, and haven't made love, and when the story of his mother isn't hanging quite so heavily, she says, "Did you love Hannah?" He's slouched at the easel; she's opposite, at the far end of the couch. He swivels slowly to face her.

"She had plenty of problems of her own, so I appreciate what she did for me," he says, "but appreciation is not the same as love, and it turned out to not be enough. She found my mother, helped me with her as she got sicker and sicker. Hannah gave up her life in Portland to follow me, but she needed more than I could give her, and it drove her crazy, crazier, the trap, there wasn't enough...affection or...unity. Our marriage was our job. She felt sorry for me, but that's not the same as love, either."

"Marriage as a job. There's more to marriage than love, but there shouldn't be less."

"A riddle?"

"My life with you eclipses my life in that big house. I get away with it. I'm shocked by how much we all get away with. But the scent of you, the smell of you, should give me away. Or the expression on my face after I've been with you. Or when I'm thinking about you while he's talking to me, and my answers make no sense. Does he just think I'm daffy?"

Daniel shakes his head. The gray cat materializes on the outside window sill. "There should be some sort of animal instinct between two people who live so close," he says, leaving the stool to sit beside her.

"Would you have known if Hannah had been...cheating?" She touches his hand, so he'll know she's curious, not judging.

"Who knows for sure, but she would let me into everything, every thought. I can't imagine her keeping a secret like that. I tried to help her, but she didn't want help. She just wanted me to see how dark she was inside. I didn't love that."

"I don't love how blind I was." A scrap of a poem crosses her mind, something that ends with "that nakedness." "Jack avoids me. Lydia keeps her distance while trying not to look too obvious that anything happened between us even though everyone knows it has. It makes everyone uncomfortable, so everyone keeps their distance from me."

"But you've always kept yours. You relied on Lydia for contact. You said so. They don't know how to approach you now. Don't take offense. You keep things from me. You even kept the masquerade a secret. You don't tell Ross anything. I told Hannah some things at least."

"But Hannah was interested. Ross isn't."

"He is. Even if he doesn't realize it. Ross senses everything but only your drawings are visible. Hannah sensed everything, but didn't really ask. And there was nothing to see."

"Maybe she and I are alike. She didn't want to know. When you contradicted yourself, or were vague, I let my questions go."

He concentrates on his hands, running his fingers across his palms, playing with his ring finger as if there were a ring. "Once…once, on my way home right after having been with you, the smell of you was still with me. I always hate washing it off, but that day, Hannah had been so manic in the morning, so angry about something, I was particularly afraid she would pick up your scent. And we usually slept naked so…" His voice is strained thin, as if tied off by wire. "I went into a gas station and tried to wash you off me, off my fingers and off my cock. In the sink. I dipped my hand under the warm water and spooned it over myself, with my pants pulled down a little. Someone came in. I didn't turn around, I stopped what I was doing, but my pants were undone, and I didn't try to cover myself up. I just stopped. He left. He must have thought I was masturbating in that sink. But what I was doing was washing you away so I could go home to my wife."

"What we've been." Even as she sits next to him in the studio where she knows every corner in every light, she feels not quite there, not quite whole, as if there's still another self, one to whom the studio will have a still different meaning. "I don't know how much longer we can go on like this. Or how much longer we should." And even as she expects him to answer with "forever" or "for a long, long time," the conversation has the peculiar feel of loose ends being tied.

"We remind me of this mythical creature I read about once," he says. "This beast who feeds on itself until there's nothing left." He looks around the studio as if it's strange to him.

"Yes," she says.

[2] And so their last night is spent on the couch in the studio, coiled limb to limb, as they had the first night in the guest bedroom. He sleeps; she does on and off while watching the light in the windows change and memorizing each detail of his being next to her, the weight, the warmth, the patterns of his breath; sometimes he breathes faster, as if there were some urgency, or a dream; other times so slowly she can count to seven or eight in between. But under this waiting, this watching, she feels raw. She's calm, and she's not. She's impatient.

She wants morning to come, because she dreads it. She wants his leaving to be over with.

At dawn, Daniel wakes up and softly says, "I hope neither one of us is ever in the situation my mother is. She doesn't know where she is. Doesn't recognize me." He sits up, disentangling his legs from hers. "I wish these two more years she and I had seemed like enough."

"Will you stay in her house?"

"Hannah called. She's with her aunt back in Portland. She sounded all right. Better than she was here with me."

Not ready to cover herself, it might be the last time she's ever naked with a man, she brings him the pitcher and bowl, puts it on the floor near them, and kneels behind him on the couch, his back to her so she can wash his neck and shoulders. Swift sudden images of long snaking limbs and bare buttocks flash; glimpses of them joined, glimpses of her watching, watching him enter and re-enter her. She slips down around him so that her knees are on either side of him. He tilts his head back to rest it against hers. She draws her hands into fists between her chest and his shoulders, thinking she'd like to pummel his bare, damp flesh. There'll be frustration today, and tomorrow, anger and frustration in having and then not having Daniel. Paring him away from her is what she most wants and most fears. And so she brings her fists down hard against his back, pounding him over and over again; he whirls around and catches her arms and presses them against her sides, presses her against him, pinning her breasts painfully.

When she stops, he casts her off. "What are you doing?"

She raises her hand, to do what, she doesn't know; he catches her face between his own hands and squeezes her cheeks and lips and features, distorting them. He kisses her gently; when she reaches her tongue into his mouth he leans back. "No." He gathers up the wet cloth and throws it against the window pane; she half expects to hear glass crack.

He stands, skin pale, thighs sleek, flanks slender, and moves away as an animal from its den. She hears him say more to himself than to her, "It's all right." He takes clothes from his pack; they're ones she'd given him, the pressed pants and new white shirt; he dresses while she puts on her own stale clothes from the day before.

He takes one more thing from his pack. A figurine. He puts it on her easel; a ballerina shaped from wood, her flesh pale, her skirt a darker shade, her face without features, but expressive just the same, and no two black dots staring out. "She's a puzzle," Daniel says. "All the pieces fit together, her skirt, her face, her slippers. You'll see."

[3] Lydia calls. "Maybe we could talk."

"Yes. Absolutely. Any time."

But days go by.

Chapter Two

[1] Her small heater made of orange coils fills the studio with heat. Late fall, the branches outside the windows stark, often black. She's numb, carefully numb in the aftermath, but the idea she'll have a new life, not something she's worked out, persists. Probably folly.

In the meantime, she counts Ross's starched shirts, keeps their social calendar full, goes back to talking to Ina about cleaning supplies and ingredients for dinner. She plays tennis. She calls Lydia at the last minute to help with some benefit event, who, to her surprise, accepts.

Still waiting to wade deep into a discussion, Lydia only tip toes. One brief foray involves her saying, "When Sarah was fourteen or so, she asked Jack if he was gay. I laughed, but he calmly asked what would make her think so. I don't remember her words exactly, but essentially, 'because you're loving but not very physical with Mom. And you never look at other women. Maybe that's why she flirts so much. But, come to think of it, you don't look at other men, either. When I'm a grown-up, I'll refuse to be mysterious.'"

Angela tries to extend this into more, with laughter, questions, but it's an anecdote, not an invitation.

[2] Late one afternoon, Angela drives by the entrance to the club where she's expected and on into Boston, to the block where Ross and she lived when first married. She walks up Boylston, her flower shop gone now, and down Newbury, where she stops in a small, dark cafe where no one she knows is likely to be. There, among strangers, mostly college students, she has two glasses of red wine and draws faces inside shapes on the paper napkins, faces with eyes closed, and then open. Sometimes the laughter at the bar is loud, a swell of joy, or inebriation.

In the back dark recesses at a table that seems set aside for employees on break, not customers, sit two men; she is slow to realize one is Sam. She stares out of surprise at seeing him, but when he turns and stares back, she realizes he's with the man, their hands lightly linked, and that Sam thinks this is why she's staring. She shakes her head to say "no problem," but realizes it probably comes across as condemnation, so she smiles, but has no idea how this is perceived. Sam and the man kiss, not deeply, but not lightly, either. Sam's companion rises and makes his way to the door, seeming to brush against Angela's table on purpose.

Sam follows a few seconds later, but stops.

"May I sit?"

"Of course. I'm surprised to see you here. In Boston, I mean." How silly, how unsure she sounds, as though grappling with the etiquette of another culture.

"It's not all about sex, you know. Being queer."

"I know."

"Do you?"

"Maybe not."

"Do you love your husband?"

There's no easy answer.

"I know he's difficult, but I'll assume you do. Did you fall in love with him, marry him, stay with him for sex? Or because you share experiences, and feel understood?"

Hyper aware of herself, her clothes, her breasts, her sex, her lover in her husband's bed, she finds nothing to say.

"I think relationships fall apart when one partner – or both – feel disjointed. 'My wife husband lover doesn't understand me.' Has nothing to do with sex – or is not decided by the sex part. Sex suffers when there's no intimacy of any other kind. And there are so many kinds. I admit I only know this now. Sylvia's great, she really is, but we were never ever on the same wave length. Never. Not her fault."

"How is she?"

"I wish you'd been nicer to Lydia."

"She didn't give me a chance. I was blindsided. I wish she'd told me. All she had to do was tell me."

"Easy to say," Sam says.

"That's not fair."

"I guess. I don't know you. But put yourself in my position. Or Lydia's. Or Sylvia's."

"I've tried."

He takes a moment to look at her, to evaluate her. "I think you have. I didn't mean to be aggressive. I've gotten this way because I feel like I finally have answers. Other people have had them all along." He knocks the table top twice with his knuckles. “Anyway, Sylvia’s expecting me. I’m picking up the kids.” He taps his knuckles again and says, “Good luck,” for what she can’t imagine.

She drives home through a narrowing tunnel.

Halfway across the lawn to the studio – she intends to catch her breath before seeing Ross, and to spread her napkin pictures out across her easel to see if there is something to salvage – she stops. The door’s open; Ross is inside. He hasn’t turned on a light, and he doesn’t seem to have touched anything, or to have looked through anything. His arms hang by his sides; he’s in the middle of the room wearing an overcoat, a black rain coat, although there’s no rain, and his back and shoulders are broad and thick and he seems weary, she can see how weary. He stands as though waiting, but is tired from the waiting, and nearly ready to accept the futility of his waiting. It hurts her, it does, her husband, standing there, some shadow having taken up residence. She doesn’t want him to see her – he seems lost in some reverie – she doesn’t want to become part of it; she’s certain he’s not going to disturb anything, although his presence there is disturbing. She turns toward the house; every shade is pulled down evenly in every window above her.

Chapter Three

[1] Still with her coffee in her wicker chair, Angela hears Lydia calling from the kitchen.

"It's so early for you." And odd. She hasn't been here in weeks. "Come on in."

"A few of us are going to try to learn how to play bridge." Lydia clothes aren't bright and her collar lies flat. Angela overheard a couple of women discussing the new sobriety in a ladies' room – their speculation was that she'd discovered Jack was having an affair – but they stopped as soon as they saw her.

"At this hour?"

"Want to come?"

"Ross didn't send you, did he?" All of the shades are pulled down, so it's quite dim with no view. "He's been complaining that I stay home too much. I suspect what he means is less interesting than ever."

"Want me to open these shades?" Lydia's already touching the cord.

"No," Angela says too quickly, too loudly. "The light hurts my eyes."

"He did call. He does say you're worse." Lydia sits on the arm of a chair near her.

"Worse than what?" He didn't come in after she saw him in the studio; he drove off and didn't come home until well after midnight. "Maybe he's having an affair. He comes home late. This coffee made my stomach feel funny." She's been feeling unusually moody; she must be suffering from aftershocks. She'd been more even keeled right after Daniel left. Maybe complete recovery isn't feasible. She's debated trying to find him, to help her with answers, but that would be foolish, and futile. But she's losing weight; food doesn't taste right, the blandest things seem strong; she'll pour wine, scotch, but can't drink it. "Does anyone still take Valium?" she says. "What do you use?"

"Right now it's Zoloft," and digs a stray from the bottom of a pocket; Angela's afraid of pills and so only holds it. "You'd need more of those to do any good," Lydia says.

"He wants me to see a doctor. 'The solution is probably simple,' he said. And nothing would be better than a simple solution. But I don't need to be solved."

"Why not? What harm would it do? I'll even take you. My doctor's wonderful, very accommodating."

"What does that mean?"

"He won't tell you that whatever is wrong with you is in your head."

Angela tries to laugh. "The two of you scheming." Angela turns to the window as if she can see through the shades, as if Daniel's at the hedge. "I'll consider it."

She feels Lydia debate what to say next. The right choice – "We've never really talked," or "I suppose I should apologize (for thinking about you naked, for thinking about your breasts and vagina and lips for twelve years,)" or "It's hard to describe what my life's been like" – might cause, would cause, Angela to share her Daniel tale, but, as is, their friendship is barely discernible. Still, in a vivid flash of imagination, she conjures up a conversation about love and sex and passion and friendship gone wrong, gone right. She herself starts to say, "We should talk."

But Lydia deflects: "No bridge?"

"No bridge."

Chapter Four

[1] Melanie calls to say, "I've found a new color! Blue! Want to see?" Once more Angela has to say she's not feeling well.

"Like a cold? The flu?"

"I don't think so." She mentions symptoms.

"And you're not pregnant?"

"Only you would think that," she says.

"Stranger things have happened."

Angela tells Ross she's willing to see a doctor. "I know that's what you want." Perhaps her mental state has suppressed her ability to ward off disease, or perhaps this is menopause, these mood swings, her late or missing periods; perhaps there is in fact some answer, some message on a prescription pad.

"Good. I'll take you myself."

[2] On their way to the low, red brick professional building, Ross talks about the weather, and about a necklace he's seen that she might like.

"Diamonds?" she asks, but is immediately sorry.

"What's that?"

"I'll bet it's lovely."

Inside the waiting room, they sit side by side on black vinyl and metal chairs; it reminds her of waiting for their marriage license. They don't speak; she wonders if they spoke back then. When her name is called, Ross pats her sleeve.

In the small chrome examining room, with a nurse standing by, her doctor confirms what Melanie suspected: she's pregnant. She sits on the edge of the table, legs crossed, arms folded, her head in one hand. "Impossible."

"But true. Congratulations."

"Don't tell my husband."

"Well I thought I'd leave that to you."

The silence is like a thick, durable shroud. The sun glints on the metal examination stirrups rising up beside her thighs. "How far along am I?" How quaint she sounds.

"A little over nine weeks."

She wants to sit in the back seat on the way home, even opens the back door without thinking.

"What are you doing?"

She's cold and still, in the front seat next to him, but tells him, before he asks, "They'll call with results in a couple of days." Nine weeks. Nearly ten.

Ross reaches his hand across for hers, and she takes it. "It's probably just some sort of anemia. That's my guess," he says. Squeezing his hand keeps her from floating through the car. Nine weeks. Daniel and she had made love with this seed of a child already between them.

[3] Termination. A reasonable, viable option. Sitting in her wicker chair, she decides on this. She's certain. She's clear. She'll notify the doctor. Dread, and the burden, lift up like a bird. She's light-hearted. Free.

And so, in a blue crisp papery gown she's about to lie back to have her baby dissolved. The nurses are calm, not quite smiling, noncommittal, it seems to her. The doctor breezes in.

"Mrs. Dunnewald. How are we feeling?"

"Unsure."

"Should I give you a moment?"

Her papery layer crinkles.

"You need to decide. Your window of opportunity is closing."

"I know that." What she also knows is she can't let go of this part of Daniel.

Walking back out through the waiting room, she's sure everyone's looking at her, sure her decision is known; it might as well have been announced. On her way home, the baby is very much with her in the car.

She tells Ross all the blood tests came back negative.

"How about a psychiatrist, then?"

[4] She hears clocks ticking even when she's not in a room with one. Ina takes to wearing slippers in order to pad about silently. She catches Angela standing sideways in front of the mirror, pulling the fabric of her skirt across her abdomen, trying to see if there's a difference yet. Seeing Ina over her shoulder, she stops, and then turns this way and that, as though checking her hem. "I thought I saw a tear." There's a little bulge under her waistband, but nothing she can't get away with.

Ina looks dubious. Nothing can be kept secret from her for long. In a mean moment, it crosses Angela's mind to fire her.

Melanie calls to see how she's feeling. "Almost back to normal." She's tempted to blurt out the truth, but it's important to her that, in someone's imagination, she remains intact. She wants someone somewhere to think of her as whole. "Well," Melanie says, "I miss seeing you. And I paint a lot better when you're around."

"I doubt that."

"Oh, it's true. Just ask my husband! He's begging you to go back to class." She hears a man in the background, agreeing with her rambunctiously.

She calls Lydia to say, "I suppose people are talking about me." Spread across the kitchen table are new sketches. Not only is she drawing, but she feels driven, driven by large, frightening figures, undefinable but with the look of gruesome fairy tales; many of the figures come from her dreams.

"Well, it is mysterious." Angela can hear her clicking her nails against the receiver as she asks, "Is it more serious than you're letting on? Tell me."

She almost does, almost pronounces the word pregnant. "It's not serious at all."

"Why did you call?"

Lonely.

Ross comes and goes; she has to think for a minute whether or not he's in the house or out of town, and Ina comes and goes, and continues to talk, although more quietly than she used to, but going on about the linens and the dust and now about how there's no milk, no sugar, no food. But Angela can't look her in the eye, as though she's the only one she's letting down.

Chapter Five

[1] Angela resides in a sort of aluminum shell. Inside, soft, vulnerable, growing, parts of her body often at odds with each other, while the outside is apparently unchanged, save for the new swelling, the new shape. To her, the very word *pregnant*, in capital letters, is visible, suspended between herself and the dry cleaning clerk, or the woman in the out-of-the-way shop where she's now buying clothes, between herself and Lydia and Beth and Emily. Between herself and Ross. She sees how her eyes look in the mirror, how they give everything away; but no one's looking.

The rims of Ross's eyes are often red. The hair behind his ears went a little gray some time ago, but now she sees how changed his hair is at the temples. He shifts his weight, and shifts it again, leaning this way, then that, in his dining room chair, one arm on the table, now both, while he plays with his fork, balancing it on its side and then laying it down, and then on its opposite side, then laying it down with important precision.

"I'll have to go to the rest of the board soon," he says. "I'd hoped Hank and I would put our finger on who was screwing with our numbers before this, and take that to them."

"The board? It's been so long since you've said anything, I thought it must have been resolved." She concentrates more intently.

He shakes his head. "It's gone on way too long, with no let up. The board's going to wonder why I waited, but it was a reasonable choice. It's best for the firm to keep it quiet."

He's on edge. There seems to be something wrong with what he's saying. She's never seen him so transparently unsure, not even back in the early days, while he waited for a verdict, for some judge to make a decision.

Ross took in a slow, deep breath, held it a second, blew it out. "It's a slow leak. Hank can see the first place it shows up," he says. "I'm sure this bores you."

"Go on."

She watches him play with his fork and his spoon, as though they were a hand of poker. "Monthly retainers come in," – he speaks slowly, as if she might not understand, but perhaps he's trying to explain it to himself – "and are disbursed, but the disbursements don't add up. It's hard to see." He shakes his head, as if excusing himself. "I don't how Hank happened to notice. The columns look fine, but the numbers do not add up. Ten thousand dollars comes in, say, and when you look again, it's only nine thousand nine hundred, or nine thousand eight. We can see that now, routinely, although not every time, and that it's never taken from the same client check twice in a row, but we can't see who is subtracting when. Without asking anybody straight out, which we don't want to do – we want to keep this thing as quiet as possible – we can't get any closer." He tilts his head, shrugs slightly. "Brilliant, really, from an accounting standpoint, but not particularly lucrative. Only thirty, thirty-five thousand gone."

"That's a lot to some people."

"But why not take more while you're at it? Real money. This small drip." Ross shrugs again, more broadly this time, as though to ask how anyone could have so little ambition. "Of course, if it hadn't been for Peterson, it might have gone on for years. But sometimes it's so few dollars gone, ten, fifteen, I'm not kidding – maybe they're after something besides money."

"What besides money?"

"Some game," Ross says. "Treating the books, the firm – like toys." Perhaps he's thinking someone's playing with him. This might be why he's held off going to the board, not discretion. "Eh. We'll smoke them out. See who quits when the pressure mounts."

"Maybe it is Peterson," she says.

Ross eyes shoot from the fork and the spoon to her, but he's still manipulating utensils, lining them up fork to spoon, now fork to knife. "Holy Jesus," Ross says.

If she could have a lover right in his back yard, and be pregnant right here in his dining room, right there in his bed, isn't it possible the thief is Hank Peterson, the one standing right beside him?

"Excuse me," Ross says, leaving her to sit alone among half-empty plates. Outside, a car creeps by; inside, a muffled clang; Ross must have dropped something, or hit something. After that, nothing. Then, "That fucking Peterson. Right under my nose. Right under my fucking nose."

[2] She dreads the meal with the Petersons. "We can't go out?"

"Not under the circumstances." Ross says this as if it were something they are in on together. "We'll see what he's made of. Can you imagine sitting in the house of a man you're stealing from?"

"He's still at it?"

"What's that word? Chutzpa? Maybe he'll confess."

The dress she bought less than two weeks before is tight through the waist. She keeps trying to pull in her stomach, like the men around the pool trying to disguise sagging bellies, but it makes no difference. It isn't stomach muscle pressing; it's baby. She'd surreptitiously checks online to see how big the baby is. Not very big at all at thirteen weeks, but big enough to press, and then there are her breasts. Ross says she looks "healthier." A few years ago, at an exhibit of Victorian dress, she saw the corsets that even pregnant women wore. It's a wonder all babies weren't born misshapen. But she wouldn't mind a corset for one evening. In any case, she won't be able to eat dinner; there isn't enough room between the baby and her dress. She'll have to tell Ross soon, but the feeling that rises in her stomach when she thinks of this is worse than morning sickness. *Hey Ross, you'll never guess.* It hardly matters, but it's impossible to determine which will hurt him more, the affair or the pregnancy. The thought of Ross hurt – humiliated – is a terrible thing; she's already witnessed his reaction to the Peterson business. She's sorry to have been the one to see the guilt first; it caused Ross to see himself the fool, but, better Angela realizing the error than a stranger. All week he's been by turns taciturn then belligerent, as he works out details, discovering, finally, exactly how it was done, numbers fudged and manipulated – she thinks of Ross's fork and spoon and knife lined up – and just how Hank Peterson has been able to distract him. Easily, she thinks. Ross thought himself impermeable, and a good judge of character. He had, after all, hired Hank. No one with brains bites the one who feeds him. All that's left is to figure out why. He never did anything to Peterson, only for him, he says. Soon, nothing will save Ross from Angela.

Angela imagines the wife, Patty, and herself retreating to a drawing room, both of them wearing corsets and long dresses with bustles, while men are left to discuss matters too heavy or too delicate for ladies' ears. Maybe she'll tell Patty she's pregnant. Strangers sometimes do better than friends.

[3] Angela bends over the directions Ina left about the dinner she started. She's disappointed to discover there's so little to do: Add sauce to the chicken, "last minute." Even the coffee has been measured out. When the conversation lags, she won't even be able to say *I have to check on the rolls* – Ina left individual baguettes.

Ross comes through the swinging door holding a half empty glass of scotch. "I was just thinking about our party."

"Tonight's?" This is no party. "Oh, you mean the masquerade." She stirs the sauce which doesn't need stirring.

"All that artifice," he says. She nods, surprised. He shakes his glass to make the ice cubes clink. "Look, if anything does happen, don't defend him."

"What might happen?"

"Nothing. You'll do fine," Ross said.

"I'll do fine?"

"It's my life he played with."

[4] Huddled arm and arm on the step are Hank, just as she remembers him, tall and thin and awkward as Ichabod Crane, and a tiny wife. Hank wears a dark blue suit nearly two sizes too big, even as the white shirt is too small, except for the sleeves, which are too long, and have French cuffs, with gold monogrammed cuff links. The wife looks older than he, late-thirties, perhaps.

"This is Patty," Hank Peterson says, extending his hand.

Patty's coat, unbuttoned, the color of pencil lead, is over a dress with a ruffle across the front, just a narrow band, but a ruffle, nevertheless, and purple against a field of miniature pink flowers. The neckline is low; she wears white shoes. The top of her head doesn't reach Hank's shoulder. Patty extends her hand, horizontally, as though she expects it to be kissed. In they come, even tall Hank dwarfed by the foyer.

"I'll take your coat," she tells Patty. They can't be looking forward to this evening either, and they're not even expecting bad news. She feels a butterfly flicker of movement in her belly, the baby, the book says, it will feel like this, but isn't this too soon? She resists the urge to touch. "Ross?" she calls, a little too breathlessly, a little too obviously not wanting to be left alone. "I thought we could have drinks in the library." She wishes she'd chosen the study; the library's too formal; they'll perch on their chairs. "Ross?" she calls again.

"What will you have?" she asks. "I don't know where he's gone off to."

"Water," says Patty. "Just water."

"Whatever you're having," says Hank.

"Scotch, then." Ross comes up behind them, shakes Hank's hand, nods to Patty; Angela is dizzy. "I'll fix you a scotch," Ross says. "My best." He pours a good portion in a glass for Hank, and hands it to him without asking if he wants water or ice.

"You're not having any?" Hank asks.

"Nope. I'm all set."

[5] The salad and soup and chicken nearly gone, Hank tells jokes not even his wife enjoys, but he keeps telling them anyway, complicated stories about huge groups of people in bars or on sinking boats, rabbis and priests and convicts.

Before Hank reaches the punch line of one, Ross leans in. "Listen." *Oh no.* Putting his elbows on the table, Ross leans forward even more, as though about to tell a secret, or to offer a plan, how they could rob a bank, or take off with diamonds. *Not now.* He seems larger than usual, something about his dark shirt looming above the white table cloth. She clears her throat, sits up straighter, tries to catch his eye, but Ross isn't paying any attention to her. The windows, four in a row, pick up some light from the new moon, making Hank squint. His mouth is still open, as though he expects to continue his story. Patty's staring at the butter dish. Hank looks as though he believes he's about to be taken into Ross's confidence. "Hank," Ross says, "it's time we got to the bottom of this embezzling business." *Please wait.*

Angela offers coffee.

"It seems to me you're protecting someone," Ross says.

Hank's features narrow, somehow become more pointed, more intent on his object of interest, which at this moment is his spoon tink, tink, tinking against the base of his water glass. "No, no. It seems to me different. If you want to get to the bottom of it, you might have to consider some motive besides money." Patty concentrates fiercely on the butter dish.

"What is there besides money?" But this is close to Ross's own speculation. He supposed Hank would come clean, or at least stumble, or twist in his seat, but instead Ross is being led down the very path he most fears.

Hank is enjoying this. "Is there anyone out there who would get a kick out of making you look bad?" He stops tapping his glass. "It pains me to have to put this possibility on the table, but think about it..."

"I don't have to think about it," Ross says

Hank, the sage now, nods. "It might be all about you, Mr. Dunnewald." Angela feels she's on a seesaw, or afloat in rough waters. "Who out there would enjoy bringing you down a peg? We both know it was set up to look like your deal. It wasn't your deal, though, was it, Mr. Dunnewald?"

"Don't be absurd." That Ross is in any way implicated is news to her. But then, again, he has taken his time notifying the board. Not guilty, in fact, but he must, she realizes, feel somehow at fault. "Patty," she says, "the men can finish up here. Come with me to the kitchen."

Patty doesn't so much as look away from the butter dish.

Hank leans back in his chair, at his ease; Ross, his face reddening some, doesn't shift his position. Now Hank's imitating the way Ross often slouches in his chair – she's seen it – this particular resting of one arm on the back of it with the other arm on the table. Nonchalantly in control. It's just like Ross, Hank's pose, when he's about to make a point that he finds unassailable; it's just like Ross to strike this seemingly casual attitude, in lieu of smirking, in lieu of actually waving away an employee, or a wife. She hates this in Ross, but it's Hank she hates now.

"Am I wrong, Mr. Dunnewald?" Hank says.

"Hank," she says, wanting him to stop. "Ross?" *Help me out here.* Looking over at her, Hank drops his Ross expression, the slightly raised eyebrows, the smile, the near-smirk, but it's not the end of the conversation: Ross still expects to win. The butterfly flicker crosses her belly again. She sees that it's her husband who's trapped, not Peterson, even though Peterson, not Ross, has broken the law.

Hank tink, tinks his spoon against the base of his glass. Then, putting down his spoon and leaning forward, clasping his hands, again like Ross, leaning forward at a critical moment, as if to question but really to condemn – it's an elongated parody, Hank with too-long, ill-fitting suit sleeves, sprouting French cuffs like blossoms – he says, "There are other people as smart as you are. We're everywhere. You just never notice. But, hey man, don't worry. We'll keep this between us." And he winks.

She expects, even wishes for, Ross's explosion, hey man, a wink. Instead Ross blinks just once, slowly, every motion considered. "When I lost interest," he says, "I hired a private investigator. One who specializes in fraud." As far as she knows, he's done no such thing. "It didn't take him long, once he stopped looking in the wrong direction. What's the expression? In the eye of the sun?"

Peterson flinches, and is once again Ichabod Crane, all traces of Ross dissolving behind his own mask. Patty shifts in her seat, crosses her legs, sighs, and seems to lose interest in all this talk about some business problem; Ross turns towards Patty, annoyed he's been interrupted.

"Patty," Angela says, standing up, "come with me to the kitchen." She's curious how this will play out, but at the same time doesn't want to witness Ross's dissolution.

"You bastard," Ross says, and for a moment she thinks he's talking to her.

"Patty, let's go."

"Think again," Hank says.

"I gave you that job."

"So what? You give a lot of people jobs." He says "jobs" like it's a dirty word. "And then you stride by our desks saying over and over how expendable we are. You don't think you're expendable?" He stands. "You do us 'favors,' a few dollars raise, you buy a box of Girl Scout cookies from an assistant, some woman you refer to as 'girl,' saying 'and I don't even like these.' You don't even know most of our names. You couldn't remember mine even though you'd hired me. I had to remind you."

"Sit down." Ross taps the table cloth with his forefinger. Hank hesitates, then sits.

"Thirty thousand bucks is small potatoes," Ross says. "Did you think you could support a wife on that?"

"It was never about the money."

Angela, still waiting near her chair, still waiting for Patty to follow, absent-mindedly rubs her abdomen. Ross sees this and frowns.

"Let the men finish up here," she says, wondering if the police should be called. Patty finally pushes herself back from the table.

"Want it back?" Hank says, taking a brown plastic wallet from his inside coat pocket. "I don't need it." As Angela and Patty go through the swinging door, he says, "I never cared about the money." From inside the kitchen, when the door swings again on its arc, she hears Hank ask, "Got a pen?"

She flips the switch for the coffee no one will be having.

What should she and Patty talk about? Fraud? Weather? Marriage? Outside the window, the studio is empty. She wishes Daniel's cigarette would flicker.

"I have nothing to apologize for." Patty's voice is loud and strained. Maybe the tone is a habit she's acquired trying to make up for her small stature. Or maybe she has to talk this way in order for tall, tall Hank to hear her. "I told him he'd been found out, but he said no, Mr. Dunnewald is completely blind, and is 'inviting me there to thank me.' We could have had a nice life. Now what? All this, just because he doesn't like his boss."

Angela sits down at the table across from Patty as if friends. "He took an enormous chance."

"I said the same thing. You don't like your job? Quit. But Hank kept saying he wanted respect, that he wasn't a charity case. I kept telling him that was ridiculous, it was networking not charity. So what if his aunt knew Mr. Dunnewald? So what? It was a good job, with a future. But he said 'Watch, watch what I can do.' And he went and did it."

Angela strokes her belly, not quite absent-mindedly.

"You pregnant?" Patty says. "Hank says Mr. Dunnewald's generosity is all show, he just wants to be able puff out his chest and act like he's better than everybody else."

"You're talking about my husband."

"Right. You don't need me telling you this. You know him a lot better than we do."

"That's not quite what I meant."

"I didn't know it had got this far, I didn't know Hank was still at it. Fifty, sixty thousand dollars is a lot of money, but I never saw any of it. I don't love him anymore. I thought we'd get married. This kitchen is huge." She turns in her chair to take it all in. "Too big for me. What are those things made out of, ceramic?" Angela actually turns to look.

"Fifty or sixty thousand?" she says. Ross said no more than thirty-five. "Yes, ceramic."

"They better not be asking me anything." Patty chews on the last of her lipstick.

"You thought you'd get married?" Patty, Hannah, herself, posing as wives, acting like wives, but never quite.

Patty laughs. "We live in sin."

The kitchen door opens. "They're leaving now."

Angela has one more question.

[6] Ross is in the kitchen, pulling Hank's check, folded once lengthwise, through his fingers.

"All this time he's been whispering in my ear," Ross says. "'I think there's something wrong, there's some irregularity here, I'll keep my eye on it for you, don't you worry, Mr. Dunnewald.'" Peterson has managed to push Ross off his two square feet of safe place. "Awhile back, I never mentioned it, I gave him more responsibility, so that he would be closer to the situation, could keep better watch. He objected. Must be it made his game too easy."

"You were busy."

"Of course I was busy. You build up a relationship of trust, you don't think you have to keep tabs all the time. Live and learn." He believed his square feet of safe space moved as he moved, a little to the right, a little to the left, even if everyone around him floundered. He could, if he chose, pull a person onto his float with him, like her, or Hank. Watching him realize this was a false impression is like watching a child lose his innocence. "People like him don't realize," he says. Realize what, she wonders. He glances out the window, at the check, at the floor, but not at her. She busies herself with dishes in the sink. "I have his admission. And his check. It's over. I can close the books on it once and for all." She doesn't ask what he'll say to accounting, to the board, a sudden deposit from Hank for thirty or forty or fifty thousand. He puts the check on the counter near her. She pushes it aside a little with her wrist, afraid it will get wet, that the numbers will run. "The board will be pleased I kept this quiet and brought it to an end by myself."

"Yes, I'm sure of that. I am so sorry."

She sees that the check is made out to Ross; it will be his sudden deposit, fifty-one thousand, three hundred and six dollars, no cents.

Her question: Did Patty ever love Hank?

Chapter Six

[1] "Lydia, I have something to tell you." In an indirect, off-center way, knowingly confusing the old Lydia's urge to be involved and at the center of things with the new Lydia of safe distances, Angela fantasizes she'll help in some way. "Can you come this afternoon?"

"My presence is requested. I'm honored."

"You'll come?"

"After lunch. But I'll only have a minute."

Angela makes them a pot of English Grey, sets out nice little cups on saucers, squares of raw sugar, lemon slices, ginger cookies. Lydia says, "What's this?" She's probably thinking, no alcohol? It's past three. "What's up?"

"You're not going to like it." Angela pours the tea, feeling terrifically and ridiculously out of place. "Come sit." She's unnerved, so much so she may not be able to say words like pregnant or lover.

"What could you possibly have to tell me that you couldn't say over the phone?" The satin edge of Lydia's red knit shirt sits perfectly against her collarbones. She sits lightly in her chair, as though she doesn't weigh a thing, and almost as though nothing that happens will touch her.

"This is hard."

"Wow. You're serious. Do you have cancer?"

"I'm pregnant."

For several seconds Lydia sits completely still, but then, "Why the mystery? Isn't Ross ecstatic? After all these years?"

"It's not his."

Lydia leans away as though Angela might be contagious. First she covers her mouth with both hands, but then her expression hardens into the same one Angela saw when a police officer refused to waive a speeding ticket after he detected wine on her breath. She has no peace or comfort to offer. Angela expected something, maybe not much, but some, some comfort, some womanly questions, some forgiveness, some understanding, but there won't be any.

"I want to slap you."

"That's not quite the reaction I was looking for." Her cheeks are on fire.

"Whose is it?"

"You don't know him."

"Whose is it?"

"I knew it wouldn't last long and never thought it would affect anyone but me."

"How stupid."

"Yes."

"You accused me of sleeping with Sam while you were sleeping with who knows what?"

"At the time – at the time – it looked like you and Sam were going to hurt Jack and Sylvia. Their kids. Sarah. I was just here, by myself."

"By yourself?" Lydia stands.

"Please don't go."

"What a disgusting hypocrite."

"I thought it would always be my secret. Just my secret. Part of your secret was me. I had a right to your secret."

"Angela shut up. Does Ross know?"

"I'm trying to work things out."

"Does Ross know?"

"Please sit down."

"How much does he know? Can't be much. He'd be apoplectic."

"Please don't say anything yet, for his sake. While we figure things out. Please."

"He doesn't know yet, does he? Little Miss Goody Two Shoes. And not going to tell me whose it is."

"There's no point." Angela crumbles a cube of raw sugar between her fingertips. "You'll give us time? For Ross?"

"This is too big to keep to myself."

"I've kept your secrets." *Hey, Beth and Emily and Rose and Susan and Althea Smythe, did you know Lydia's lesbian? Has had a serious crush on me? All these years?*

Lydia's face hardens. "You think you're better than me."

"Of course not."

"Definitely. 'Art.' What a lot of bullshit."

"I thought I was protecting you."

"From what?"

"Shattered illusions."

"There you go again. No wonder Ross thinks you're insane. Where did you do it? When?"

"Do it? Afternoons. Here. In the house. In my studio."

Lydia steps away from the chair as though there's sex on the cushion. "Was I ever here when he was?"

"No." Close, though.

"And now you're pregnant."

"Yes."

"No birth control? No precautions?"

"Not enough, obviously. I felt sterile. Ross made me feel sterile."

"How long have you known?"

"It doesn't matter."

"How long have you known?"

"A few weeks."

"You're disgusting."

"I don't think so. I did try to tell you. I tried to tell you how I'd kept every wedding vow except one while Ross kept only one. And maybe that one isn't the most important. This wasn't the right solution. I didn't think it through, I didn't think at all. I just opened a door."

"You're not making any sense."

"I am."

"None. No abortion?"

"I want the baby."

"What for?"

"I want the baby."

[2] Ross will come into their room late at night when she's finally asleep, and turn on the overhead light. "Someone has to make a living around here," he'll say. "Have you seen that brief I was working on?" The flood of light, the burst of it, makes her eyes ache, and speeds her heart rate. What does this do to the baby? Leaving the room, he'll ask "Do you want this light off?"

Or he'll tell her to do some errand, take care of some largely unnecessary detail, like having the knives sharpened. "Just so you know, I couldn't even cut my steak last night." It isn't true. The knife slipped through the meat. "I know how busy you are," he'll say, shaking out his paper over breakfast, one large sturdy shake of the financial page, rattling his coffee cup and causing toast crumbs to scurry, "but you can at least attend to this. Try not to run into anything with your car." The mention of the damaged car, long since repaired, snaps a picture of the decaying green and white house into her brain. She relives finding Daniel's house the first time. The battered car in the driveway, the ramp, the wheel chair, her lover, the sad, sad mother, Hannah and her bleeding vine.

"Angela, I asked you about dinner. Do you want to go to the club or not?"

"Dinner?"

"You look drugged. Most of the time, you looked drugged. Are you on something?"

"The club. Why not?"

"Wear something pretty."

"Pretty," she says to the ballerina on the windowsill. The wooden ballerina is in a vanity drawer upstairs. She likes having it in the house with her, even though it's also with Ross. She's taken it apart, and put it back together, the pieces warm, and smooth, like fine fabric, linen or silk, but the last time she took it apart she'd been unable to bring herself to put it back together, to have all of its solid pieces touching.

[3] She acknowledges people with a wave of her hand, but notices how no one comes over to see her. Ross has them seated at the table he likes in the center; she'd prefer being off to the side, out of sight, near the windows. She's ready to leave before she has so much as unfolded her napkin. The button at the waistband of her skirt is undone, and it's a new skirt, a size larger, with elastic at the back, but while putting it on she discovered it's already too tight; so now there's a safety pin holding the zipper, all of this hidden under a long loosely-knit shirt.

"That would look better tucked in." Ross is waiting for the waiter to come with another drink; his first scotch has gone watery, the cubes thin. Ross insists that scotch itself tasted thin. "I'll bet this is Dewar's, not Glenfiddich."

Pressing the tines of her fork into the leaves of the white tablecloth pattern, her breasts feel swollen as though twice the right size; she thinks of unwed girls who used to disappear into homes for nine months; perhaps there are places like that for wayward wives.

The food in the dining room makes her stomach flip flop, the meats, the fish, the oil from the roasted potatoes; she can even smell the salad dressing, the goat cheese, the balsamic. "Excuse me," she says.

Out through the double glass doors into the air. It's cold and clean and snowing a little; there are thin wisps in the headlights. She could leave – there's a cab now, bringing Sylvia and the kids. She raises her hand to call it, but there would be too much to explain.

"Lydia's gotten it into her head she wants a new car." Jack's at their table. "How do you like yours, Angela?" Both he and Ross have fresh drinks. "She's off tonight playing bridge. Her new craze. Not for you?"

"No, I'm afraid bridge is over my head, all those numbers and decisions."

"Her lease isn't close to over, but her birthday's coming up."

Ross nods. "A new car?" Ordinarily, he'd have launched into a discussion about leases and the unreliability of dealerships. Jack considers Ross and Angela over the rim of his glass. He raises it then, for a one-sided toast. "Women." He smiles and leans back a little, but he's still watching.

"Excuse me," Ross says. "Phone call to make. Too noisy in here. Be right back."

"I guess you know about Sam," Jack says the second Ross is out of earshot.

"I think everybody does. Sylvia's amazing."

"I shouldn't have blamed you. I was out of line."

"It's okay. We all seem to be out of our depth all of a sudden." She breathes a thank you for Lydia; clearly she's kept quiet. "I had no idea what I was supposed to do. Am supposed to do."

"I shouldn't have said anything. I made things worse."

"It'll be better in the end."

"I don't see how."

Ross heaves his body into his chair, like luggage.

"I'll leave you to your dinners. Good to see you, Angela. Ross."

"Just so you know," Ross says, so quickly Jack glances back thinking he's talking to him, "I've had enough."

"Enough?"

"When are you going to tell me what's going on?"

"Going on?"

"People are gossiping."

"About what?" Sam? Lydia? The Peterson deal?

"About you. You're beyond weird."

"Is that what you're worried about? Gossip?" She puts down her water glass. Ross leans in close, his tie touching his glass full of scotch, his hand outstretched.

She thinks he's going to take her arm, crush it with his fingers, leave bruises there, or shake her, in front of everyone, like a child.

"I'm not very hungry," she says. "I saw a cab out front. Finish your dinner, have another drink." She stands, and is surprised that she stands, and is surprised that she leaves. People watch. She's surprised Ross doesn't follow.

[4] The red voice mail light blinking blinking blinking. Ross, no doubt, angry and complaining. She crosses the lawn to the studio, snow swirling and beginning to accumulate. In the studio, she turns on the heater but no other light.

She sits on the white couch, lies down, pulls the comforter over her, and sleeps, feeling safe. In a dream, Daniel appears, or in a half-conscious state she conjures him up, the peaceful part of what he left behind. When she comes to completely, it isn't Daniel, it's Ross; she's so much in Daniel's mind, she doesn't immediately recognize her own husband. "What is it?"

He stands over her. He's never hurt her before, but he's a different man tonight. She sits up. He's so much bigger and taller and angrier than she. She crosses her arms over her belly.

He lumbers about the small room. He touches things. It would not be any worse if he were touching her. He lumbers out. She shivers uncontrollably.

Eventually, she'll have to go inside, she needs to go to the bathroom, she's hungry, thirsty. She has a baby to think about; she imagines it parched. Has he locked her out? She turns off the heater.

She's surprised the back door knob turns easily. No lights are on, not in the back hall, not in the kitchen. She switches on one or two, but the house feels mysterious, not theirs. Everything seems out of place. The colors are all off.

Ross is in the study. The only light is the one on his desk and it's turned down very low. He's sitting there, doing nothing. She's never seen him doing nothing before. There are no papers on the desk, no cigar lit, no drink of any kind. It's as if someone has died.

"What's going on, Angela?" he says. "I always feel Ina knows more than I do. Should I ask her? Oh God damn it. Why don't you get it over with and leave me? What's taking you so long?"

"Leave you?" She hasn't considered this is what he's been waiting for; she'd only thought of how he wouldn't be able to get her out of his sight fast enough, once he knew. "Ross, we'll talk soon, I promise. We should have long before this." But her reluctance in telling him has as much to do with her dread of having to watch him realize that his own area of safe space is even smaller than he thought as it does with the jeopardy she'll put herself into. Yes, he'll be angry, but most of all it will be the end of the illusion she's helped him to keep for so long, the same one Peterson helped to diminish. "Tomorrow," she says. "First thing."

Before going upstairs, she goes back to the kitchen, wanting something warm to drink. She needs to eat. Prays Ross won't follow.

She imagines sitting with Ross in the morning over coffee, just like any other day, as though nothing unusual has happened; imagine, using Ross to make things seem normal, right, safe, the man she thinks she might despise.

Waiting for the water to boil – she put in just enough to cover the bottom of the kettle – she stands in the light of the refrigerator door. There's very little to eat. Some cheese, she bites off a hunk, finds it bitter. She breaks off a stalk of celery and eats it without washing off the grit.

She feels Ross before she sees him. She closes the refrigerator door and turns to face him with her back against the white panel. She feels she's about to be sacrificed.

He comes closer. He spoons his words out. "No, I want to know now." The whistle on the kettle howls. She almost laughs with the ordinariness of that, the shock, the kettle boiling. She tries to get by him to turn it off. She thinks about the kettle boiling dry and being ruined. He moves slightly, just enough that to get by him she would have to touch him. She does not want to do that.

Midstride she looks at the space he's left for her while he looks at her. Finally, he moves to the stove himself and picks the raucous thing up without a pot holder – he knows the handle gets hot, has told her to replace it – and flings it across the room. The top comes off and the boiling water washes in an arc between them, almost splashing her face. The kettle hits the wall and knocks down two ceramics. They clatter to the floor and then there is silence. She hasn't screamed.

Expecting him to strike her, the skin on her back rises up when she turns to walk out. She's disappointed when nothing happens. He could make something happen. She wants the violence, some discovery, a passion to peek through, desire out of whack.

Upstairs, she starts to lock herself into the guest room, but then leaves the door ajar.

It takes a few minutes for Ross to follow her; she hears him push the door open. She sits on the chair near the window, quietly watching the backyard. It doesn't feel like a room in their house with Ross in it; it could be a stranger's borrowed room, in a hotel, or an inn, somewhere that's well-furnished but not theirs.

"Everything is about to be played out," she says.

"You're crazy."

"There is so much that no longer matters." She opens the drawer to the vanity, for some reason thinking the pieces to her ballerina puzzle will be missing, but no, there they are, the head next to the wings of the skirt. She slides the drawer shut.

"I've had a lover," she says.

The room is bathed in the softest of gray. Outside it's lighter than inside, what with the snow, and moonlight, the little storm over. But inside it feels soft, romantic, even; everything is the way it's supposed to be for this drama.

"You're unbelievable," Ross says.

"He's gone now. I don't know where. But he would come here, right here." She gestures to the room, sees just how it was. And sees just how Ross is, attentive, disbelieving. "Remarkable, isn't it? It even seems remarkable to me."

"You expect me to believe this?"

"How long have I had the studio now? He wasn't inside the house much after that. He would never tell me where he stayed in between, or what he did when he wasn't here. He led me to believe he lived with friends, that he got odd jobs, but for the most part, I don't know what he did, or who he was. He was, well, different. Magic. It's what I wanted."

"You're making this up. You're making this up as you go along. You want to hurt me. For some reason, you want me hurt."

"As it turned out, he only lived a few miles from here. I was at his house once; it was a little ramshackle. He lived with his mother, who was ill, dying, she may have died by now..." She won't admit to Hannah.

"You're delusional."

"Is that what you need? Delusions?" Not ready or willing to accept a lover, it seems he's ready and willing to believe in dementia. But then Ross sits down on the floor and leans his head heavily against the white bedcovers.

His eyes seem too bright; she manages to look at him in order to let him see her. He doesn't blink. She thinks she sees, or wants to see, tears on his cheeks. His eyes are round, bright, still. He's very much with her in that moment; for the first time in their lives together she feels seen. "There was a point when I thought all I would ever feel was guilt. And I expected to keep that to myself, when it was over, and I knew someday it would have to be over." She says, more quietly, "I didn't know if I loved you anymore. I didn't expect it to come to this."

"To what?"

"I'm pregnant."

The word sits in the air as though it in itself is with child. It hangs, a bloody ball, between them.

Ross stands. He shifts his weight as though falling, takes two steps toward the door, stops, his face as solemn as a death mask. "You're telling the truth."

"Yes." She feels strong, and unexpectedly free, and she softens a little as their silence grows deeper.

There's a light on at the neighbor's through the trees, a light that wasn't on a few minutes ago. She hears his breathing. Her belly softly growls. And there's exhaustion. An exhaustion descends over both of them.

"It was a shock," she says, "but I'm not sorry. I'm scared, but I'm not sorry."

He stands at the door for a long quiet time, his back to her; perhaps he wants to say something else, but he simply stands there. She'd touch him. She'd be willing to reach out. She wouldn't mind if he stayed longer.

"I'm shaking," he says.

Chapter Seven

[1] Morning, a still pale gray and looking as though it's about to snow again. From the window in the guest bedroom, she sees Ross outside, dark against the snow. He walks to the studio where the door has blown open.

Then she sees the glow from the heater, the same color as the glow of one of Daniel's cigarettes, only there's more of it, and it's dense, and never flickers.

Ross on the couch. The stool. The small chair by the door. She thinks of him looking at the room from a number of angles, and sees how he'll run his fingertips along the walls, across the tacked-up pictures. He'll touch these, and it will be as though he's running his fingers along the inside of her heart, or her womb. The room pulses, and is full of things he doesn't understand, but which he will no longer try to keep from her.

He must have placed the heater face down.

Flames rise, small ones, and Ross leaves the small white shed with his arms awkward and full of white sheaves and canvases; she sees the orange glow behind the windows, hears glass break.

She runs down the stairs, a long journey, feeling each step through the soles of her slippers; her hand touches the banister as if counting out quick beats. Does she think she can save it? But then Ross, in the study, near the desk, his hand on the phone.

"Call. It's my studio." When he doesn't move, she takes the phone out from under his hand and dials the emergency number herself, already knowing nothing will be saved.

A faulty heater, Ross tells the men who soon stand in their yard in huge rubber boots and bright rubber coats, walking them back around to the front, the new snow churned into gray and brown slush. "My wife," he shrugs. "Hopelessly careless."

To the neighbors who have gathered at the end of their driveway, she says, "Don't worry. It was only a gardening shed after all."

Later, inside – she at the study door, tears falling freely, he near the window looking out over his handiwork, shoulders back, chest puffed – Ross says in a harsh whisper, "If I could, I'd burn the whole house down."

[2] Every morning, even weekends, Ross leaves early. She stays in bed in the guest room until Ina is due, or until she's simply too restless to stay any longer. She pulls what's become a melodrama up over her like a cover, the story, her story, a lover, a wronged husband, a baby. Perhaps she should swoon. Ina creeps around the house as though Angela and Ross are in mourning. And just as she knew about Daniel without Angela saying anything, she knows Angela is pregnant, even as Angela can't say this out loud. She's still in some odd state. Lydia stays away. And since Angela's not involved in any projects, or luncheons, or plans, and since the undercurrent of every conversation and every thought is the baby, distances are inevitable. Angela will stop by the club, to keep up appearances for Ross's sake, but never stay long; she feels swollen, noticeable. "I'm anemic," "I'm on all sorts of medication," she insists. "It's making me gain weight. But don't worry. A few weeks, I'll be fine, the doctor says. Rare, but treatable." How easily the lies slip out. Hillary and Susan seem convinced, but are more interested in knowing what happened between her and Lydia. "Did you have an affair with Jack? Lydia with Ross? We can't think of anything else." Angela laughs, mostly from relief that Lydia has so far kept quiet, in and of itself remarkable, remarkable that Lydia can keep quiet, and remarkable that she sees Angela capable of retaliation: Didn't you know? Lydia's lesbian. Thinks she's in love with me.

[3] Ross spends evenings alone in the library or alone in his bedroom; her downstairs domain is the study now. Sometimes she feels him listening for her down a hallway. It seems after all these years that he wants her, but it's also possible he only wants what he'd come to expect. When it happens that they're in the same room, which happens only by accident since they carefully choreograph, the only part of her that seems to be truly there with them is the baby in her womb. Her mind, her face, the rest of her, what she's saying, where she stands, all this is subsumed by their awareness of the baby, its presence so loud, it might as well be crying.

Late one night, in the dark, she sits resting in her wicker chair –she's so very tired all the time; the doctor gently says her age is a factor. Ross, not seeing her there, comes in to the desk, but doesn't sit; he sighs, almost a cry. She shifts in the chair, a small sound, to warn him; she feels him realize she's there. He coughs, clears his throat, rustles papers loudly, and then, when she moves again, adjusting a pillow, he says, "How do you know the baby's not mine?"

Her breath is forced out of her lungs.

"No one ever said it couldn't happen," he says, with more strength.

She turns. His eyes are bright. Her first impulse is to say, yes, anything's possible, but in the end, this would be the crueler choice. "I don't see how."

"We made love, didn't we?'

[4] Ross finally says what she's been expecting him to, but over the phone from his office downtown instead of face to face: "It's time we agreed on terms of separation."

"Of course." She wonders where his assistant is, whether she's listening in, or at his elbow, waiting for his signature. Outside she notices buds on the tips of tree branches for the first time.

"Something has got to be done," Ross says, as though trying to convince her.

"I know."

She has tried to figure out what should become of her, what she deserves, but the problem and the options are so large and so foreign, the future continues to be amorphous. She finds it impossible to imagine herself with a baby, sees other women holding them, carrying them, pushing them in strollers, but when she tries to see herself in their position, fails. She still thinks of foundling homes, those old fashioned places, and does now, without any sense of disgrace. She looks out across the charred lawn.

"Ross?"

"What?" he says.

"We were happy once?"

"Don't start."

"I just wanted to know if we were ever happy."

The ballerina's eyes seem straighter now.

Chapter Eight

[1] Her new drawing is of some winter woods, but looking at it from different angles, in the shadows, and in the sun, there seems to be a wolf. Quite late, she's gone to the study where she keeps her drawings, no longer putting her things away every night; this is the drawing Ross holds in his hands.

"Your lover," he says. "This is his picture. I smelled him, there was something wrong, unclean, I thought it was Ina slacking off." He carves each word, syllable by syllable. "But, in the back of my mind, I felt invaded, I felt the intrusion on my privacy. I've been thinking I should have known, but I did know, didn't I? I trusted you. I took care of you. You never asked for anything, because you never needed more than I gave you. I gave you everything. That's what you led me to believe. And I believed nothing about you would ever worry me. There wasn't that much to you, and that made things easy, the way they should be."

Not much to you. "Please. Put the drawing down." She realizes, standing there, that her father had seen her mother like this, as a little, uncomplicated thing, a source of amusement, her simplicity, a woman without any secrets.

"You think I never wanted some of my own excitement, some little fling?" Ross says. "I thought about it once or twice, never with a plan, but I thought about it. I had all this energy. It seemed wasted on you, your ballet benefits, your garden club. You were always here waiting for me, no problems, no suggestions, no anything."

"I realize the failure isn't yours alone." She hadn't thought of her mother as simple, but she had, also realizing this only now, thought of her as hidden.

"Failure? Life with you was dull, believe me. But I didn't cheat on you, Angela, I didn't. But you did. And with this guy, this tramp, this derelict. He was dirty, I can still smell him."

Her father, though, and her mother had loved each other.

Ross drops the drawing onto the desk; she turns to leave. "I'm going to bed," she says. "I'll start packing tomorrow."

"Angela." He runs a finger down the drawing, a damp finger, to smudge, to obliterate, some part of it.

"What is it?"

"Nothing," he answers.

"We'll talk more after I'm gone, when things seem less…urgent."

But he's about to say more. He draws in a breath, seems to be considering his options, but then lets it all go, shakes his head, turns away from her, the drawing, and whatever he was going to say. Going up the stairs, quietly, quickly, but also worrying about leaving him alone, she feels some new destruction possible, another shed burning down.

In bed, there's panic in the bottom of her belly, beneath where the baby lies. Something in Ross is coming to a head; she can't put her finger on a clear definition. When Daniel is mentioned, not often – they're so rarely in the same room together – it isn't as Daniel, or as her lover, it's "your friend." "I suppose you wish your friend were here." "Where's your friend now, doesn't he even care?" And when she thinks of Daniel herself, it's as a body, a being, like the drawing downstairs, his name has lost its shape in her head. A distance has come between her and memory, between her and longing, but now as the day comes closer when she'll be leaving this house, both longing and memory are crowding back in. She isn't sure, though, that the longing is for Daniel. It might be for Ross, for what he was once, or for what he might have been. Or for something altogether different.

[2] The terms of separation are so generous, she doesn't understand. She's had no say in what was to become of her, wasn't once asked what she wanted, but could hardly consider this unfair, and thought that whatever Ross decided, she'd manage. Ross's lawyer contacts her to say Ross has found her a house, a small house in a smaller town, farther from Boston, where she can live until the baby comes, maybe longer, and he calls again to let her know Ross is making arrangements for Ina to help.

"It's not necessary to do so much, Ross."

"You're going to take care of a baby alone?"

"It's a lot to ask for."

"You never asked."

When she goes in to sign papers, his lawyer says, "He seems to feel in some way responsible. He isn't blaming you for everything."

"What did he tell you, if you're willing to say?"

The man hesitates. "As a friend, not an attorney. He told me the baby could be his."

"Oh."

"I'm not prepared to say more."

"There's no more to say."

Ross's in the study when she gets home. He's smoking a cigar, looks comfortable, or, rather, looks as though he has designed himself so that she'll believe he's comfortable. There's an edge in the air, but he says, as though asking if she bought butter, "They're all signed? We're all set then?"

"Ross?"

"Something not to your liking?"

"No, no, of course not." Perhaps she should say something about his lingering hope, the baby moving now even as she speaks; being his wasn't impossible, only highly improbable. Still, she isn't always certain what she herself believes. "I'll make us something to eat," she says.

"Don't bother."

Chapter Nine

[1] Dozing in the guest room in the middle of an afternoon, always tired and often irritable now, Angela surfaces through a half-dream – some notion involving feathers and candlelight – to realize Ina's calling her. Her insides, her guts, the baby, her breasts all fight with each other for attention. She thinks Ina's waking her to say she's leaving – "Why not just leave a note?" – but Ina's in the doorway saying, "It's Lydia. Lydia's here."

Angela thought she might only ever see her again by accident.

"Should I say it's a bad time?" Ina raises a window shade.

Angela squints even though the light is weak. "She didn't call first?" Ina shakes her head. "Does she look angry?"

"Not angry. Upset, though. I'll bring her up here. And stay close."

In a moment, pushing the door open with so much force it bumps against the wall, Lydia. "All right."

"All right?" Angela pulls the pillows behind her in order to sit up straighter, in order to meet this woman head on.

"Ross says he's some homeless guy." The words themselves apparently taste badly.

"It's not true."

"Then where did he live?"

Angela hesitates. "With me."

Lydia flicks this answer away with her hand.

"I have something to say." When Lydia perches on the edge of the small upholstered chair near the window, it tips forward slightly; Lydia catches herself, throwing her arms out wildly, and tips it back. "You were sleeping?" She cranes her neck to get a look down the hall. "Can Ina hear?"

"I doubt it." She's seen Lydia agitated when the cleaners failed to get out a stain, and impatient when tennis lessons were running late, but never quite this unnerved, not even in Jericho's, or when she told her she was pregnant. And she has on a pink blouse and blue pants; her hair looks uncombed. Angela wishes Ina had lifted the window shade higher. "Jack's all right?" she says. "Sarah?"

Lydia says in a single sputter, "I had an affair, too."

She's here for one-upmanship?

"A serious, long-term affair." Lydia concentrates on her nails. "Two years. With a woman."

"I see." Ina passes by carrying an armload of tightly stacked linens.

"You're not surprised?" Lydia whispers.

"I'm just listening."

"It ended right before I met you."

"Why are you telling me now?"

Lydia tilts her head back, crosses her arms, stares off at the ceiling, strokes her throat with her fingers, and says, "Jack knew about it. Sam's sister. Julia."

"Sam's sister? Oh my God."

"Why oh my God? I met you right after."

"I wondered how Sam knew to confide in you."

"I remember sitting on your packing crates talking about dry cleaners, or florists. In any case...Julia had left me less than a month before. I was reeling. I was in free fall."

"Are you still?"

"I loved her. So much. But I couldn't bring myself to leave Jack. Everything I had. All the *normalcy*. The way people saw me. I'd worked hard for that. But Julia finally couldn't have it any other way. Can't blame her. Somehow thought I could have both Jack and Julia. She wanted a family, for us to have a baby. I wanted us to have a baby. I actually thought we could while I stayed with Jack. And of course there was Sarah. An imbecile. I was naïve." She hesitates. "Just like you were here, apparently." She waits for Angela to react. Angela decides not to. "I was never in love with Jack the way I was with her." She picks at a cuticle with such tenacity Angela waits for it to bleed. "I knew when I married him there wouldn't be any sex, or not much. Asexual. Do you know about that?"

"I don't."

"It's why I married him. I wouldn't have been able to handle a man fumbling at me all the time. And he understood me. And it worked for him. So we thought it was a perfect solution. Two aberrants living together."

"Aberrants?"

"That's how we thought of ourselves. We could both pass as straight. We were so young. But then I met Julia, but then she left, and there I was, staring down the rest of my life. Then you moved in."

"Did I mislead you in some way?"

"You were wonderful."

The chameleon, changing shape and colors to fit the situation. "Not that wonderful." And Jack, wanting everything and nothing all at once.

"You act like you already knew all this."

"No." Only some.

"You were so delicate, so reserved…"

So malleable?

"So contained, so opposite of me, spilling out all over the place. Julia and I were more alike. You were different."

"Malleable?"

"What? I could see you didn't like Ross very much. I thought maybe for the same reason, and that Jack knew but Ross didn't. It's amazing what we talk ourselves into. I didn't want to be a lesbo. Never wanted to be. I never wanted to be an outsider. My father was brutal. Called all women with short hair dykes. All female athletes. Made fun of their husbands. Can't begin to tell you what he had to say about gay men. Once a guy wearing a little make-up and an ascot got on a bus with us; Dad made us get off, but not before calling him a fag to his face. I was mortified. To this day I think about what it was like for him after we got off. How the other people must have looked at him. I still wish I could apologize. But I already knew I was what my father hated. Hated the most. What I hated. 'If I ever found out one of my kids was gay…' I was relieved when he died. I thought it would be better. It wasn't. I wasn't."

"You've never talked about your father like this."

"Who would?"

"I wish you'd told me."

"How? How would I? I cycled through acceptance and rejection. Still do. Schizo. Made me loud. I thought I was too much for you. But you hung on. Which let me think…whatever I wanted. Kids have it so easy now."

"I doubt if they all do."

Lydia slides down a different hill.

"Julia. She showed up out of nowhere. With Julia, things changed. I felt myself. For the first time ever. She made it seem easy. I thought you were going to make it easy. When that didn't happen, I pretended. Pretended we understood each other. That we were secretly in love." She says these words with silly exaggeration. "But then I'd forget I was pretending. Jack would remind me and warn me. But it got so I couldn't stop. I was so lonely. I am so lonely. Do you know what it's like to never be touched?"

Angela starts to say oh yes, but Lydia interrupts. "Let me finish. I love Jack, but what good is water when you want wine? All my life things had pretty much fallen into place. I pretty much got what I wanted – everything but this – without trying very hard. So, just when Julia leaves, someone new? Divine intervention."

Jack's words. "It's a lot to take in."

A deep blush spreads from Lydia's chest up her neck across her cheeks.

"You don't have to tell me more," Angela says.

"Right after Julia left. I forced Jack. Into sex. He felt raped. Something I promised I would never do. It was the worst night. I don't think we ever really got over it. The worst. And I got pregnant. Had an abortion."

"I'm so sorry."

"Aren't we all." Lydia stops, thinking, perhaps, of loss. "And in the middle of all that, I kept imagining us – you and me – physical."

Angela feels she's naked while Lydia is dressed. "I must have done something to make you think you could."

"You almost never said no to seeing me. You agreed with everything I said. Until the art thing."

"I thought that's what friends did." Eliminate friction.

"And the lover thing. Jesus."

Angela feels singed.

"And a baby. I would have liked another baby."

"I didn't know that."

"But Angela, sex with a woman is so easy. So much easier than being with a man. When men and women have sex it's competition. When same-sex people have sex it's about communication and communion. The sameness comes alive. Why would any man and woman want to be together? What could they possibly ever know about each other? Queer sex is the only sex that makes sense."

"I don't think that's true with all men," not Daniel, "but I see what you mean," with Ross.

Lydia almost smiles. "Maybe you're queer after all."

"Maybe there's a little queer in all of us."

"I wish you meant that. I don't know how Julia knew she could hit on me. I'd never had the nerve, not even in college when other girls were experimenting. You've never been tempted? Never thought about what it would be like?"

"My mind always comes up blank." *Not quite true.* "Well, it stops short."

"Sorry to hear that." She does smile. "I tried for a while to believe I'd made being lesbian up; that it was just Julia, something about Julia. After all, how could I have done without for so long? I kept thinking about that Jessica Stein movie. Do you remember it? I tried to convince myself that I hadn't really been in love with her, that the phase was the delusion."

In Angela's brain, tiny vessels seem to burst like little clarifying fireworks. "I understand." The first weeks with Lydia had been odd; she'd often felt like a ping pong ball, back and forth over rough ground. She'd blamed her inexperience with lofty social circles.

"Do you? Before and after Julia, I was just…waiting. For something. I felt superior because I had this secret. I had this great secret that set me above and apart. I've felt that way all these years. Everyone else was so satisfied with their little lives, but I had this grand secret. But then it's you, of all people, you who find exactly what I want." Lydia voices catches. "You find somebody and that somebody's not me. Until then, I'd consoled myself thinking at least you weren't happy, either. That at least we were in it together. I knew how selfish that was. I didn't care. But all of a sudden you were happy. I could see it. And I didn't know why, only that it had nothing to do with me. I was insanely jealous, and I didn't even know what for."

Ina appears just outside the door, to ask if anything is needed, but Angela shakes her head discreetly, points outside to signal she can leave, but when Ina disappears, she wishes she'd had her stay.

"Well." Lydia crosses her legs and jiggles her foot, re-crosses her legs, runs her fingers through her hair. "That's everything." Her restlessness makes Angela feel brittle; under full breasts and pregnant belly and swelling hips, she feels bone-thin. And vulnerable, sitting there against pillows while Lydia sits in the little chair, jiggling.

Angela touches her abdomen just below her breasts, right where her belly begins to swell. She strokes what she thinks must be the baby's head, it's so firm and round, but perhaps it's a bottom!

Lydia blows out a quick puff of air, and, with a big sweep of her arm, resorts to theatrics. She stands, smoothes her hair down, straightens her rings. "To think all I thought I needed way back then was a fresh face." She enunciates "fresh" and "face," opening her eyes wide, thrusting her shoulders forward. "Yours."

"Have you talked to your therapist?" A tepid response. Angela puts her legs over the side of the bed to get away from it.

"I've only ever told her how frustrating it is to be married to a guy with so little interest in sex. But it's like being tone deaf. You can't understand music if you can't hear it. Maybe I should have left him. Maybe we'd both be better off. Julia's married. Two kids with her partner. Could have been me. But I couldn't see getting trapped in that life. I thought it was small. I could never figure out how somebody *got* into it – how they found it – in the first place. I met Julia completely by accident. Now her life is bigger than mine. Certainly more real. But how was I supposed to know that? How was I supposed to get out of the one I had? The one I'd been raised to fill? It turns out this is the small one. And you turned out to be the brave one. I've dreamed of getting swept off my feet again. Is that what happened to you? You got swept off your feet?"

"More than that. Surprising intimacy. Like you had with Julia. I didn't know I was waiting for anything. I thought I was just fine living inside my head, dealing with Ross, making do."

"Dealing with me."

"Yes. Dealing with you. I was brought up to believe rewards are in heaven." She smiles, but she's not thinking of Lydia; she's thinking of the minister in the little gray Protestant church in which she'd spent her childhood Sundays; he hadn't demanded Catholic confessions, but, any sense of worth, or of an inner self that was powerful or important, was the sin that would send her to hell. "Now I think my sin was pretending parts of my mind didn't exist."

Lydia looks at Angela at length, finally. "Yes."

Part Four

Chapter One

[1] A few boxes full of this and that sit on the lawn getting damp in the thin skin of early spring frost. Angela's surprised how little she wants to take with her. All of her drawing things, of course. The ballerina from the kitchen window. The ballerina from her vanity drawer, reassembled. In time she'll replace the drawing table and the easel lost in the fire. Not the small square of charred wood from Daniel's bookshelf. Two men with a truck, the same men who came to take away the debris from the gardening shed, have already left with the wicker chair, the couch from their first apartment which had been stored in the attic, her vanity table and mirror, the white guest room bed, on their way to her new house. Inside this house one more time, she walks past the library where Daniel lit that small, warm fire the first night, and across the carpeted foyer where the parquet was laid for the masquerade ball; stops at the study door for just a moment, the space where her wicker chair stood now vacant. Through the window she sees the lawn, the hedge, the ruins of her studio. She has the sense she's never quite lived here. The memories are thin; the house feels borrowed.

In the kitchen, Ross stands near the sink with an empty glass.

"I didn't hate you," he says.

[2] Her new little rented house is made of wood, not stone, and there are green working shutters that open and close. The kitchen is small and rather musty, but she opens all the windows; it will air out. In a different year, another year, perhaps she'll repaint, and plant a garden out back. She'll buy hanging baskets of white blossoms for the porch.

The houses of her new neighborhood are close together. There's rhythm to the street; in the mornings garage doors open, and men leave for work almost always in the same order; kids climb onto buses at the corner, some moms waiting until the bus is out of sight to leave for their own work, while others have children too young for buses or seem to be in charge of car pools. She feels nosey, looking out the kitchen window all the time, but it's irresistible; the life that seems routine to the husbands and children and wives seems new to her. One woman, about Angela's age, wearing jeans and a t-shirt with the name of a college on the front, stops by with a cake – "Oh, no, I don't need to come in," she says. "Just wanted to let you know I'm right across the street." Inside this woman's house and all the other houses, Angela understands there's love and anger, frustrations and doubt, but there's also activity borne of itself, people waking up mornings with purpose, a plan, days to be put one in front of the other.

[3] Ina, scrubbing out the kitchen sink while Angela sits by with her lunch, the soup, and the eggs, all growing cold, says, "I knew you were pregnant."

"I tried to be so careful. How could you tell?"

"I had two babies, and my friends, my son's wife, you get so you know."

In the face of Ina's straightforward life, she feels some failure. *Mr. Dunnewald wants to believe it's his.* Did she know this also?

"My daughter wants babies, lots of them, and my son had his first last year." Ina's life seems to have followed a natural selection; now there are grandchildren, and no separations.

"And where is your husband?" she says.

"He's home. Sick, bad heart. He can't work."

"Why haven't you ever said anything?"

Ina takes off her yellow rubber gloves, shakes them out and hangs them over the faucet. "In your house, I worry about your family."

"And what did you think about my being pregnant? That I was horrible?"

She waits a moment before saying, "Some things aren't meant to be reasoned out."

Ross was right. Angela couldn't have managed without her. At the same time she's consumed by her baby, and what's ahead, she's a little lost in this new, odd isolation; this new, odd neighborhood that actually resembles the one she grew up in, as though she's moved backwards, not forward; and this new odd way of thinking about what's ahead.

As much as she savors severing ties to her old, false life, there are strings attached. The old monotony has been replaced by a new one, but one which, at seven, eight, nine months pregnant, she can do nothing about.

She misses Lydia. She could have used the Lydia of grand entrances, lunches out, chats about things that do and don't matter.

She calls Melanie.

"I'm so glad to hear from you. I was so worried. What's happening?"

All Angela manages to say is that her marriage has crumbled.

"I thought as much. I'm sure you have friends right close by to talk to, but let me know if you need someone else. Absolutely any time. Promise?"

"I hope you're still painting," Angela says. "Are you still on blue?"

She thinks Daniel will find her, but he doesn't and he doesn't and he doesn't.

[4] The baby moves almost constantly, even as there is less and less room; sometimes it's painful, like an alien being wanting out, likely to burst through her belly button any minute.

It must be easy for Ross to believe he's shrugged her aside, the woman who's fallen off a precipice, a woman he would not save, did not want to save, and has discarded, the only viable option, although he has to realize, even if only at odd moments, that she did the discarding.

But Ina, who's dividing her time between their two houses, tells her, "Mister Dunnewald. He sits down, he gets up, he paces from window to window. Like he's expecting someone. I know that he sleeps downstairs in that chair in the library. It's not very comfortable. I put different pillows."

"How long have you been married?"

Ina waves her hand. "Thirty-five years. But Mister Dunnewald. He locks the doors and the windows, keeps checking them, and turns on the alarm. I thought he didn't like the alarm. But nothing does any good. It's like he's being watched. And he doesn't go to work every day."

"He doesn't?"

"Once he pulled all the blinds in the study down to the sills and told me to leave them that way, but when I came back a little later, they were all up. And once, he saw something at the corner of the hedge. He made me go outside and stand with him, wouldn't even let me take my coat. It was beginning to rain. I caught a cold. But we never saw anything."

A chill runs from the base of Angela's spine across the top of her head. But Ross must only be imagining things; recreating her life in his mind makes him think he sees things, shadows. It can't be Daniel, only a shadow in Ross's mind.

But, also, Ross's idea that the child could be his continues to surround her pregnancy with a mystery even if she doesn't believe in this one. After signing the papers and before moving out of the house, she'd felt his belief and desire hanging between them, seen it, like a curtain. They both must have, but neither said a thing, save the time she heard him say as he had to her once before, but apparently thinking she wasn't close enough to hear, "We made love, too, didn't we?" She hadn't answered, but had wanted to go up to him and put her arms around him and share their circumstances – just once – as a husband and wife should. This belief, his desire for it to be true, makes the baby ambiguous, less flesh and blood and doctor's appointments; sometimes, she wants it to be only that: flesh and blood and doctor's appointments.

She wonders if Ina has seen Daniel, but can't bring herself to ask. It would sound like begging. She rarely thinks of him standing in one place. Instead he'll be in a car, or on a train, or walking, sometimes towards her, sometimes away. She'd wanted passion. She'd wanted to find it in herself, that profound feeling that at the bottom, things matters, that there is a source, a font, a flowing out, that she's not like the gray cat wandering through its life, in and out of the studio door. And, once passion had introduced itself, she'd hoped for no fear, no fear of herself and anything she might find there. And, despite the pain and despite the delusion, Daniel had shown her and given her what she'd wanted. In the middle of lies there's purity. She'd been afraid of being found out, of finding it over, of having it brought to an end by things outside her volition, but she hadn't been afraid of the love, and what was discovered there.

Chapter Two

[1] The afternoons are warm. She opens every window of her little house. Some days, she can't exactly remember what Lydia looks like. Some days she can't quite remember Ross. Or Daniel. She doubts they remember her clearly. She sees a notice for the annual ballet benefit, and photos, one of Althea Smythe receiving a special award, and another of Susan, reading to a group of children in a classroom. Some days she imagines Daniel working in strangers' yards, or high up on rafters; she thinks of him carving and polishing the pieces for her ballerina; she thinks of him making love to her, even as the cunt he so loved feels nearly turned inside out with the baby's pressing.

The baby will kick a rib, or do what can only be somersaults; this idea of a body bound by hers makes her queasy, and so much upheaval, her own skin and muscle rippling over someone else's bottom and shoulders and head. Once she woke up in the night with the sole of one tiny foot pressed into the palm of her hand. She's as anxious to be free of the bound body as she fears the labor which will deliver it.

She suffers through pregnant dreams, violent dreams violently colored. Large fluid objects will be drawn through spaces smaller than the eyes of needles; pink and purple octopi force their suction cups through coral slits.

She eats well, craving what children do. Dollops of peanut butter on crisp white celery. Omelets dripping with cheeses. Soft breads. Ice cream, always vanilla; she pictures her baby drenched with it, the cream and the pureness of it. Her arms and her belly are now eight months round.

"Mr. Dunnewald calls," Ina tells her. "He calls me at my house. To see how you are."

"I'm surprised. No, I'm shocked. What do you tell him?"

"The truth. Getting fat."

"Isn't that what I'm supposed to be doing?"

One Saturday, she and Ina drive to a farmer's market. Angela's enjoying the mountains of gorgeous color, and wishing she'd brought her sketch book, when over the tops of big red tomatoes, she sees the heads of Lydia and a woman she doesn't recognize. She goes around the stand to find them arm in arm. Lydia doesn't seem to recognize her at first, because they are so far out of context, she supposes, and because she's so huge. Making a show of it, Lydia comes forward and touches her cheek to Angela's. But then, the grand mask drops, and Lydia is smiling and seems real, there, honest. "Sally, this is Angela, the woman I was telling you about. Angela, Sally."

"Very nice to meet you."

"And you." Angela thinks to ask about Jack.

When Sally says she's off to find avocados, and Ina goes off to find basil, Lydia stays. Asks about Angela's due date, and passes on some non sequitur gossip about Susan, and Beth. But then she says, "I'm *with* Sally. I never would have believed this could happen."

"I'm glad."

"We met online."

"I think it's wonderful. You look happy." She feels an odd stab of jealousy. Of displacement. "And Jack?"

"Still there. Sally understands. He understands. But it's not permanent. I don't know what will happen. People are going to catch on that Sally's not just a bff. Not just your replacement." Angela cringes. "I have to decide how much I care. I'm afraid I still care a lot. I'm not like you."

"I hope it lasts. Try to make it last."

"I am."

And they hug, like any two friends after a separation.

"Will wonders never cease," Ina says.

[2] Ross, or the idea of Ross, his single-minded stability, his inability to be diverted from a set course, has become a central strength for her. It isn't that she wants him with her, but there's comfort in the thought of him, and his sort of stability, or single-mindedness.

"I'm going to be able to do this, right?" she says.

Ina's in the tiny back hall fussing with the baby carriage. "Give birth? No choice. You don't have enough blankets."

It's impossible to ever be comfortable – her doctor said, "You're my oldest patient right now" – she spends a lot of time on the living room couch. The television sometimes on, mostly off; a book sometimes in her hand, mostly closed. Her sleep resembles the half sleep of an afternoon on a beach, that half-consciousness bathed in sunlight. She'll wake from this, or half-wake, thinking of Daniel, of holding his hands, of the way his shirt felt, or sometimes she wakes thinking of Ross, or Hannah, all of them in the same room. She imagines all of them dancing through the sprinklers of her childhood lawn. But then the face of Daniel's mother will press against a window pane, as her car dips against a wildflower bank.

Ross surprises her out of a baby daze: "I thought I should see how you're doing," he says on the phone.

"Nice of you, Ross. I appreciate it. I'm okay. Very tired." She's trying to read a novel Ina brought, one written by a woman about love and redemption. Its first words are "The only truth..." "I'm so glad Ina's here. Thanks for that. Thanks a million."

"It takes two," he says.

"What's that?"

"For you to go to such...lengths...there must have been something...wrong. With us."

"Ross?" Quietly, then, and perhaps still something of a secret to himself, Ross is entertaining the idea that all that happened might be partly his fault, that it's possible her choices grew out of some failure in their marriage, although he can't yet name the failure.

"That doesn't mean I excuse your behavior," he says.

"Of course not."

"Just that, like they say, it takes two." Swelling, breathing, a certain guilt; he feels it.

"I never meant to hurt you," she says. Her voice skirts over the top of other words. "I didn't think you cared, so I wasn't thinking about how what I was doing would hurt you." If she lands on them with any force or speed, Ross might spin out of control.

"Didn't care? That you were sleeping around?" He might spin out of control anyway.

"Didn't care if I was...happy, or unhappy." She can't bring herself to mention love or need. "I was selfish, but so were you."

"Selfish? I gave you everything. Everything I had was yours."

"That's not what I meant."

"Well, that's what I mean."

"Yes," she says. "I'm a disappointment."

"That's putting it mildly."

"But so were you," she says, quietly, though, too quietly for him to hear, because after all this time she's still protecting him; he can't endure much truth, never has, and it's this, she now knows, that first came between them.

"Excuse me?" he says.

"Nothing." She's still afraid for him; should he ever look at himself right in the eye, he might crumple, disintegrate; he's that fragile. "I appreciate your calling," she says.

Ross hangs up first, saying only, "Okay," as though something has been determined; hanging up releases him; his small confession is all he can stand. But, perhaps someday he will find himself thinking of his sin, or sins, as being great, as great as hers, even if he can't quite name them; it's unlikely he'll ever forgive her, and he wants that made perfectly clear. She simply wanted all their wedding vows to matter.

But, while making love to her, Ross lifted her blue nightgown over her head, so that she disappeared.

[3] Her skin takes on a different hue as it fills with baby and fluids and breast milk. The touch and texture is rich, not soft, but protective, firm, unyielding. And what sensations! She feels close to orgasm just washing her breasts with a sponge, or just feeling her nipples brushing against the fabric of a blouse or dress, however soft the fabric. As her baby grows and her belly grows until her navel is turned, strained, inside out, her vagina, also, feels spread and open and short, as if the path from the outside world to her womb, and her pleasure, is very short. A touch of fingers would bring her to climax, but she doesn't do this for herself. She feels it would be a sacrilege, and feels some ancient superstition that pleasure will damage the fetus, that her worldly joy will somehow become the fetus's only memory. And she's heard that sex, orgasm, pleasure sometimes brings on labor, and she's not ready for that. But there's frustration in her denial, because her desire is as close to the surface, as close as sweat and pore, and she sometimes catches the sight of her face in a mirror, in a store window, passing some random mirror of her desire and her pain and her refusal and self-denial as if she were at that moment in the throes. She laughs. It's all so absurd.

[4] She wakes up shivering. Maybe the furnace isn't working; she doesn't want to have to go down to the basement to try to figure the thing out. Ina tried to tell her what to do, which button to push, if it ever needed restarting, a red

button, Ina said, on the left, but she never went down to look; when was the last time a furnace went out? But worrying about the furnace is ridiculous. It's July. When she gets to her feet she finds the pressures in her belly different, and urgent. She expected another few days to prepare; Ina says first babies are usually late.

It doesn't seem to be her in the driver's seat; instead it's as though she's in the middle of the car, with the car propelling itself forward, her pain bigger than the car. Inside the great glass sliding hospital doors she's surrounded – there's a wheelchair, an attendant in baby blue scrubs – she feels she's being sucked in. Her body becomes their body; they do what they want with it, *you're alone?*, explaining things, but giving her no choices. She's a stranger, with no access to their vocabulary or their knowledge. The birth is drenched by waves of pain and discomfort that seem impossible to be coming from her. Her doctor says, "You'll have a baby by dinner," but a nurse says, "No, this one's quick." She's aware of being more alone than she's ever been in her life, and less so. The nurse is dark-haired, not pretty, not young, her eyes, large and brown. She hangs on to those eyes, and won't let that particular nurse leave the room. A baby, then, a pale opalescent slip of a daughter.

[5] In a hospital bed in a hospital room, her child beside her in a plastic bassinet. She loves the child, but can't quite fathom in her exhausted half sleep how it came to be with her or what she's to do with it now. The baby's fingers curl, uncurl, still thinking she's floating in fluid. Angela hasn't held her very long or many times yet; her arms seem incapable of bearing the weight. She can't think of a name, the right name, any name; she'd considered Tess or Isabelle or Sophia, but decided to see the child first, to see if she could tell what name was needed.

Nurses come and go all afternoon, all night, sometimes taking the baby for measuring and monitoring, they say, then bringing her back to put her to her breast. The surreality is in part due to there being no one she knows, only strange faces, strange voices and unfamiliar pain. If Lydia had been there, or even Ross, and she thinks of a crowd, Hillary and Susan and Althea Smythe, the people against whom she'd measured herself for years and years, she might have a better idea what to say, what to do. If Daniel were there, she believes she'd be very sure of herself. Instead, it's a foreign place.

Daniel once said he liked the name Adira – "for having strength, wisdom."

[6] She doesn't recognize the woman in the doorway.

"You scared me," Ina says. "Why didn't you call me? When I got to the house and the door was wide open, and the car was gone, and not even a note. Why didn't you call me?"

"I should have." Oddly, she'd felt too alone to call.

"I called here. But they wouldn't tell me at first." She lowers her voice. "I told them I was your aunt. How are you? Oh, the baby," and Ina rushes in, with a bouquet – daisies – and warmth.

"She's beautiful, can I hold her? What's her name?" And in the flood of newness and the flush of motherhood and after the hours of isolation, Angela smiles, and then laughs and then cries a little. Ina says nothing, overlooking the fact that Angela's sitting in a hospital bed, in a hospital gown, weeping, from joy and relief.

Ina brings her fresh water, and adjusts her pillows and helps position the baby while she lies on her side so that she can look at her without holding her weight; she's weak, and her back aches, but she's much less fearful with Ina there.

Quietly, Ina says, "I think I should call Mr. Dunnewald."

"How long are you staying?"

"As long as you like. I can turn on the television? I brought my knitting."

Angela tries to doze during the drone of soap operas – "My stories," Ina says – but she's so relieved to have Ina there she doesn't suggest changing the channel. When Angela wakes up more fully, she says, okay, Ina, why not call Ross, he might want to know.

"She's had her baby," Ina whispers into the phone, as though she's sharing a frightening secret; it's Ina who now seems close to tears. "I didn't know who else would tell you. I'm here with her now."

Ina nods, as though Ross can hear that, and then says, "Yes. Okay, okay."

"What did he say?"

"He wondered whose house I was due at tomorrow."

But Angela knows him now. She sees him at his desk in the city and knows that pain grows out of him. In this moment, a live thing is pulling his insides out. Perhaps he's forgotten about this possibility, this sure thing, Angela and a baby, not only a pregnancy. He won't picture a pure pale child swaddled in a hospital gown; he'll picture his wife writhing in the effort of spewing forth her lover's daughter, or his daughter, is it a daughter, he hasn't asked, and the baby's small and red and angry. Ross will cry out. She moans a little herself.

"Do you need a nurse?" Ina asks.

[7] Later, in the night, still so tired she's not sleeping well, her body still inside out, her breasts are painfully swollen to near bursting with more milk than her baby could ever want. Coming through her door, Daniel, over and over pushing open her door and over and over dissolving, but it's his touch, his words she wants, his voice saying he'll love her and the baby, even as she knows it's a fairy tale.

From her childhood she'd looked ahead with a certain separation, a certain waiting, believing that when she was an adult, she'd have more control, find her soul mate, have children, find those confidantes who would help her through her life, and she theirs. But she hadn't. Reserve and separation became entrenched. And one day the truth of this broke through, and a sort of insanity formed at the edges, because it was as though she were in solitary confinement; her flurry of friends and activities; her husband and her quiet house. Those walls.

And then, for some reason, Daniel.

The sounds in the hospital hallway increase; natural light replaces the fluorescent blue glow.

How good it would be if she could be in her studio with her baby beside her, and with Daniel, but not Daniel, Ross, with some Daniel inside, a Daniel with Ross's ambition, his desire to carve out a life, so as to exert some control over the chaos, to provide trust and faith, but all this with Daniel's capacity to love her. She'd been after love. She'd wanted to love and be loved. But what this longing brought her was herself.

Daniel's face hovers near the hospital bed, a dream, but the voices in the hallway are not dreamlike; there're real, even harsh. Someone's laughing, and a baby's crying, not hers. She tries to straighten out, to separate herself from her dream but it isn't a dream. Daniel is very close to her bed. She sits up. *How do I look?* Thick, matronly; a new nightgown, but the ribbons are untied; her breasts are showing.

Her hands shake as she tries to tie the ribbons, her whole body; she doesn't know what to do.

"Angela." His voice is soft and lyrical. "Ina told me you were here, but I needed to see for myself that you were all right."

"Ina?" He looks no thinner, no older; his eyes are as clear, his hands as fine; but it also seems impossible that she's made love with this man. He's been gone so long, he's a stranger, and she isn't calm; she doesn't know what to offer him. "Ina's known where you've been?"

"Only the last week or so."

"She never said."

"I asked her not to. But then I couldn't stand the way things were any longer. But I was afraid to show up; it's not what we planned. A baby!" He puts his hat down on the bed; still facing her, he rests a little of his weight on his hands, which shifts her body slightly towards him. "I don't know what to say."

Her own hand rests near his. She does nothing. Tries to do nothing. But then, his hand, smooth under hers, cooler. "It's been hard, but I'm all right."

He cups her face in his palm; he looks at her from the same depths he had when about to make love.

He closes his eyes briefly and takes his hand from her face; sitting down on the very edge of the bed makes his hat topple to the floor. He bends to pick it up, and she sees him, sure of himself, lean, easy; this is the man she'd made love to, for weeks, for months, in the white studio. She touches his shirt, his shoulder. He turns his hat over and over, watching it, not her.

"The baby," she says. "Adira. You told me once you liked that name."

He bows his head, and then lifts the end of one of the ribbons on her nightgown with his fingertips; she feels connected to him as if by a thread of electricity. "Ross thinks the baby's his," he says.

The current now a shock down her spine. "I know that." She sits up straighter. "But how do you?" Ina and Daniel and Ross all in touch? Only she left out?

"I went there. Yesterday. I was surprised to see he'd done nothing with your studio. He hasn't so much as cleared it away. He came outside. Told me you were here and shouldn't be disturbed."

It's easier than she thinks it should be imagining them face to face in the ruins of the shed.

"And he told you the baby was his?"

"Not really. The tone of his voice, it was proprietary." Daniel hasn't so much as looked toward the bassinet. "He can't bear the thought that everything was taken from him." Daniel takes a deep, deep breath. Letting it out, he says, "You don't need…this. We all know there are tests that would make things certain. But we don't seem to want that."

Her heart fills up as if with some liquid, some gold; it's a feeling she hasn't had for months. "Hold her," she says. "Hold the baby," she says with much more force than intended.

Daniel's as startled as if she'd unexpectedly clapped her hands. He turns to her with a hand raised as if to ward her off.

"Hold her," she says again, more softly.

Finally he stands, moves, steps around her bed to the bassinet; there's dread. In the faint morning light, she sees tears. Daniel lifts the baby with his hands, his arms, as though lifting the baby with his whole body. He holds Adira, that small being, that small life, those tiny hands, that tiny heart; he holds Adira to his chest and presses his face against the baby's tiny blanket.

Angela feels softly, completely, released.

"Enough," Daniel says. He places the baby next to her, near her breast.

"Stay longer," she says. But he's already beyond her reach. At the door he pauses but only to look back. He closes the door gently. Cradling Adira, she throws off the covers, she puts her feet on the floor, she should follow, he should stay longer, but she doesn't follow.

When the door opens again, it's Ina. "What do you need?"

Chapter Three

[1] Before feeding Adira, already three weeks old, Angela picks up the phone to discover someone already there. "Hello?"

"He still loves you."

"Lydia? Is that you? I was hoping you'd come out to see the baby."

"I went to see him."

"Ross? At the house?" How busy Ross has been, meeting up with both Daniel and Lydia. She imagines him just home from the office, his tie still knotted but not pulled tight against his collar points, at the desk in the study, or perhaps he's been asleep in the cramped library chair, where Ina has thought to put extra cushions. "How was he?" It would have been awkward, he and Lydia, acquaintances for years and years, but rarely without spouses, or some crowd, always barriers, buffers, something, not necessarily friendship, between them.

"We had a drink. I didn't even tell Jack I was going. I just got into the car and drove over. It was obvious he didn't want me there."

"What's wrong?" She wonders if Sally has already left her. Or she Sally. The phone caught between her chin and shoulder, she rocks Adira in her arms. She had little idea how to do much, change a diaper, give a bath, but with Ina's help, she's learning. Still, she's afraid of the baby, so small, so dependent, so much, and, right now, needing to be fed.

"Regardless of what he says, he still loves you."

"Maybe."

"I pretended at the farmer's market that it's been easy for me. But it hasn't been. It hasn't been. I'm not sure why I called."

"I'm glad you did. I've been wanting to tell you a couple things. Like I miss you."

"And?"

That's it? "That I treated Ross badly, and you badly. And that I'm sorry. And that I might never forgive myself."

"Don't expect me to."

Angela nearly laughs. "The baby's fussing. Hang on. I need to feed her."

"You're not breast-feeding, are you?"

"I am."

"Figures."

Angela puts down the phone, opens her blouse, adjusts Adira to her breast, the bundle that surprises her every time. When she and the baby are settled: "Ross called to say it takes two. Maybe it takes all of us. How else would so many of us have ended up in the wrong lives?"

"You're blaming me?"

"All of us must have been complicit in each other's..." Daniel's word, "fabrications."

"I don't know anything about that. I just don't understand how you could have done this to me. Lied so."

As though she and she alone. "Or you to me."

"My situation was different."

"Was it?"

"I didn't know you at all."

"I didn't know you."

"If I had..."

"If you had...?"

"I wouldn't have liked you."

"I would have been kind."

"I had reason to be circumspect," Lydia says.

"We're all convinced our excuses are valid."

"If he wasn't homeless, where did he live?"

"I told you." Angela smells the paint, the chalk, the scent of the studio; she can feel her hand pressed against the fair white bones of Daniel's breast. "He lived with me."

The silence is long and Angela grows hopeful but no: "I'm late for garden club. And my other phone is ringing." Not yet.

"Lydia."

But Lydia's gone.

Chapter Four

[1] "Melanie. Let's have lunch." And so they meet at a little place near Angela's house. This time, the grand entrance will be hers.

Already seated when Angela arrives, Melanie's looking over a menu and chatting with a waitress. When she sees Angela, she glows; when she realizes she has a baby, she gasps.

"Yours?"

"All mine." And Angela tells Melanie everything. She tells her every truth.

They're still there when dinners are served.

[2] Ina practically pushes Angela out the door to take walks: "The baby loves it." Why Ina believes this, she doesn't know; Adira eats, sleeps and cries in cycles, often unpredictable, completely unaware of her surroundings. But Angela goes around a block or two. There's the house with lace curtains, and another with a sculpture in the garden, a sort of stencil of a hovering bird. The woman who brought her the cake might be digging in the soil of her small plot and wave and say, "Nice to see you." Another woman, this one with a young baby of her own in a carriage, will stop to compare notes – Have you gotten any sleep? How much is she eating? This is still so new to her, questions from strangers. She's not sure she likes it, but Ina's right. It's good to be outside, and good to see other mothers. Along benches in the small town park, they all line up with strollers, and juggle juice boxes, bottles, containers of Cheerios. It takes her a long time to take a seat alongside them. Older children play on slides and seesaws, and the mothers seem content, even when their children come running to them in tears, crying over some bruise, some injury. She goes more and more often, but doesn't know if she'll ever be one of them. She feels set apart; her story is different.

She's nearly back to her normal size, although her belly still feels padded, and her breasts loom, and she still aches deep inside. Her arms and shoulders and even her hands still feel stretched. She doesn't see how she'll ever recover completely. Only her mind sits intact. Small, clever, utterly contained, its own power brought her to this point, its own choices, and sequencing of events. This mind of hers might not be especially beautiful, but it is as sure of itself as a small metal ball.

Adira wakes two or three times every night. Once, when she was a girl, Angela fell from high up on monkey bars. Her body fell through the scaffolding of metal and hit the ground hard. Nothing had been broken, but she spent the next few days in bed, every muscle and every bone a separate ache. Sleep deprivation feels just like that. Ina wants to stay over more often, but she's bent on doing as much as she can on her own.

Chapter Five

[1] In the hard rain during the night there were sounds, and lights flashing by from cars; she'd thought of her pencils and paints; how good it would be to pick them up again. No particular drawing had come to mind, but a strong urge.

Now at the kitchen table, considering her missing wedding ring, and thinking about drawing, imagining paint, thinking of Melanie's yellows and blues, she's aware of the traffic outside; she hears tires on the wet pavement; a car slows at the stop sign and pulls away every few minutes. She's mildly aware that the last one hasn't pulled away, or that it has parked; there's someone outside. It's too early for Ina, but she doesn't want to stand, afraid her chair on the linoleum will wake the baby up and she doesn't want the baby to wake up.

Without planning to, she stands and goes to the kitchen door which faces the side yard that runs along the street. There's an older couple jogging; she's seen them before, dressed in identical outfits, aqua and orange. And there's a black car, Ross's.

She pushes open the screen door; there's a baby stain near the knee of her white pants; her green blouse hangs out.

"Do you want to come in?" she calls. He gets out of his car and crosses the lawn. Months ago, she'd called the same thing to Daniel.

Once inside, she sits down where she'd been and says, as though continuing a conversation they'd already been having, "I wonder what it would be like to make a living from my painting. I couldn't, I know, don't worry, having a baby hasn't made me delusional, but people do. I never really thought about what that means. Does one decide to do it? Or is it something that just has to be? What a great risk. I'd be afraid of running dry, of having nothing more people wanted to see. Or, if I were that good a painter, could I part with what I'd made?" She glances up at him. "I was just wondering. How are you?"

He looks as though he hasn't shaved for days, or washed. He seems to be all jowly and dark, and discouraged.

"What's wrong?" she asks, as though this is how they are with each other, straightforward, and familiar, and in full view when things aren't going right. It seems easy and right to do this, even though for all the years of their marriage their method had been to pretend otherwise.

He stays standing. "It was time I checked in on you."

"Okay." She nods, doubting that this is why he's come. Driving out to her little house at that hour would be a spur of the moment decision, not a planned responsibility. "Lydia says she saw you. I don't hear from her very often. Have you seen Jack?"

Ross shakes his head. "Only Daniel."

His putting this name between them makes her feel lightheaded. "He came to the hospital for a few minutes." She wants to stay a step ahead of him.

"We've been talking."

"In person?" she says. Ross must only mean he's thinking about what he would say if they ever met again, or about what he should have said, the way one does after a lost opportunity.

"Yes, in person. I recognized him right off, the first time he showed up after you moved out," Ross says, a little explosion, a child saying "Hey, look at what I did." "He was the one I talked to about my puzzles at the masquerade party. The one you said was there to give someone a ride home. I'll never get over how easily you lied." But his eyes reveal nothing. There ought to be some reaction, some state of mind showing through. He might as well have been on the phone, canceling the newspaper subscription. But then again, the control, the lack of expression; maybe that is expression itself. On the shelf beside him, the wooden ballerina, her eyes facing Ross. She looks capable of pirouetting.

"I need to check on the baby," Angela says, but without moving, wanting to seem nonchalant but overwhelmingly curious about what else might be between Ross and Daniel.

"You invited him?" Ross says. "To the party?"

Her studio, white bones, music, a glass of champagne in her hand, Lydia the flapper dancing with the Tin Man; Sylvia dancing with Abraham Lincoln; Merlin head to head with her lover. "Of course not."

"You didn't discuss it with him at all?"

Only for fun, not as a plan. "I suppose he wanted to meet you, and the people I had told him so much about. Lydia, and the others." Discussing Daniel with Ross feels like a sacrilege.

Ross pulls out a chair. "You talked about me?" He'll find the chair too small.

"We talked about a lot of things." She pushes her own chair back a little, as if to face him, but it's to put a little space there. The choice Daniel and she made was to separate, and to not subsist on memories. But Ross's speech makes her feel possessive; he's trying to make himself part of Daniel's and her affair. She resists the urge to stand up, walk away, exclaim, stop talking. She doesn't want him to see he has an effect.

Ross adjusts himself in the chair, but it's unlikely he'll ever get comfortable. "The joke is definitely on me." He gives out a short laugh. "I stood with him in the library talking about woodworking. He explained how the construct, that was his word, construct, of the puzzles allows the wood to swell or shrink, but that the pieces would always fit together. He said the puzzles were 'honest,' that there was no cheating on the wood, nothing false, no fillers to make it work. I stood there thinking you would like him. The word that came to my mind was – I'm not kidding – genuine." He laughs again, his laugh this time sounding like a cough.

Daniel might as well be in the room with them, sleek, sure, his white shirt, his pack on the floor near the door, and a puzzle, the globe or even the ballerina, resting in his hands.

"Angela?"

"The baby," she says again, standing up. On the other side of the kitchen doorway, out of Ross's sight, she stops. The moment seems pure, drenched, she wants to be alone in it, as if she can both see and touch the pleasure and the loss, but already Ross is there with her, his dark suit and day old beard, the smell of scotch on him, and something else that's stale, like sleep, or conversation.

He says, "You're fine here, aren't you. I might as well go," but she distinctly feels he intended different words.

She's about to say thank you for dropping by.

"Look."

Should she?

"Daniel comes to talk about your studio." What would he possibly have say to Ross about that? How they'd made love on the couch, how much she must feel the loss of her easel, how much she must miss her colored crayons? Maybe he criticizes Ross for burning it down. "He wants us to rebuild it." She looks directly at him now, at his skin, his eyes darker than she remembers, his mouth less set. "Adira," she says, moving away, although the baby's not making a sound; Ross takes hold of her arm. "Your lover wants to rebuild your shed." A skeletal shape made of lumber rises up in her imagination, and also objects made for an absent mother, the shelves, the bowls, the porch, in the hope she would come home. The moment at hand divests itself of sense and sound.

"Your studio, if you..."

"I didn't think you loved me. All those years, I never thought so. Is this about love? Or something else? Pride? Control?"

He lets go of her arm and, taking a step away, says, "I'll go." She stays where she is until Ross is gone. He closes the kitchen door gently, as though to be careful not to disturb anything more. After a minute, two, she follows to watch him from the window. Ross is slouched forward a little in the seat of his car; perhaps he's put his key in the ignition, or is about to, but has stopped, to wait, to wait for what, some decision, to come back inside, perhaps. She doesn't want him to come back inside, doesn't know why he would, what else is there to say? Her breathing is audible, in and out, as if to measure how things stand.

Back in the living room, with Ross just outside, still in his car, but pressing in, it's almost as though she were back in his big house, with Daniel waiting somewhere outside near the hedge or in her studio. She sits down on the couch, but only on the edge of it, unable to settle back; Ina says it needs softer cushions. She hears Ross's car, but it goes away slowly, lacking conviction.

She wishes the telephone would ring, that Ina were here, that she had a drawing to finish; she wishes she had her easel, or somewhere she needed to go. Instead all she has are words. *Your studio. Daniel wants to rebuild. Would you...* Daniel, sitting on the edge of her hospital bed, saying that she doesn't need either of them, but now, it seems, they need her or want her.

These streets, the park, the other moms, might not be a final destination, but she feels no urgency, no panic, only the knowledge that she doesn't yet know where, eventually, she'll belong. There's time; Adira is so young. But now Ross, and Daniel, making plans; she feels as if her eyes and her mind and her body are wrapped in something she can't understand. Only a little while before she'd been at the kitchen table, thinking only of paints and canvases and missing wedding rings.

Ross again, at the kitchen door knocking on the little window, or maybe it's Ina. No, Ross, his knuckles tapping. He opens the door a little. "Did you love me?"

"I still haven't fed the baby." Down the hallway and into the tiny bedroom, she lifts her small daughter as though she's lifted her a thousand times before.

She sits in her wicker chair and folds the blanket back from her baby's face; Ross has followed as far as the doorway, and she knows he sees the face, and her face, and that he watches her unbutton her blouse and offer her breast, ripe and discolored, to the infant; his? She leans her head back and closes her eyes, and feels the baby's mouth. Ross doesn't want to watch, but won't walk away, he'll stay where he is, his head also back, his eyes also closed.

"Why would I go back to all that we didn't have?" She's not sure if Ross will see what she means, if he'll be thinking of the carpets and the furniture, the mahogany table, the carved library chairs, and so question, still be questioning, what else it is she could possibly want. He says, "It wouldn't be like that. Ever again." He isn't thinking of carpets and furniture.

Still. "Why not? Nineteen years aren't easily dissolved." Because Ross doesn't have a quick, ready answer, perhaps she'll trust some part of it. The baby suckles, a sensation almost sexual, certainly sensual, the attachment, the activity, the nurturing; she feels this, and says, "I wanted someone to love me. Just once."

"I loved you."

"I was lonely, Ross. Isolated and lonely. You never knew I was there. One's life ought to be noticed between spouses." Even Jack and Lydia knew each other.

Ross covers his face with his hands.

"I'm exhausted, because of the baby," she says, "but I'm content, even happy."

Ross is thinking of making love; she feels this as surely as if he has said it. But it isn't for love, or only love; he wants to repossess her, bring her back to his side; to him love is still partly possession, even now. She sees how he watches her switch the baby into her other arm, sees her offer her other breast, and she sees that he knows all she has is Adira's.

"I never dreamed nursing had to be timed," she says. "I wanted to be loved. I didn't realize I needed *to* love just as much."

And Ross thinks of dying; she knows this, too, as clearly as if he has said it, but he's thinking of death as one might think of peace, or release, not agony. However willing – or reconciled – he is to a new studio rising up in his backyard, peace will not come easily. She can only envision it half-built; once complete, what would it mean? Who would they be?

"She's fallen back to sleep already." She holds Adira a few moments more before standing up to put her in her crib, adjusting her to rest on her side, as though Angela knows how to do everything.

When she passes by Ross in the narrow hallway, she's buttoning her blouse. Ross stops her, covers her hands with his, then brushes her blouse off her shoulders, sees the swell of her breasts, and she stands, not questioning him, not wanting something else. Ross draws her blouse back over her breast bone and closes the tiny pale buttons, saying, "Come sit down. I can see how tired you are." He takes her hand and leads her to the living room where they sit side by side on the couch. He leans back and is quiet for a moment, and his voice is quiet when he speaks. "We were two people knocking against one another who didn't know one each other very well. I know you a little better now, not perfectly – I'll never think that again – but well enough not to hurt you anymore. Or, I'll try my best."

White walls rise up.

"Daniel describes a place for you to work that's better than before, better than a gardening shed," Ross says, "bigger, with a little porch, large windows."

She considers her hands in her lap; how chapped, how useful. "I never needed a better one."

Ross starts to answer but hesitates; she thinks he's going to object to her resisting his plans, but instead he says, "I'd like to see the baby close up." She hesitates; giving her over to anyone but Ina seems too much to let go, but she nods and leads Ross into the baby's tiny room. When Ross puts his hands under her baby to lift him, she takes a step forward, where's he going, but Ross merely lifts the child and holds her close; Angela's never seen a baby in his arms before.

"I've agreed. Go ahead, I said, rebuild. He comes every day to talk to me about it. Or, he just sits in the backyard, smoking near the hedge." Ross sways back and forth, slightly, just enough to rock the baby. "But he warns me, that afterwards – even when it's finished – that even with your studio, you might not come back."

Daniel sits on what's left of the broken cement step while he speaks, turning one of Ross's puzzles over and over in his hands, the globe, or the bear. She, feeling the fine grain against her own palm, sees how patient Daniel is, how calm, saying these things to Ross, to Ross, the less experienced one.

Angela listens.

E.V. Legters comes from the far western reaches of New York State. After working in advertising, traveling widely, and raising three children, she earned her MFA at the Vermont College of Fine Arts. She lives in Connecticut and teaches writing and literature at local colleges and writing studios. Her stories have appeared in literary journals including *Glimmer Train*, *Alaska Quarterly Review*, and *StoryQuarterly*. Her debut novel, *Connected Underneath*, was published in the Spring of 2016.

CPSIA information can be obtained
at www.ICGtesting.com
Printed in the USA
FSOW01n1401220417
33327FS

9 781590 216477